ADORKABLE

Cookie O'Gorman

ADORKABLE

Ordering Information:
For details on quantity orders for educational or business purposes, please visit the author's website at http://cookieogorman.com.

ADORKABLE/ Cookie O'Gorman. -- 1st ed.
ISBN 978-0-9978174-0-9

To My Aunt Pat

I love you more than cheese my dear

Adorkable (ah-dor-kuh-bul):
Descriptive term meaning to be equal parts
dorky and adorable.
For reference, see Sally Spitz.

CHAPTER 1

My mother thought I was a lesbian.

Terrific.

After she'd set me up with her boss's nephew—who, by the way, chewed with his mouth open, tucked his napkin into his shirt bib-style, and stole the last dinner roll—I hadn't thought it could get much worse.

Guess that's what I get for being an optimist.

"Never again," Mom had said after the Bid Incident last summer. It hadn't ended well. "I'm never setting you up again."

"Do you solemnly swear?" I'd asked.

She'd nodded. "When it comes to you, Sally Sue Spitz, I am done. I'm hanging up my matchmaking gloves as of today."

Too bad she'd handed those gloves down to someone even more meddlesome.

Daisy Wilkins rang our doorbell at precisely 7:30 p.m. Mom let her in with a huge smile and introduced her as the daughter of Stella Wilkins, my mom's eccentric hairdresser, adding "She's from New York." I didn't know everyone in our small town (though it felt like it sometimes), but I'd have known Daisy wasn't from Chariot just by looking at her. That Mohawk screamed big city.

"Nice hair," I said as we sat down for dinner. The pink tips were pure punk, but the bleach blond roots were positively Malfoy-esque. Not just anyone could pull that off.

"Nice smile," she said back—which I thought was sweet. It wasn't everyday you got a compliment like that and from a complete stranger, too. Mom seemed pleased, and I'd assumed it was because she'd put an awful lot of money into my smile with the braces and headgear I'd worn for three years.

We were nearly done with dinner when things took a turn for the weird.

"So Daisy," Mom said, "do you have a date for prom? You know, Sally still doesn't have anyone to go with."

I did a mental eye roll. Thanks, Mom. Let's just advertise it, shall we: Sally Spitz, salutatorian of her senior class, President of the German Club, voted Most Likely To Be Terminally Boyfriend-less until the end of time.

"Not yet," Daisy said, picking at her mashed potatoes.

She didn't say so, but I suspected Daisy was a vegetarian. She hadn't touched her steak, and her purse had a bright pink patch with the word PETA on it. That plus the dirty looks she kept throwing the beef on her plate were pretty big clues.

"You hear that, Sally?" Mom raised her brows. "Daisy doesn't have a date either."

"Hmm," I said, reaching for my water, glancing again at the clock.

When was Hooker's latest matchmaking-disaster going to get here? My bestie, Lillian Hooker, had dreams of becoming a professional matchmaker—which unfortunately meant I was her special project. Boys would do anything for her. This included having dinner with her BFF and said BFF's mother on Sundays. Tonight's "date" was already an hour late. Not that I wanted to meet another guy in the long line of setups, but the Southern part of me revolted at the thought of his rudeness. The girly part of me was just ticked at being stood up.

"Maybe you two could go together?"

I choked, eyes watering. "*What?*"

Mom shot me a stern glare. "I said, maybe the two of you could go together. I mean, if Daisy's not going with anyone, and you're not going with anyone..." she trailed off, looking at me expectantly. When I just stared, she added, "Oh, come on, Sally. You both need dates, right? Why wouldn't you go together? I think you and Daisy would make a cute couple."

I simply blinked. At the time, I was incapable of anything else. She'd said "couple" like she meant...

"Very cute," Daisy agreed, and when I looked to her, she winked. Winked!

I swallowed. Good grief, that was *exactly* what she'd meant.

"Mom, can I see you in the kitchen?" I was out of my chair and steamrolling toward the door before she could answer.

When Mom came in behind me, she sounded put out. "That was very rude, Sally. Now Daisy's going to think we're in here talking about her. What's so imp—"

I rounded on her, voice incredulous. "Mom, you think I'm a *lesbian*?"

"Well, aren't you?" she said confused.

"*No!*" I shot a quick glance at the door to make sure it was still shut. Seeing it was, I repeated, "No, I'm not. Not even a little bit. Mom, what...what would make you think something like that?"

"Lillian asked, and I couldn't rule it out." She shrugged, looking down at her hands. "I don't know."

"It had to be something," I persisted. I needed to know. If Hooker and my own mother had gotten that impression, maybe other people had too. Just how far did this misconception go?

"Well," Mom said finally. "First, there's the fact that you've never had a boyfriend."

"A lot of people don't have boyfriends."

"You're going to be eighteen."

"And?" I retorted. "What else?"

"There are those rainbow stickers you always carry around in your purse—"

"Those are for the kids at work!"

"—and then there's the whole Becks issue."

"What Becks issue?" I said.

"Sally, that boy is prime real estate to any female with eyes. You've been best friends with him since grade school, and never once have you said a word about how attractive he is."

"Becks is Becks," I said diplomatically. "And don't think I'm not going to tell him about the creepy comment you just made. Please, go on."

"You never go for anyone Lillian sets you up with," she huffed.

As soon as she said it, I knew this was the real reason.

"That's because they're either criminals or total idiots," I pointed out.

"That's not true," Mom argued. "There was Oliver Morgan—"

"Who constantly referred to himself in the third person."

"Devon Spurrs—"

"Currently in ISS for trying to steal Funyuns out of the school vending machine."

"Andy Archer—"

"He couldn't remember my name, Mom. Kept calling me Sherry, even after I corrected him—eight times."

Mom would not be sidetracked. "Then there was Cromwell Bates."

"Well, there you go," I said, and she pursed her lips. "The name alone makes him sound like a serial killer. I mean, who knows? Maybe his parents know something we don't. Besides, he spit on me when we first met."

"He didn't do it intentionally." Mom lifted her hands in a helpless gesture. "Sally, the poor boy has a lisp."

I shrugged. The feel of Cromwell's spittle on my cheek still gave me nightmares. At the time, I'd been afraid of hurting his feelings, so I'd just let it stay there, forcing my hands not to wipe at my skin as I felt condensation settle into the pores. First thing I did when he left was wash my face, three times for good measure.

"You know...it wouldn't bother me if you were." Mom hesitated, tone shaky but sincere. "Gay, I mean."

"But I'm not," I said again. "Just because I haven't gone for any of the loser guys Hooker's sent my way doesn't mean I'm into girls."

Mom laughed suddenly. "No," she said, "no, I guess it doesn't." She took my hand and met my eyes. "I just worry about you, Sally."

I gave her hand a squeeze. Mom had been saying that since my fifth birthday when I'd asked for a light saber instead of a Barbie doll.

"And don't be too hard on Lillian," she added. "She reminds me of me at that age, always trying to get people together."

"I wish she wouldn't," I muttered.

"Her heart's in the right place."

"I don't know why she feels responsible for my love life. Mom, I'm only seventeen. There's plenty of time for me to find the right guy...and it *will* be a guy," I reiterated just to be clear.

She shrugged. "One of these days, it could be The One, waiting right out there on our doorstep."

"Mom."

"I know, I know," she said, waving me off. "Occupational hazard, I guess. I'm a servant of true love; it's what I do, Sally."

I'd heard that one before. As a wedding planner, Mom really couldn't help herself. It was natural for her to want to put soul mates together. Her job was to give couples their happily ever after. She and Hooker were like two peas in a pink-heart-shaped-love-drunk pod. I just wished they'd use their talents for good instead of trying to match me up all the time. "Don't go planning my wedding just yet, Mom."

"Oh, please, I've had your wedding planned since you were in the womb."

I couldn't hide my look of horror.

"Relax, I'm just kidding," she laughed. "The truth is I don't want you to be alone." Her eyes went from sparkling to hollow. "Believe me, it gets old after a while."

It was moments like this that reminded me how much I despised my father.

"Better than being tied to a lying, cheating son of a b—"

"Sally," Mom said on a warning note.

I widened my eyes all innocence. "What? I was going to say banker."

"Sure you were." Mom shook her head, looking toward the kitchen door. "Poor Daisy, I feel terrible about all of this. I think she really liked you, Sally. She's going to be heartbroken when she finds out. What should we say?"

Daisy and I had gotten along fine, but I wasn't so sure about the whole heartbreaking thing.

I gave Mom's hand a pat. "I'll let her down gently," I said as we walked back into the dining room.

Daisy was typing something on her phone, texting someone. When we came in, she looked up and said, "Sorry, but I've gotta go." She stood, and I followed her to the door. "Mom just confirmed my flight. It looks like it's been moved up a few hours, so we're going to have to leave really early tomorrow. It was good meeting you, Sally."

"You, too," I said, noticing only now that Mom had somehow managed to disappear. Apparently, she was leaving this up to me. Well, I supposed there was only one way to say it. "So Daisy, there's kind of been a mistake. As much as I liked talking to you, I'm not—"

Daisy placed a hand on my shoulder, giving me a sympathetic look. "Listen, no offense, okay? You're cute and everything, but you're a little...dorky for my tastes." I opened my mouth, but she went on, "Oh, don't get me wrong. I'm not saying that as a bad thing. It's just not what I'm looking for right now. You understand, right?"

I swallowed then said, "Of course."

She leaned in and gave me a peck on the cheek. "If you're ever up in New York, give me a call, okay?" As she opened the door, she glanced back over her shoulder. "We'll do lunch or something."

I stood there stunned, watching her taillights disappear around the corner, until Mom came up behind me a few minutes later. "So, how'd it go?"

"She said I'm not her type."

"Oh." Mom shrugged. "Well, that's too bad."

I was indignant. "She called me a dork. She just met me. How could she possibly make that call after only one dinner?"

Mom eyed my outfit critically and then said, "You do realize you're wearing your Gryffindor jersey, right?" I opened my mouth to tell her it was a collectible straight off the Harry Potter official clothing line, but Mom cut across me. "And you know that when Daisy walked in, you had your right hand up, fingers splayed in that strange *Star Trek* signal."

Yeah, I thought, but that was just because I'd assumed it would be my date walking through the door—which I guess, it actually had been—and I'd wanted to scare him off. In my experience, boys didn't look twice at girls who employed Trekkie references, let alone wore Potter memorabilia.

"It was the Vulcan Salute," I muttered.

"Okay," Mom said, "but did you have to say 'Live long and prosper'?"

"I wasn't sure she knew what it meant." Daisy might've thought I was shooting her the bird in another language or something. I lifted my chin. "And you know what? I've gotten quite a few compliments on this shirt."

"From who, ten-year-olds?"

I flushed. "Becks said he liked it, too."

"Becks doesn't even care that you're a girl." It only took a second for Mom to realize what she'd said, but by then I was already heading up to my room. "Sally, I'm sorry."

"It's alright," I said, waving over my shoulder so she wouldn't see just how much she'd hurt me. "Night, Mom. Love you."

"Love you, Sally," came the solemn reply as I shut my door. I could tell by her tone that she already regretted it, felt sorry for speaking so bluntly. But how could I be mad? She was just speaking the truth, and I knew that as well as anybody. Still didn't take the sting out of it, though.

Plopping onto my bed, I dug into my nightstand and pulled out my journal. Blogging wasn't really my thing, and for the yearbook, my senior quote would read, "Facebook steals your soul." Twitter wasn't my bag either, as I considered it one small step away from legalized stalking, so for me social networking was pretty much out. But then, I'd always been a fan of the classics anyway.

The first page was dedicated to Date #1 Bobby Sullivan. Hooker had met Bobby at a wedding last spring, where they'd gone to second base in the church. He'd agreed to go out with me only after she promised not to tell his grandma. Catholic guilt, still alive and well today. But the worst was still Cromwell "The Spitter" Bates, Date # 7. I was officially scarred for life.

Flipping to my latest entry, I started up a new page. At the head I wrote, Mystery Date # 8 Daisy W. I followed it up with a short summary of the night, starting with how I'd been completely oblivious of the fact that she was my date until the talk of prom, followed by Mom's reasons for thinking I was gay, and ending with our little conversation by the door. At the bottom, as I'd done in each of the previous entries, I gave the night an overall success rating of six—notably my highest rating so far. It didn't surprise me that the date I'd rated highest had been with a girl who'd called me a dork. The others were simply that bad.

My phone went off beside my bed. I swung up to sitting and looked at the screen. There was a new text from Becks.

It said: "Scary Movie marathon u up 4 it?"

I sent my own back. "Not 2nite."

It took him less than a second. "Bad date?"

I couldn't help but smile at that. Becks had always had the uncanny ability to read me, even through the phone. I thought it over then sent, "Not 2 bad. Tell u about it later?"

"Can't wait ;) Night, Sal."

"Smartass," I mumbled and sent him a "Night" in return. Hopefully, Becks wouldn't give me too much grief about the whole Daisy thing.

CHAPTER 2

Okay, so I knew there would be some grief. But seriously, was that grin really necessary? Becks was leaning against my locker, all six foot two of him relaxed, wavy black hair brushing the tips of his ears, watching me as I walked toward him down the hall. It wasn't like I could just turn tail and run. I had to get my books for next period, and he was in the way. His eyes, the ones I knew nearly as well as my own, were swimming with mirth, his expression expectant.

Determined to wipe the grin right off his face, I said, "Hey there, Baldwin. How's it going?"

He blanched. "Jeez, Sal. Not this early in the morning, okay?"

I smiled to myself. Baldwin Eugene Charles Kent, aka Becks, had always hated his Christian name. With a name like that even I wanted to hate him—and he was my best friend. Luckily, Becks had escaped that clumsy mouthful with a killer nickname. Born with the last name "Spitz," there'd been no hope for me. From the first grade on, my peers had refused to call me anything else.

"So, what happened?" he said, straightening as I reached past him. Becks ducked down looking at me, but I avoided his gaze. "Oh please, it couldn't have been that bad. What, did this guy have webbed toes or something?"

I laughed despite myself. "How would I know?"

"You get another spitter?" I shook my head. He ran a hand through his thick hair, but, as usual, it fell right back into his eyes. "Honestly Sal, I can't imagine what could be worse than that. What did he do? You know, I'll keep asking every five seconds till you give it up."

I sighed. Might as well get it over with. No amount of stalling was going to change the facts, and Becks was stubborn enough to make good on that threat.

"*She* didn't do anything," I said. "It was the situation that was awkward."

"She?" Becks repeated and broke into a wide grin. "What's her name? Is she hot? Do I know her?"

Typical Becks, I thought. Only he would ask those questions, in that order, after hearing something like this.

Slamming my locker closed, I set out for my first class. With his long legs, Becks caught up in no time.

"Sal," he coaxed, nudging my shoulder. Left and right people called his name, but after acknowledging them, Becks turned back to me. "Don't be mad, Sal. I've always been overly curious. You can't hate me for that; I was born this way."

And that right there was why I couldn't stay mad at Becks for long. It was simply impossible.

"Her name," I said in answer to his first question, "was Daisy. And how should I know if she was hot or not? She had a pretty cool mohawk, though. As to whether or not you know her, she's Stella's daughter."

"The hair lady?" I nodded, and Becks's look turned thoughtful. "I think I might've seen her once or twice. Tall, decent figure, nose ring? Dang, Sal. What made Lillian think she was your type?" He laughed. "Do you have a secret bad boy fetish I should know about?"

"Don't you mean bad girl?" I muttered.

Becks shook his head. "I don't get it. What's the big deal?"

"The big deal is Hooker set me up with a chick."

Becks shrugged. "Could be worse."

Frowning, I sent him a glare. "I'm serious."

"Me, too. Sal, these things happen."

Was he joking? "These things happen. That's the best you've got?"

"Well, it's true."

"*Wer—?*" I threw up my hands. "*—Sag es mir, Becks, sag es mir sofort, denn ich will es wirklich wissen.*"

"English, please, Sal. I have no idea what you're saying."

And I had no idea I'd slipped into German; that only happened when I was upset. "Who exactly does this happen to?" I repeated.

He shrugged again. "To you, apparently." When I went to pinch him, he laughed and jumped back.

"This isn't funny."

"It's pretty funny, Sal. I, for one, think—"

Before he could complete that thought (and most likely earn himself another pinch), Roxy Culpepper and Eden Vice stepped into our path. The way they eyed Becks was enough to darken my day, but watching Roxy cock her hip, nearly popping the thing out of socket, was at least entertaining.

"Hey, Becks," Roxy said, giving him the head tilt and hair twirl. "Nice shirt."

"Yeah," Eden said eagerly. "The cut looks great on you. And that's like my favorite color."

Becks and I both gave his white Hanes a dubious once-over.

But unlike me, Becks didn't roll his eyes. Oh no, that'd be too impolite. Smooth-talking, woman-loving charmer that he was, Becks simply tucked his hands into his pockets, flashed them a wink and said, "Thanks, I've got four more just like it at home."

They laughed like a pair of hyenas, and Roxy reached out to run a hand over Becks's scruffy cheek.

"I see you're still keeping with tradition." As her fingertips lingered at his jaw, I had a real urge to smack her hand away—or stick gum in her hair, but I thought that sounded a little too grade school. Best stick with the smacking. It was considerably more adult. "Think we're going to win tomorrow?"

"You know it," Becks said.

"Oh, Becks, it's senior year. You have to win." Eden gave his other cheek the same treatment. "You just have to."

"I'll do my best."

"You'll win," Roxy said with certainty, hip out so far I was shocked to see it was still connected to her body. "Score a goal for me, okay?"

I glared as the two slinked away, but Becks couldn't have looked more satisfied with himself.

Watching him watch them was so not my idea of a good time.

Shifting around, I said, "Becks, how do you stand it? They come up to you and pat you like a dog. It's degrading."

"Is it?" Becks was still looking after Roxy and her amazing swaying hips. I swear that girl was born double jointed.

"Yes," I said. "It is."

Becks's tone was dry. "I feel so used."

Rolling my eyes, I walked away just as another girl came up to fondle his face.

Due to a rumor started last year, it was now acceptable for people to come up and pet him out of the blue. When Becks had first told me about the ritual—how he'd stopped shaving three days before a game to avoid bad luck; he'd read it in some sports article—I'd written it off as superstition. But then again, last year was our first season going 23-0, so what did I know? Personally, I hated the five-o'clock shadow. Not because of the way it made Becks look—believe me, Becks was a stunner with or without the facial hair—but people thought it gave them the right to touch him. And everyone had at some point or another.

Except me.

That was just not the kind of thing best friends did—and even if it was, I didn't have the cojones to do it anyway.

"Wait up, Sal!"

I slowed. "Finally got away from all those adoring fans?"

"Don't be like that," Becks said, sidling up to me. "They're just excited about the game."

"Yeah, right."

"What's really bothering you? And don't tell me it's the fan thing, I know you too well."

He was both right and wrong.

"It's just...I can't understand what gave her that idea," I said, going with the least complicated of the two things bothering me. "My mom, I mean. What'd I do to make her and Hooker think...well, you know?"

"Parents," Becks said, as if it was some great mystery. "Who can say what makes them do what they do."

Stopping outside my first period, I tried to make my voice sound ultra-casual. "You never thought that, right?"

"Thought what?" Becks waved as someone called his name.

"That I was, you know—" I swallowed. "—gay?"

Becks gave me a half-smile, looking completely unaware of how much his answer mattered—to me, at least.

"Sal," he said as I held my breath. "Gay or straight, we would've always been best friends."

I exhaled. Wasn't exactly the answer I was looking for, but I'd take it.

"I'll see you at practice?"

"Of course," I smiled. "Someone's got to write about the early years before you went pro. Might as well be me."

Shaking his head, Becks said, "See ya, Sal," and then kept going down the hall. As he walked, people—girls mostly, but a fair share of the boys—greeted Becks with catcalls, pats on the back, more cheek rubs. He took it all in stride, even when Trent Zuckerman gave him a chest bump that nearly sent him sprawling.

"So Spitz, you coming tonight?"

I turned and came face-to-face with my self-appointed matchmaker. Lillian Hooker was the only person who had permission to call me that name and my closest bestie right after Becks. On paper, she and I looked a lot alike: same height, same pant size, same long hair. In reality? Hooker's hair was dark chocolate, mine sandy brown. Confidence and curves-in-all-the-right-places set her apart. The caramel complexion didn't hurt either. She was exotic while I was ordinary.

In other words, Hooker was the Amidala to my Hermione.

"Don't know, Hooker." We'd bonded in the seventh grade over a great love of superhero movies and a deep hatred of unfortunate surnames. That first sleepover made our bestie status official. Hooker and I had been stuffing our faces with popcorn and watching TV when we flipped to a cheesy Western called *Tombstone*. Instant obsession. While other girls were dressing up like pretty princesses, we were Doc Holiday and Johnny Ringo for Halloween. "I'm still recovering from last night."

"I heard it went well."

I cocked a brow. "Should I even ask?"

She shrugged. "Martha texted me. She said you and Daisy really hit it off."

The fact that my mom and Hooker were texting buddies...well...I guess, I should've seen that coming.

"Did she also tell you—" I lowered my voice. "—that I'm not batting for the same team?"

Hooker laughed as we walked into our class.

"And by that, I mean: I like boys."

"I knew it was a long shot. If you were gay, there's no way you could've resisted all *this*." She gestured to herself, and I couldn't stop my smile. "But you haven't responded to any of my guys. Stella's been doing my hair for years, and when I saw Daisy the other day, I figured why not?"

"Hmm, let's see...maybe because I'm. Not. Gay."

"Yeah, sorry about that," she said. "I'll make it up to you, promise. Anyway, you are coming tonight, right?"

"I've got some reading to catch up on, so I might have to pass."

"But you can't!"

I was immediately suspicious. "Why not?"

Once seated, she waved me off. "Oh, no reason," she said, her face completely guileless. "I was really hoping you'd come, though. It's going to be a lot of fun tonight. You just have to be there."

I narrowed my eyes. "Why?"

"Oh now, what kind of question is that?"

"A good one," I replied, watching her closely. "This isn't another setup is it, Hooker? I told you I'm through with that. No more mystery dates."

Instead of answering, Hooker gave a long-suffering sigh and started chipping away at her nail polish. Today's color was a bright sea blue that perfectly matched the color of her eyes. The same eyes that, at the moment, wouldn't meet my own.

"I mean it," I insisted. "I told you before: I'll start dating when I want to."

"And when might that be?" Hooker was pushing back her cuticles with short efficient jabs. "Before or after the day of reckoning?"

I crossed my arms, refusing to let it go.

"Okay, okay." She stopped the assault and looked me in the eye. "Opening night, new X-Men. You in or out, Spitz? I thought you'd like to go to the midnight show and see Storm kick some evil mutant ass. Excuse me if I was mistaken."

Letting out a breath, I finally relaxed. "Rogue has it all over Storm and you know it."

"Puh-lease," she said, rolling her eyes, "Storm could cause a hurricane that'd knock Rogue back to last week."

"Yeah, and all Rogue would have to do is touch her, and Storm'd be out like a light, transferring her powers to Rogue in the process." Right as Ms. Vega was walking to the board, I asked once more, just to be sure, "So, no mystery men...or women?"

Hooker held out her palms. "Just Xavier and his crew."

"Then I'm in," I said back, and Hooker smiled.

Being so dateable herself, Hooker always seemed to have some guy on the side. For the past three months, it'd been Will Swift, a college boy fresh out of Chariot and attending UNC. Boys were just drawn to her. They'd been calling her up since middle school, and she couldn't understand why I wouldn't want her cast-offs.

As my best girl friend and an aspiring professional matchmaker, she felt it her duty to "broaden my romantic horizons." She typically arranged meetings with guys who were either hot and/or experienced—the bad part was she never actually told me beforehand. Sunday guess-who's-coming-to-dinner was just the start. I'd show up someplace (a restaurant, the mall, a football game) at a time we'd agreed to meet, and instead of Hooker I'd find Joe Piscotti, the second guy she'd set me up with, who I admit had been easy on the eyes—but who had also been twenty-six to my seventeen. Thankfully, Mom had never found out about that fiasco. Or Connor Boone, a nineteen-year-old self-proclaimed artist who'd offered to paint me in my birthday suit. I'd respectfully declined.

It wasn't that I thought I was better than them (except, well maybe, in the morality department). In fact, on the whole, it'd been the guys who'd ended the dates early. They hadn't been interested, simple as that. Honestly I hadn't been either, so it'd worked out great for everyone except Hooker, who'd taken it personally. I was now her mission.

Hooker had upped the amount of setups this year, determined to have me matched by graduation.

"Senior year, Spitz," she'd said on our first day back. "I have to find you a guy."

"You really don't," was my response.

"Yes, I do." Her eyes were bright. "I want to be a matchmaker. What does it say if I can't even find my own bestie her man? Unacceptable."

"But—"

"No buts, Spitz. I'll find you a guy or die trying."

Too bad I couldn't tell her I'd already found one, *The One* as a matter of fact.

But that was a secret I'd sooner take to the grave.

Still, I'd asked Hooker countless times to stop fixing me up, but she never listened. She had to know it was a lost cause. Didn't she realize I was best buds with the Adonis of the school? The only girl in Chariot never once chatted up, picked up, or felt up by the town's best-loved playboy? There had to be something wrong with me. Not pretty enough, not girly enough, something. I'd accepted it a long time ago, so why couldn't she?

My classes went by quickly. After school, the German club meeting ran a little long—which hardly ever happened since there were only two other members—so I had to sprint out to the bleachers to catch the end of practice. I swiped a hand over my forehead, and the back came away damp. Apparently my glands had missed the memo about how girls aren't supposed to sweat, because I was definitely sporting more than a glisten.

My eyes wandered to the sidelines of the soccer field, catching Becks flirting with yet another legs-for-days cheerleader, his second of the day. Coach Crenshaw yelled his name, voice slicing through the air with all the finesse of a foghorn. Becks didn't even flinch. He was sweating like a fiend, but Miss Double Back Handspring didn't seem to mind.

Crenshaw called Becks's name again, turning red in the face, which was around the same time he noticed me. Ignoring the coach, Becks jogged right over.

"Enjoying the show?" he asked, tugging the bottom of his shirt up to wipe his face.

A bout of girlish squeals erupted.

"Sure," I said, cocking my head, "but not nearly as much as they are."

"Ah, Sal, give me a break. I'm working my butt off out there. Are you going to write me a prize piece or what?"

"Oh yeah, definitely," I nodded, tapping at my notebook, "Don't you worry. It'll be totally Pulitzer-worthy."

"Hey, listen." He cleared his throat as Crenshaw bellowed his name a third time. "If you can't stand the heat, get off the field." He paused, smiling wide. "So, what do you think?"

"About what?" I asked.

"I'm thinking that's going to be my quote for yearbook."

"Seriously?"

His face dropped. "Too obvious?"

"Yeah, just a little." Unable to stand that look, I added, "But for you, it kind of works."

"Really?" His face suddenly brightened. "Then I'll go with it."

"Take it off!" The shout brought on another round of feminine laughter.

Turning toward the giggling mass of girls, Becks grinned. "Only if you say pretty please."

"Pretty please," they replied in unison, and I nearly gagged. When he didn't immediately strip, the girls started up a chant of "Take it off! Take if off!" This was why they shouldn't let cheerleaders hold practice next to the soccer field. The words got louder and louder as they got bolder, an unruly mob of hormonal teenage girls with megaphones. It was a scary sight.

"You're not seriously going to listen to them," I said flatly.

"What else can I do?"

"Becks, beware the dark side."

"What's that supposed to mean?"

"It's a Yoda-ism," I said, "and you know exactly what it means. Becks, have you no shame?"

"Nope," he said, lifting the jersey over his head in one swift pull, causing a mixture of applause, scream-ing and appreciative sighs.

I shook my head, struggling to keep my eyes north of his jaw line.

"What can I say, Sal?" he said, backing away. "It's like that line from that show *Oklahoma.* I'm just a guy who can't say no." Flicking his jersey at one of the cheerleaders, he hot footed it out to center field, grinning all the while. He gave a frowning Coach Crenshaw a swat to the backside, and then the team got down to business.

I wrote down Becks's quote, making a side note to include it in my next article, while the girl who'd caught Becks's jersey gripped the shirt to her heart and pretended to faint.

At least, I hoped it was pretend.

CHAPTER 3

"Becks, not so high! You'll drop it."

An eye roll. "Relax, Sal, I do this every night."

Looking at the frilly cooking apron he wore, I raised a brow. "You wear pink lace every night? Wow, Becks. After all these years, the truth finally comes out."

"If that's a dig at my masculinity, you know it won't work." Becks tossed the dough higher, grinning as I gasped. "Why do you make me wear this anyway?"

Because only one thing beat a shirtless Becks: Becks wearing a hot pink number, featuring "Kiss the Cook" on his chest, making pizza for me and my mom. After practice, he'd followed me home so we could hang out before he went to work. Mom wouldn't be back for a couple hours because of a consultation in Bixby. Becks made dinner for us at least once a week. The apron was just a bonus. It'd been a gift to Mom, but even she'd said it looked better on Becks. Which reminded me...

"My mom thinks you're hot."

He almost missed the dough for real this time, saving it just before it hit the ground. The look on his face was priceless.

Recovering, he said, "That's nice." Dropping the dough on a pan, he pushed at the edges and started rolling the crust.

"Nice?" I repeated. "Don't you mean weird? Creepy? All kinds of wrong?"

Cutting me a sideways glance, he said, "Why are you getting so worked up?"

"I'm not," I lied. My mother was hitting on the one guy I'd secretly loved forever. No big. Who'd get upset over a little thing like that?

"At least we know Martha has good taste."

"Becks!"

He laughed as I crossed my arms. Once he'd sauced and topped the dough off with cheese, pepperoni and pineapple, Becks popped it in the oven, set the timer, then came over and mimicked my stance. He was grinning, but I refused to crack.

"Speaking of taste," he said after a beat, "what's with this music?"

"Classic '80s," I sniffed. "If you don't like it, feel free to switch the station."

"No, I like it." Becks nudged my shoulder. "Brings back memories, doesn't it?"

"It does," I agreed, a smile touching my lips. Becks and I had gone through the same '80s phase every kid goes through. A lesser-known rite of passage.

"I seem to remember you having a thing for that guy in that dance movie."

"I had a thing for his *dancing*," I snorted. "And don't act like you don't know his name."

Sighing, Becks ran a hand through his hair. "I won't deny it. I wanted to be Swayze."

"Hmm," I said, taking in Becks's Swayze blue eyes, the thick dark lashes. "I seem to remember you wearing black t-shirts and slacks for two months straight. I'm thinking you were the one with the crush."

"I—" Becks froze as the song that was playing ended and a familiar one began. It was as if the radio was tuned into our conversation. "Wanna dance, Sal?"

"You sure?" I said back. "Sixth grade was a while ago."

"Yeah, but you forced me to practice every day for four months straight." Before I could remind him that he'd been the one to insist we practice so much

(Becks'd always been a perfectionist; one of the reasons he rocked in sports *and* academics), he smiled, held out a hand. "I think I can manage."

Taking his hand, I assumed the position. Becks at my back, he placed my arm behind his neck, fingertips doing a slow glide down my arm, the side of my ribs, to my waist. I tried (and failed) not to shiver. Maybe this hadn't been such a good idea.

Learning the final dance from *Dirty Dancing* had been tough. We'd practiced long hours at my house until we had the moves. The difference between the sixth grade talent show and now, though, was embarrassingly obvious. I hadn't expected his touch to affect me the way it did. I mean, I'd always been in love with him, but when you're eleven things are just different. Mom had had to skip the naughty bits so we could watch the movie for goodness sake. The lyrics to "Time of My Life" were as innocent as ever. But I was so aware of him. His grip on my hip, the way he led me across the kitchen floor. Those eyes. The dance had been PG in the sixth grade, but with Becks's sure touch and my stuttering heart, we were definitely approaching an R-rating.

When he pulled me to his chest, I jerked away.

"What's wrong?" Becks said, reaching for me. "You okay, Sal?"

"Fine, fine." I jumped back again, watching his hand fall, wishing my voice didn't sound so breathless. To cover, I said, "Just out of shape, I guess. Maybe I should start working out like you."

"Nah." Becks leaned against the counter. "You're fine."

"Says the guy with a six pack," I said, trying to get hold of myself.

"No, really," he said. "I like girls with a little meat on them."

Good to know.

"So, what's your type?"

The comment was so out there I looked up. "What?"

"Earlier, at school, you said you weren't into bad boys…or girls," he added with a wink. "Just made me wonder who you're into."

You.

No joke, it was the first thing that popped into my head. Good grief. Not only would it end our friendship, Becks'd run for the hills if I said that to him. Get it together, Spitz.

"Don't know," I said. Afraid of the answer, I asked anyway. "What's your dream girl like?"

"Freckles," he said not missing a beat.

"What?" I scoffed, secretly pleased. I had freckles! "Way to narrow the field, Baldwin."

"You didn't let me finish." Eyes moving over me with a focus that made my breath catch, he said, "*Cute* freckles, wavy brown hair, about five six, hazel eyes. Naturally beautiful."

"Becks—"

"She's smart—," He talked right over me. "—can quote *Star Wars*, curses like a German sailor when she's mad. Someone who makes me laugh out loud, a girl who's herself and lets me be me. Sounds pretty great, right?"

I stared at him. A moment, two hours, I didn't know. He'd sounded sincere, but he couldn't be. I wasn't that lucky. "That's not funny."

"You see me laughing?"

"Becks..."

"Yeah, Sal?"

"You are joking...right?" I had to ask. Even if the hopeful note in my voice revealed too much, I had to ask.

There was an awkward silence.

Then Becks's smile broke through, eyes bright.

"Man, you should see your face right now," he laughed while I tried to recover. "Priceless."

Well. That answered that.

"You want to know my type, Sal? Female."

"That's it?" I asked.

Becks shrugged. "I'm a guy. I love women," he said and shot me a grin. "Some more than others."

Shaking out of it, I punched him, popped him right in the arm. "You jerk. Why'd you say all that? Was it to embarrass me or what?"

He laughed the whole thing off like nothing happened. "It's true, Sal. You've ruined me for other women."

"Yeah, right."

"Where am I going to find another girl who throws a punch like that?"

"Haha, good joke," I said, throat tight. I knew better. Becks hadn't said anything, never made a move in all this time. But as he'd described me, his eyes softened—or had I imagined that?

The timer went off, and Becks pulled the pizza out of the oven. The crust was golden brown, cheese spread evenly over the top.

"I better get going," Becks said, setting the tray down, grabbing his bag off the floor. "See you later?"

"Probably." I swallowed and forced a smile. "May the Force be with you."

"You, too."

Becks waved as he walked outside, and I waved back, trying to ignore the ache in my chest.

"Mom, have you seen my gloves?"

I'd looked all over my room, under the bed, the nightstand, even checked the bookcase. The search had started over an hour ago after I finished my homework. The Calc questions were always a breeze, but the reading had taken longer than usual—mainly because I'd kept replaying that talk with Becks. My hair took more time tonight. Despite what Becks had said, it wasn't wavy. It was downright unmanageable most days. Sprinkled over my cheeks and the bridge of my nose, I'd made peace with my freckles over the years. But they weren't cute; they were just *there*. Looking back on it, I should've known it was a joke from the get. I shouldn't have spent so much time over thinking. Maybe then I wouldn't be running late.

"Mom?" I said again, stepping into the kitchen.

"What gloves?" she asked, head down, looking at a layout of bills while she compared cloth swatches. The bride must've chosen orange and bright green for her wedding colors. I shuddered. My eyes hurt just looking at the mix.

"Um, the only gloves I own." I tried not to sound too sarcastic. It wasn't her fault the stupid things were missing. "The short yellow ones. Bright, stretchy, kinda cheap-looking."

"Oh, those," Mom said, discarding amber for vermillion, "Did you check the hamper?"

Jogging to the laundry room, I rifled through the basket of dirty clothes. "Not here, either." I'd known it was a long shot. I hadn't worn them out in a while—not since my X-men themed eleventh birthday party—and besides, I suspected the shoddy material wouldn't hold up in the wash. Walking back, I muttered, "I could've sworn I laid them out last night on my dresser."

"Did you look to make sure they weren't on the floor somewhere?"

I nodded. "Yeah, even checked behind the headboard." Sighing, I slid into the seat opposite her. "Guess I'll just have to go without them. Hooker's going to be disappointed. You know she goes all out for this stuff."

"Don't worry," Mom said as she bound a few squares together. Looked like she was going with shamrock and orange peel with an accent of deep gold. Not bad, considering what she had to work with. "Lillian won't—"

"Won't what?" I mumbled, picking at the table as I waited for Mom to answer. When she didn't, I looked up and caught her staring at me. "What's wrong?"

She shook her head. "Nothing. Sally...what happened to your hair?"

"Oh." I instinctively raised a hand to my brown locks. "I just used some hot rollers and teased it a little. Put some baby powder on the front strand to look more Rogue-ish—Rogue circa the '90s cartoon series not major motion picture Rogue. Do you like it?"

"I'm not sure," Mom said with a small frown. "It makes you look...older, somehow."

"Thanks a lot," I said, not bothering to hide the sarcasm. Over the hill at seventeen. My life just kept getting better and better. Standing, I brushed the remaining wrinkles out of my black X-Men tee. The gloves would've completed the ensemble, but oh well. This would have to do. "Alright Mom, I'm gonna head out."

Mom glanced at her watch. "But it's not even eleven yet."

"Hooker wanted to meet early to get good seats."

"But what about the gloves?" Mom said, following me to the door. "Don't you want to check again?"

"No, that's okay." I gave her a peck on the cheek. "Hooker will just have to deal. Love you, Mom."

"But Sally, can't you just wait..."

Before she could say more, I opened the door...and saw the boy with the sky blue Scion striding toward our house.

Through clenched teeth, I hissed, "Mom, tell me you didn't."

"I didn't," she said, but I wasn't buying. Her smile was too bright, her manner too content, to be some innocent bystander. Then the truth, "Lillian did."

"I told her no more dates."

"She's just trying to be a good friend, Sally. Who knows? He could be your soul mate."

"If the first eight weren't my soul mates, the odds aren't in his favor," I said. "Plus, I don't want Hooker feeling like a third wheel."

Mom's look was shrewd. "And since when does Lillian go anywhere without a boy on her arm?"

She had a point, but...

"I'm not doing this." I shook my head. "Not tonight."

"Oh yes, you are," Mom said, pushing me onto the porch as I tried to back away. "His name is Austin Harris. He's a good boy, according to Lillian, and I promised I'd make sure you left together. Now—" She slipped something into my hand. "—go out and have some fun."

The door slammed. Unbelievable. Mom had literally thrown me out of the house. As I heard the lock click into place, I looked at what she'd given me.

The yellow gloves. She must've taken them out of my room sometime this afternoon while I was at school.

My mom, the calculating mastermind.

The thought nearly made me grin, but by then Austin had made his way to the door.

"Hi," he said smiling, reaching out a hand, "I'm Austin. I ran into Lillian at the bookstore, and I guess she thought—well, yeah."

"Sally," I said, shaking his hand. Austin had the body of a surfer/swim model with a face to match. I couldn't figure out why he was being so nice. Boys who looked like Austin rarely were. But after eyeing him more closely, I noticed...was that a pocket protector? I'd thought those were a myth. And his dark blue tie, which he wore loose over a white, untucked button-down was actually imprinted with the Hogwarts seal. "You like Harry Potter?" I asked, nodding to it.

"Hell yeah," he said enthusiastically. Then, like he'd caught himself, he said, "I mean, yeah. Harry Potter's pretty cool. If you're into that sort of thing."

I grinned. "I wear my Gryffindor jersey at least once a week."

"Really?"

"Really."

"Oh. That's good." He looked relieved. "I thought I'd blown it in the first five minutes."

"No, you're doing fine," I said then took a peek at my cell. If I wasn't there in ten minutes, Hooker would be shooting lightning bolts out of her eyes. "Listen, Austin, I don't know what my friend told you, but we're meeting her at the movie theater. If I'm not there in about ten minutes, it'll probably be sold out."

"X-men, right?" Austin fished two tickets out of his pocket. "I already got them. Lillian sent me a text a couple of hours ago."

"Wow." I was honestly impressed. Hooker's deviousness had suddenly reached an all-time high. "So, you won't mind hanging out with the two of us?"

"Not if she's as cool as you are." He flushed a little but gestured in my direction. "I like your hair by the way."

"Thanks," I said.

And that's how I ended up going to the movies with Austin Harris, a boy I barely knew, who'd already given me more compliments than any of my previous dating disasters combined, and was a surprisingly cautious driver.

Too cautious. He drove like a ninety-year-old man with cataracts. If he stopped at one more yellow, I couldn't be held responsible for my actions.

When we walked in, Hooker was propped up against the snack stand, tapping her foot impatiently, clad in full-out Storm paraphernalia. The white thigh-high boots she was wearing looked painted on, but that was nothing in comparison to the white Lycra bodysuit and cape. My favorite touch was the frosty bob wig she'd donned just for the occasion. Classic Hooker. She never did anything by halves.

Spotting me, she pushed off.

"Hey, Spitz," she called, waving wildly. "Sally Sue Spitz, over here!"

I gave a smaller wave back and tried not to be embarrassed as every head turned my way.

The ticket taker stopped mid-tear. "Spitz?" he said and then smiled. "Great God Almighty, you must be Nick's kid."

I fought down my grimace and nodded.

"Well, how about that." The guy's nametag said Eddie, and he was dressed in a suit. I assumed he was the manager. "You look just like him you know."

Actually, I thought I favored my mother, but whatever.

"Your dad's a great man. He really helped us crack down on illegal activity here at Regal Cinemas."

"Hmmm," I said and tried not to roll my eyes. If selling popcorn and candy at such high prices wasn't a crime, I didn't know what was.

"You be sure to tell him Ed said hi, next time you see him."

"Sure." As I walked away, I added, "But you'll probably see the jerk before I do."

Though we lived in the same town, I didn't see much of my dad. He was like one of those zits that popped up when you least expected it. A nasty surprise that made life hell until it cleared out. To most people, he was Nick Spitz, Chariot's favorite cop. I knew him as the guy who'd gotten caught banging the babysitter—while I was in the other room watching cartoons. Mom filed for divorce the next day.

"Finally." Hooker was hands on hips when I reached her, the timeless superhero pose. I didn't even think she realized that she was doing it. After the talk about my dad, the sight made me smile. "I was beginning to think you wouldn't show. Will's up there saving our seats. What took you so...oh hey, Austin."

Offering his hand, Austin said, "Hi again, Lillian, and thank you. Sally's great."

"And don't you forget it, bucko." Tugging me around, Hooker bent her head to mine and said, "So, what do you think?"

"He's really nice," I said. "I don't appreciate you enlisting my mom's help and springing him on me as I was leaving the house. But he seems okay."

She scrunched her nose. "Just okay? That's it?"

"Yeah, he's actually not so bad."

"Spitz, the guy's wearing Chinos, and he tried to shake my hand." She tugged at one end of her bob. "I found him bent over a book bigger than my head in the sci-fi/fantasy section at Barnes and Noble."

That sounded suspicious. "And what were you doing in Barnes and Noble?" I asked.

"Isn't it obvious?" she laughed. "I was looking for the male version of you."

I laughed despite myself.

"Glad you think it's funny," she said. "I always say it's the polite ones you've got to watch out for. Also, please don't kill me."

"Kill you for what?" I said.

"Hey Lil, I see you found my date." Turning my head, I caught Chaz Neely checking out my ass.

Hooker glared at Chaz while I glared at her. This couldn't be happening.

"I told you not to call her that," she said.

Chaz held up both hands. "Sorry, man, I forgot." To me, he said, "Love the hair by the way. It really gives you something, almost makes you look hot."

I glared harder as Hooker slammed a palm against her forehead.

"She's actually *my* date and she's already hot," Austin said a little red in the face. "Don't listen to him, Sally. You're definitely hotter than most, if not one of the hottest girls around."

As much as I enjoyed hearing Austin defend my level of hotness, I was ready to end this conversation and go watch the movie. I didn't think Hooker could top the Daisy fiasco, but it was no contest. This was officially my most uncomfortable date ever.

"Shall we? It's nearly midnight." Not waiting for an answer, I dragged Hooker to the second theater on the right, my two dates trailing after us. "Tell me you didn't."

"I wanted you to have a wider selection," she explained. "Two guys, one date, double the chance of success. Isn't it genius? This way you can choose: smart and dorky—again, basically you in boy form—or hot and...well hot."

"You so owe me for this."

"I know, I know," she said, eyes sparkling. "But it'll definitely give you something to put in that journal of yours. And hey, kudos on the sex hair. I'm so jealous. Mine would never do that."

I nearly tripped. "What?"

Hooker nodded. "That's a great look for you. Now all we need to do is find a better bra to give the girls a little pick-me-up, and you're home free."

Rolling my eyes, I walked down the aisle, feeling queasy. Bra support was the least of my problems. That much was clear even before the previews started.

I ended up seated between Austin and Chaz. The first offered me the armrest, asked if my seat was comfortable enough, wanted to know if I needed anything from the concession stand. By the tenth question—

Why do people like the X-Men, anyway? Justice League is so much cooler—I'd had about enough. Movies were not talk time, and the incessant questions had to stop. Besides, everyone knew there was no comparison. Members of the Justice League were just X-Men wannabes, plain and simple. With him whispering in my ear every five seconds, I could barely hear the movie.

Chaz, though not as loquacious, was just as exasperating but for different reasons. He kept trying to put his hand on my thigh no matter how many times I swatted it away. His constant attempts to try and look down my shirt resulted in me leaning so close to Austin that, at one point, we'd ended up bumping heads. Thwarted, Chaz slumped back in his seat and told me to go buy him a large coke and popcorn with extra butter. Hearing him, Austin got upset, called him a douche, and the two started arguing back and forth with me trapped in the middle.

The fighting didn't stop until one of the security guys came over and threatened to throw us out. After that it was, thankfully, quiet. But by then the movie was almost over.

As the credits rolled, Chaz stretched then said, "So, I guess it's true what they say, Spitz. You really are uptight."

I whipped around. "I'm sorry, what?"

"Uptight," he said again. "You know, frigid."

"Who says that?" I asked in disbelief. I was glad Austin was somewhere down the row looking for his cell. He'd dropped it during the movie. I didn't want anyone else hearing this.

"People." Chaz shrugged. "Lillian said you were pretty desperate."

Hooker had some major explaining to do.

"*Ich bin nicht das, was Du gerade über mich gesagt hast,*" I hissed. "*Und Du bist ein Idiot.*" Going by the confused look on his face, I may or may not have said all that in German. Plus or minus, a few swear words.

"Whatever."

And then he was gone. Good thing, too, because I was about two seconds away from using that left hook Becks had taught me.

"So," Hooker said, gliding up to me, "how'd it go?"

Brows raised, I rounded on her. "You told him I was *desperate*?"

Her eyes widened. "He wasn't supposed to tell you that."

"Hooker," I groaned.

"Alright, alright," she said. "I'm sorry. Chaz was kind of a last resort. Great hair, tight butt, but not much going on upstairs. What about Austin?"

I shook my head. *How was this my life?*

"Not him either, huh?" she said. "Okay, no problem. The next one will be better, I promise."

"There's not going to be a next one. I'm done." As she walked away, locking arms with the Wolverine look-alike standing at the end of the aisle, I made a last ditch effort. "You hear me, Hooker? Done. I'm serious this time."

"Yeah, okay," she tossed back. "Later, Spitz."

"Sally?" Austin was waiting patiently near the door, phone in hand. "You ready to go?"

"Yeah," I replied, feeling sort of bad. I hadn't even remembered he was there. "Sorry about all this. I had no idea Hooker was going to bring me another date."

"That's okay," he said.

"Thanks for understanding." Reaching him, I shook my head. "Austin Harris, you are too nice for your own good."

Austin was silent at my side, looking deep in thought, and I was scared I'd said something wrong. We'd both already had to suffer an entire two hours of Chaz Neely. That was enough to put anyone in a bad mood.

As we stepped outside, he stopped me with a hand on my arm.

"Sally," he said hesitantly, "there's...something I want to say...but I don't want to upset you."

So polite, I thought. "Okay, I'm listening." Whatever it was couldn't be that bad.

Taking a deep breath, he said, "I think I'm in love with you."

My breath left me in a whoosh.

"I know it's sudden," Austin said, taking my hand. "I know we only just met, but...I also know how I feel. I've never met a girl I could talk to so easily. Sally, I can just feel it. You're the one for me."

It took me a beat. My shock was so great I was surprised I hadn't swallowed my tongue.

"Austin," I said, trying to remain calm. The situation required delicacy.

"Yes, love?"

Oh, that was it. "Are you crazy?!"

"But—"

"No," I said, taking a step back. "You can't possibly be serious."

"But Sally, I love you!"

His face was so open, he looked so sure. Besides being totally freaked by his confession, I actually felt sorry for the guy. Austin Harris was clearly a wackadoo, but a wackadoo with a heart.

"No, Austin—" I shook my head and made my voice as gentle as possible. "—You don't. You hardly know me."

"I know how I feel," he said, tone resolute. "I love you, Sally Spitz, and that's all there is to it." He paused to meet my eyes. "Do you...feel anything for me?"

"Yes, friendship," I said. "I'd love to call you my friend, Austin, but that's as far as it goes. I'm sorry."

Watching the hope in his expression disappear was like a slap to the face.

"I get it," he said, scuffing the toe of his shoe against the pavement, looking anywhere but my face. "I really made an ass out of myself, didn't I?"

"No way," I said. "You're a nice guy, Austin. There's someone out there for you. It's just not me." I held out my hand. "So...friends?"

"Friends," he agreed, and we shook on it. "Are you ready to go?"

Remembering his safer than safe driving, I thought quickly. "You go on. I think I'm going to stop by Paula's for a slice. They stay open late whenever there's a midnight release."

"But how will you get home?"

"I'll catch a ride." I shooed him toward his car. "Go ahead, I'll be fine."

"Alright, if you're sure." Austin took my hand again and kissed the back. "It was nice meeting you, Sally."

"You too," I said surprised.

On my way next door to Paula's Pizzeria, I reviewed the events of the night. Chaz had been a complete bust, but Austin was okay. Why couldn't I just go for someone sweet like him? I mean, sure, he was a little nuts, telling me he loved me after only one date, but there were worse things. As I watched him still navigating oh so slowly through the near-empty parking lot, though, I knew it would've never worked.

I liked to drive fast, five miles over the speed limit at least, and Austin was a by the rules kind of guy. If I ever got behind the wheel, I was sure he'd have a coronary. And I wasn't sure I could date someone who preferred Justice League over Rogue and her crew. That right there was the definition of incompatibility.

Paula met me at the door. "Hey, Sally. Oooh that hair should come with a warning: Large and in charge and too hot to handle. You go girl, never knew you had it in you. What'll it be?"

"Water and a slice of pepperoni with pineapple, please." I smiled as she led me to my usual table. "Thanks, Paula."

"Sure thing, sweetie."

A few moments later, Becks came out with my water and plate, set them down and sat across from me. The first thing he said was "What's with the hair?"

"Just trying something different," I replied. "You like it?"

He shrugged. "It's cool. So how was the movie? Was it as mind-blowingly awesome as it looked in the trailer?"

Figures Becks would be the only one to write off my so-called sex hair.

"Don't know." I popped a piece of pepperoni into my mouth. "It was kind of hard to pay attention."

Becks smiled. "Well, this sounds interesting."

"Don't you have to get back to work?"

"Nope." He untied his apron and laid it in front of him on the table. "I'm officially off the clock. Spill it, Sal."

By the time I was through, Becks was laughing so hard he had tears in his eyes.

"Chaz Neely?" he said, breathless. "What was Lillian thinking? That guy is such a tool."

"Yeah, I know." In my re-telling, I'd left out the frigid bit. Partly because it was embarrassing and partly because I didn't think Becks would find it funny. At all. Standing, I asked, "Could you drop me off? I didn't want to go with Austin, thought it'd be kinda weird."

Still grinning, Becks stood as well. "Yeah, like the most awkward car ride ever. He really likes Justice League over the X?"

I shrugged.

"The guy is either seriously deluded or straight-up crazy," he said. "My vote's for crazy. He really told you he loved you? That's just ridiculous."

"Gosh, Becks," I said, masking my hurt with sarcasm, "I'm so happy I told you."

"Ah, Sal, you know what I meant."

"You really know how to make a girl feel special."

"Never had any complaints before."

I went to stalk past him, but slipped on a wet patch instead, wincing as my ankle rolled. With cat-like reflexes, Becks's arms shot out to catch me. If he hadn't been so close, I would've definitely faceplanted. Knocking out a few front teeth would've been a perfect end to this crapshoot of an evening.

"You okay?" Becks said.

"Yeah," I mumbled into his chest. His arms were locked around my waist, mine resting on his forearms. After such a trying night, his familiar scent, the comfort I found in his nearness almost undid me. I was so tired of surprises. If I had to meet one more blind date, I would literally go insane.

"Jeez, Sal," he laughed, resting his chin on my head. "If you wanted a hug, all you had to do was ask."

I slapped his shoulder. "Jerk."

"I'm just saying."

Despite my protests, I stood there, embracing him longer than necessary. It'd been a hard night, and I didn't even get a chance to really watch the movie. Lucky for me, Becks gave the best hugs on the planet. Even Austin's kiss, sweet as it was, had nothing on the feel of Becks's arms around me. It was exactly what I needed to clear my head.

These surprise dates had to end.

They just had to. Since demands and pleading hadn't worked, I'd have to try a different approach. What I needed was a plan, something failsafe, something to get both Mom and especially Hooker off my back. A sure way to end the matchmaking forever. The answer didn't come until much later, but when it did, the solution seemed so simple, so perfect.

Now all I had to do was find the perfect guy.

How hard could that be?

CHAPTER 4

"How's that article coming, Spitz?"

I mentally counted to ten.

"Hello," Priscilla said, rapping her knuckles twice on the table. "Earth to Spitz? It's October, mid-season for God's sake. I need an ETA on that sports article like yesterday."

Taking a deep breath, I gave up the counting. Numbers wouldn't numb the pain. Priscilla Updike's annoying voice was like listening to fingernails on a chalkboard, enough to make my ears bleed and set my teeth on edge.

Looking up, I forced a smile. "It's coming along, should be ready by Saturday."

"You just make sure it is." She fluffed her hair which was already over the limit on the fluffiness scale. Blonde, busty and a big fan of Mary Kay, Priscilla was the image that came to mind when most people pictured the Southern bombshell. "And don't skimp on the word count. Everyone knows they only read our newsletter to check the scores and see highlights. Make sure you include those this time instead of going off on one of your silly human interest slants."

The bossy attitude, though, was why I called her Pisszilla—only in my head, of course.

As Pisszilla moved on to her next victim, I looked down at the list I'd started at the beginning of the period. Journalism was the sole writing class Chariot High offered, and I usually paid extra-close attention. But since our evil editor was the only one talking, I didn't feel the need. She wouldn't even notice if I left the room. Now that she was busy biting someone else's head off (apparently each of the horoscopes last week had ended in gruesome death, a detail Pisszilla was none too happy about), I could turn my mind to more important matters.

It seemed so obvious. I didn't know why I hadn't thought of it before. Last night at 3:42 a.m., when I'd been half-asleep, half-delirious, I'd come up with the perfect solution to my matchmaking blues.

A fake boyfriend.

Hooker couldn't set me up if I was already set up, so to speak. All I needed was someone to play my boyfriend for a while, and I'd be golden. The key to success was finding the right guy.

On the sheet of paper I had stealthily tucked beneath the crook of my arm—in case someone decided to be a real jerk and snatch it—I'd outlined my criteria under the heading:

THE IDEAL F.B.F.

1) Must be able to keep a secret.

2) Must not be afraid of Hooker.

3) Must be MALE (no more misunderstandings)

4) Must be willing to work cheap and agree to a month's worth of service

5) Must be able to keep hands to themselves and separate F.B.F duties from reality

Numbers one, two, three and five were the most important, but four was nonnegotiable. The timeframe of a month would make it more believable, especially to Mom. Then when the guy called it quits, there'd be no question of me dating again. I'd be too heartbroken, too devastated at the loss of my so-called first love. The plan was so freaking perfect. I barely stopped myself from busting out the maniacal laughter as the bell rang. Hooker wasn't the only scheming mastermind in this school.

Now, if I could just find someone who met all the requirements, I wouldn't have to go on another blind date for the rest of my life.

The thought had me smiling so hard, my cheeks hurt.

"Spitz."

I turned and found Ash Stryker, soccer star and fellow news staffer, staring at me, frowning.

"Something wrong with your face?"

Trust Ash to ruin my good mood. Dropping the manic grin, I deadpanned, "No. Something wrong with yours?"

He shook his head, still looking at me like I was the strangest thing. "Listen, I wanted to give you a message. The team doesn't appreciate you focusing all your stories on one player. There are ten other guys out there besides your boyfriend. It wouldn't kill you to quote one of them sometime."

"Wait—" I couldn't believe this. "—you can't be saying what I think you're saying. Have you actually read any of my pieces?"

An eyebrow raise was all I got from number forty-three.

"Ash, you do know I was the one who gave you your nickname?" I'd christened him The Whip last year, describing his quick dribbling and the sound his foot made as it connected with the ball. That was when he'd been an up-and-coming sophomore. Now, as a junior, The Whip was a starter on varsity, not quite as good as Becks but definitely talented—and arrogant. "I mean, seriously, The Whip? People didn't just come up with that on their own."

"My mom was calling me that way before you ever wrote your little article."

And did I mention cocky as all get out? Sweeping blond hair, lean frame, easy smile. The guy had most girls falling at his feet—lucky for me, I wasn't most girls.

"Yeah, whatever," I said, walking past him and patting his shoulder. "Good talk."

"You're an odd one, Spitz."

"That's what they say." Stopping in the hall, I turned back around. "And by the way, Becks and I are just friends."

Ash grunted and slipped past me, the back of his shiny white and green jersey dissolving into the mass of students on their way to first period. Shrugging, I went to my locker.

I got about ten steps before some girl I didn't know grabbed me.

"You and Becks?" She laughed, looking me up and down. "Most hilarious thing I've heard all day."

"Huh?" I said, confused.

As she rejoined her giggling group of friends, another girl (Shelia, Shelly...something like that) came up to me as I reached my locker.

"Ignore her. She's just jealous." She rolled her eyes. "Personally, I knew it all along. Y'all are just the cutest couple I've ever seen in my life."

"Okay..."

Shelia/Shelly/something-or-other smiled conspiratorially. "He any good?"

"Who?" I asked.

"Well, duh," she laughed. "Your boy Becks."

Oh, I thought, soccer. Finally catching her drift, I said, "Oh yeah, he's phenomenal."

"I'll just bet he is." She winked. "Body and face like that, how could he not be, right?"

I didn't see what Becks's face had to do with him being good at sports; but I didn't want to embarrass her either, so I just nodded. "It should get him into a good college."

Her jaw dropped. "They give scholarships for that kind of thing?"

"Oh, yeah sure," I said. "Tons of them."

"Well," she muttered, turning away, "learn something new every day. Bye, Spitz."

"Bye." Well, that was weird, I thought, putting in my combination quickly. The warning bell had sounded sometime while Shelia/Shelly was talking, and I didn't want to be late. Opening my locker, I found a box of Goobers with a little note attached. It said: Sorry about last night. Hope you accept my peace offering, Hooker. And right below her name, there was a P.S. Heard something, *really* need to talk to you. The last part was scribbled, almost illegible, looking like it'd been hastily tacked onto the end.

Scooping up my books and the Goobers, I hurried into first and made it to my seat seconds before the final bell. Across the classroom Hooker tried to flag me down, but after a glare from Ms. Vega, she settled down. Her eyes were tense as she locked gazes with me from across the room.

I didn't know why she was taking this so seriously. Goobers were my favorite, but she had to know that I'd forgive her. Chaz Neely was not about to end our friendship. There was no reason for her to look so anxious.

I smiled at her, making a big show of hugging the candy to my chest, but her expression didn't change. The whole class she kept shooting me uneasy looks. And that was strange because Hooker never got anxious over anything.

She jumped out her seat when class was over and was next to me before I could shut my textbook.

"Tell me it's not true," she demanded. "Tell me this whole freaking school has gone bat-shit, taken too-many-happy-pills bananas because I'm about to have a heart attack over here."

"What are you talking about?" I said.

Hooker looked at me like I was the one acting crazy. "I'm talking about—"

"Sally, can I see you for a second."

It wasn't really a question. Ms. Vega's tone said she expected you to do what she asked, right then, to her complete satisfaction, no buts about it. My German teacher was an assertive, take-charge kind of woman and my favorite because of that. I was her best student; we'd become friends over the years.

Hooker looked pained, but she said, "We'll talk later. Don't avoid me," then left.

I rolled my eyes. Avoid her? What was up with everyone today?

Ms. Vega was sitting at her desk, head down, brandishing her red pen like a sword till the essays before her were bloodied and bruised. I sincerely hoped mine wasn't one of the fallen. Skimming the pile, I noticed my cover page sticking out near the bottom and heaved a huge sigh of relief.

"Yes, Ms. Vega?"

She took a final stab, crossing through a sentence three times, and looked up at me, eyes enlarged by coke bottle glasses, silver gray hair catching the light. "How are you, Sally?"

"Fine," I said, "And you?"

She sat back in her chair, rolled the red pen between her fingers. "I have been hearing some things."

With her unique accent, a mixture of Spanish, French and German roots—all three subjects she taught by the way—the "things" sounded more like "tings."

"Like what?" I asked, hoping it wasn't anything bad.

"You have yourself a new boyfriend."

Taken aback, it took me a second to reply. "Oh really? Who told you that?"

"I hear things." She shrugged, but her eyes were shrewd. "Many times I hear the new rumors, the gossip flying about. You are not usually the topic of such talk. Today was different."

I wasn't sure how to feel about that. On the one hand, people typically didn't bad mouth me behind my back. This was a good thing. On the other, they might've been recently. Not so thrilled about that.

Standing, Ms. Vega came around her desk and put a hand on my shoulder.

"You are a good girl, Sally. Never late to class, always do your homework, assignments turned in on time." She ushered me to the door as the first bell rang and class started filling up. "Just be sure this boy is worthy of you."

The conversation was peculiar on several levels, but I appreciated her comments even if I didn't actually have a boyfriend. It reminded me to start thinking about who could play my F.B.F.

"Thanks, Ms. Vega," I said. "But—"

"And you make sure this Becks person knows that you are his girlfriend and no one else." She pursed her lips as I stood there speechless. "Men seem to have trouble with this concept—just ask my first two husbands."

Turning away, Ms. Vega started mumbling to herself about the many odd names today, but I was still in shock. Did she just imply that Becks—*Becks* of all people—and I were going out? How ridiculous. Why would anybody believe such an obviously made-up story?

The shock lasted until about the time Hannah Thackeray, a fairly good friend of mine, nudged my shoulder. "Hey Spitz, glad you finally got your guy."

"What?" I said dumbly.

"You and Becks," she said, smiling. "I'm happy for you. It was inevitable, really."

Was everyone here delusional? "Hannah, that's absurd. Who told you that?"

"Absurd?" she repeated, her smile faltering. "But I saw the two of you...at Paula's last night."

"And?"

Hannah blushed. "Well, you guys looked pretty cozy. Becks was holding you like he might never see you again."

I remembered Becks hugging me, but Hannah's view was completely different from mine.

"He just caught me as I fell," I explained. "I slipped on some water, and he grabbed me so I wouldn't hurt myself."

She looked unconvinced. "It looked pretty serious to me."

"Well, it wasn't." At her frown, I immediately regretted my tone. "Hannah, I'm sorry. But really, what you saw was nothing more than Becks saving me from a busted lip. We've been best friends since grade school for goodness' sake. Becks would never even look at me that way, let alone ask me out."

"Whatever you say," she muttered and walked past me into the hall.

"You'll never be able to keep him, you know."

Quinn Howell, queen bee and Varsity cheer captain, was suddenly there, her long blonde hair tied together in a loose braid, her makeup perfection. Becks had told me they made out last Friday, but there wasn't any "chemistry." Sounded like she disagreed.

"He'll figure it out sooner or later," she said, a curl to her lips. "I mean, how could Becks go from me to someone like you? It just doesn't...make sense."

"I have no idea what you're talking about," I said.

Quinn shrugged her lean shoulders. "Just remember I called it first, Spitz. You and Becks? It'll never last."

"Okaaay," I said. That'd been the weirdest interaction yet. Quinn was your classic mean girl, but she wasn't stupid. She couldn't truly think Becks and I were together.

As she walked off, I caught other people—most everyone—looking at me, or whispering to someone else and *then* looking at me. A strange sensation, having that many eyes on you at once. It made me wonder if this was the way Becks felt every time he was on the field.

Becks, my boyfriend? Now that was a laugh.

Like anyone would ever believe that.

And yet—the thought struck me as Quinn and her crew kept shooting me the stank eye—people had believed. Bought the lie, told it to their friends and their friends' friends, repeated it so often that it had even managed to reach the ears of Ms. Vega.

The effect of one small, innocent hug was extraordinary.

And I'm not going to lie and say it took me a long time to come to a decision.

Nope. The light bulb hit about thirty seconds later when Becks called out, "Sal" and I saw Hooker striding toward me from the opposite direction, face pinched.

I didn't think. Acting on impulse, I grabbed Becks by the front of his jersey, dragged him to the storeroom not far away and pushed him inside, which earned us a few catcalls.

"Sal," he said again, laughing, but there was no time.

Hooker had stepped up the pace and was nearly upon us.

Without a thought, I threw myself in right after Becks and jerked the door shut behind me, heart pounding as I heard the final bell ring.

"Lillian, are you coming to class?"

The voice was Mr. Caroll's, the Political Science teacher, and I'd never been so happy to hear it in my life.

Hooker mumbled something back that I couldn't quite make out. Through the little window in the door, I saw them arguing, Hooker pointing toward our hiding place, Mr. Caroll's frown getting more and more pronounced. With one final glance, where Hooker and I actually locked eyes but only for a moment, she turned stiff-backed and walked to class.

I exhaled.

"So, you want to tell me why you're running away from Lillian, not to mention pushing me into old storerooms? What's the deal, Sal?"

"The deal," I said, placing my back against the door, "is I need a boyfriend. And everyone thinks you're it."

"Oh yeah, I heard that." Becks made his way to an overturned bucket and took a seat. "Don't worry, I told them it wasn't true."

"No!"

Becks gave me a look.

Taking a moment to order my thoughts, I placed my books on a nearby desk, making sure they were perfectly straight, grabbed the Goobers off the top for moral support, and then returned to my place by the door.

"What I meant was you don't have to do that. There's no need."

"Sal, they're saying we're together." He paused to make sure I was getting it. "Like *together* together."

"I know," I said.

"Correct me if I'm wrong, but didn't you just say you need a boyfriend? This isn't exactly going to help your cause."

"Actually, it'll help a lot."

He crossed his arms. "How?"

Ah, and wasn't that the question of the day. Popping open the Goobers, I poured a handful, chucked it into my mouth and chewed slowly. Becks met all my criteria, exceeded it. With this new rumor going around, it was almost like it was destiny. It had to be him, that's all there was to it.

Deep breath, I thought. Then I let the dice fly.

"Becks, I need you to be my fake boyfriend for a month."

His semi-hysterical laughter was not encouraging.

"I'm serious," I said. "I can't take another mystery date, and Hooker refuses to give up. Help me, Obi-Wan Kenobi. You're my only hope. This is the only way I can think of to stop the madness."

After he got himself somewhat under control, he said, "Yeah, okay. A fake boyfriend, great plan, Sal. I'm sure that'd solve all your problems."

"You don't get it." I slumped. "I can't take it anymore. I've reached the end. It's getting to the point where I can't go anywhere without being scared. Everywhere I go, she's trying to fix me up. Hooker's telling people I'm desperate." Shaking my head, I forced myself to rally. "These dates have to end, and they have to end now."

"Why don't you just find a real boyfriend?"

"Of course," I said sarcastically, "Why didn't I think of it before? Thanks to Hooker, I've got my choice of guys who either a) end the date when they realize I don't look anything like Hooker and am, as we've established, quite the dork or b) start decent but turn out to be I-love-you-even-if-I-don't-know-you crazy ala Austin. Come on, Becks, be serious. You've got to help me." Taking one last shot, not caring if he laughed in my face, I simply spoke the truth. "Becks, you're all I've got."

Instead of laughing, he frowned. "Sal, you could get a boyfriend if you wanted to. You're a great girl, the best. Who wouldn't want that?"

"Yeah," I said, "because there are so many guys willingly lined up to go out with a girl everyone calls Spitz."

Shaking his head, he said, "A fake boyfriend, huh?"

Hope ignited in my chest. "Yeah," I said, "a fake boyfriend."

"So, what would I have to do?"

I couldn't help but be incredulous at that.

"Do?" I repeated. "You'd do what you always do. Pretend I'm your latest girl Friday."

Becks's brow furrowed. "You want me to French and feel you up in the janitor's closet?"

Maybe, a treacherous part of my brain whispered, but I swallowed the impulse, afraid I'd scare him away. "No. We'd just have to play for the crowds, parents, friends, etc. In private, we'd be just like we've always been."

"Just friends?" he asked.

I nodded. Just friends.

"You said a month?"

"Yeah," I swallowed again. Man, even with Becks—*especially* with Becks—this was embarrassing. "At the end, we'll just tell them we decided to call it off because of irreconcilable differences. I'd pretend to be devastated. The dates would end; you'd be off the hook. No harm done. So—" I tried not to let my nerves show, hoped my voice wouldn't waver. "—what do you think?"

I held my breath the entire time Becks thought it over.

Finally, he said, "Okay, I'm in."

I blinked. "You're in?"

"Yeah, I'll do it."

"You will?"

Becks looked up at me and grinned. "Sure. You didn't think I'd say no, did you?"

"No," I said, but it came out more like a question.

He laughed. "Sal, I just want to help. You're my best friend. How could I possibly refuse?"

"So, that's it?"

"Well, yeah," he said, and I began to breathe a bit easier.

Good old Becks. A guy any girl would want in her corner. My entire body was floating on a cloud of relief. The best friend I could ever ask for...

"Now, about what I'm getting in return."

That put an end to all the light and fuzzy.

"I thought you said you just wanted to help," I said incredulously.

He shrugged. "You know what they say: You can't get something without giving a little something, Sal."

That wasn't quite what "they" say, but I got it.

Cutting him off before he could get going, I said, "Okay, Becks. You now have ten seconds to tell me your demands."

His jumped off his bucket in protest. "But, Sal, you can't—"

"Eight seconds," I said, looking at my watch.

"But—"

"Five, fo—"

"A month's worth of Calc homework and hand over the Goobers," he said in a rush.

I gaped at him, forgetting the counting altogether.

"But you're great at Calculus, nearly as good as me."

"So?" he said. "It was the first thing that popped into my head."

"Becks, it's unethical."

"Sal, I'll check over the work. I just want you to do it first."

"Why?" I asked, truly dumbfounded.

"Like I said," he repeated, "you've got to give a little. It's only fair."

"Okay," I said, picking up my books, turning to the door in a daze. I couldn't believe we'd skipped half of second period. I'd never played hooky a day in my life. Even more unbelievable I'd just gotten my first boyfriend for a month's worth of Calc and a box of Goobers. The whole thing seemed surreal. The fact that the boyfriend, real or fake, was Becks was just too impossible to take in.

"Hey, Sal."

When I turned back around, Becks was holding his hand out, palm up.

"Goobers?" he said.

Still reeling, I handed them over, watching as he emptied the entire box into his mouth in one go. I was seriously considering the possibility that this was a dream when I opened the door and saw Hooker scowling on the other side, bathroom pass dangling from one hand.

"Spitz, you cannot be serious," she said flatly. "This is *Becks* we're talking about."

And that's when I knew it was real.

CHAPTER 5

Could this situation be more awkward?

Answer: Yes.

Backing away from Hooker, I nailed Becks right in the chin. He groaned and stumbled, tripping over the bucket he'd been sitting on, taking out a few mops along the way. Luckily, Janitor Gibbens showed up, drawn by all the noise, and told us to get to class.

"This isn't over," Hooker had warned. But I'd dodged that bullet. At least for now.

Becks was waiting for me at the end of second period.

"What's up?" I asked as he walked over.

"Want me to carry your books?"

"Huh?"

Grabbing my binder and books, he grinned. "I'm your boyfriend now. Remember?"

"Oh." He said that so easily.

"Girls let their boyfriends carry their books," he said slowly as if I needed it explained.

"Sure," I said. "Okay, then. Have at it."

Hooker knew my schedule, but I knew hers, too, so I led him the long way to my class. The upside was we didn't run into Hooker. The bad part? We walked right into Eden Vice—or rather, she nearly knocked me over in her haste to get to Becks. Fingers gripping the front of his shirt, eyes wide, the girl was in a state.

"Becks, it can't be true," Eden said. "This is just some lame rumor, right? You're not really dating that Spitz girl."

"Her name is Sally," Becks said. I jolted as one of his hands landed on my waist, drawing me to his side. Crossing her arms, Eden pouted while I tried to ignore the warmth of that hand. "And yes, I am."

"But why? I don't get it."

"You don't have to."

"But *Becks*," she whined, "I don't understand. Why her?"

"Nothing to understand really," he said, smiling down at me. "Sal's my girl. Always has been."

As he squeezed my hip, I swear I stopped breathing. Eden was a dip, but she walked away at the clear dismissal. I was having trouble getting my lungs to work. And Becks was just standing there, smiling like all was right with the world, like this was all normal.

"Man, I tell you it's a lie. Becks wouldn't waste his time."

I was so close I actually felt Becks's body stiffen. Loud and obnoxious, the voice brought back bad memories of last night's wandering hands. I knew I should've punched Chaz Neely when I had the chance.

"Spitz is an ice princess," Chaz continued, speaking to the two guys at his locker. They were a little ways down the hall, backs to us, but their voices traveled.

"I don't know," Rick Smythe, goalie for CHS, spoke up. "They've been friends a long time."

"Yeah, friends with benefits," J.B. Biggs laughed. "There's got to be something in it for him."

"We went out last night," Chaz said. "Lamest date I ever had. She wouldn't even let me get to second base. Way I figure it, Spitz is a prude."

I blushed furiously as we walked up behind them. I couldn't believe Becks had heard that.

"Either that or she's not into guys."

"Maybe she just wasn't into you," Becks said.

"Who the hell—" Chaz's big mouth snapped shut as he came face to face with Becks's glare.

"You are such a sleazebag," I spat.

"What was that you said about my girlfriend?"

The way Becks so casually called me his girlfriend distracted me.

"Apologize," Becks said.

"What?" Chaz tried playing dumb. "Becks, you heard wrong, man. What I meant was—"

"Apologize," Becks repeated, stepping closer, "or I knock your teeth down your throat. Your choice."

"Sorry, Spitz," he said, still looking at Becks.

"Sally," Becks said lowly.

"Sally," Chaz squeaked. "Sorry, Sally. God, I'm sorry."

"Better." Becks nodded. I started when one of his hands gripped mine. "Sal's my girlfriend. You mess with her; you mess with me. Got that, Neely?"

There it was. That word again. As Chaz scurried away and the warning bell sounded, the hall cleared pretty fast. Everything that'd just happened hit me full force.

"How do you do that?" I asked after putting some space between us. It was impossible to think with him so close.

"Do what?"

"*That.*" Gesturing to his face, I laughed uneasily. "All that stuff about me being your girl, laying it on a little thick there, don't you think?"

"Sal," he said, "you are my girl."

I waited for him to explain, but he didn't. Instead he reached out to grab my hand again, and (of course) I jumped about a foot.

"So, what's up with the jumpy thing?"

"What jumpy thing?" He cocked a brow, and I flushed. "I don't know. Just not used to you touching me out of the blue, I guess."

"We'll have to work on that."

"How?" I asked miserably. If I was this awkward when Becks held my hand, what chance did we have at making people think we were dating?

"I'll have to think on it." When I lifted my head, Becks's eyes were lit up. "There are so many possibilities."

I didn't know what he meant, wasn't sure I wanted to. His face was full of mischief, and, for some reason, his earlier comment replayed in my head: *I'm a guy. I love women.* Ugh.

<hr />

Football was a religion down South, but in Chariot, North Carolina, soccer reigned supreme. Forget helmets and all that padding; our boys played sans cups, preferring the less restrictive, less protective jockstrap. Greater risk of injury, but they were unwilling to sacrifice range of motion. I'd always thought that a tad shortsighted, but when I'd asked Becks about it, he'd said, "Long as you know what you're doing, there's no need." When I'd given him a skeptical look, he'd tacked on, in his infinite wisdom, "Cups are for pansies," and that put an end to it.

Cups or not, Chariot High was known for its soccer. We'd taken the state title home the last two years running. College scouts attended nearly every game; the cheerleaders cheered; parents, teachers, students, everyone showed up to watch the Trojans decimate their opponents.

But they were really there to see Becks.

Only one Trojan consistently made headlines. Only one held the school's official records for most goals in a season, most minutes played, most penalty kicks taken and scored. And only one had already been offered scholarships to the top ten collegiate soccer programs in the nation.

Everyone called Becks "The Second Coming," obviously a reference to his British predecessor, David Beckham, one of the greatest names in soccer history. But Becks never bought into the hype. He knew he was brilliant on the field, was confident enough not to compare himself to anyone else, and outspoken enough to tell others not to—but they continued to do it anyway.

Becks was actually the reason I'd gotten the sports beat in the first place. He refused to talk to anyone, wouldn't give quotes to any of the local papers or media, until he'd talked to me first. As much as I adored him for it, I knew I wasn't exactly qualified for the position. After four years, I still carried my soccer-slang cheat sheet tucked in the front pocket of my jeans just in case.

"Am I seriously supposed to believe this?"

I sighed. Here we go again.

"Believe it or not, it's true," I said, studiously watching the players sprint across the field, making a real effort *not* to look at her.

"So, what?" Hooker said. "You're telling me you just woke up this morning and realized you're into Becks, a guy you've been friends with since second grade? A guy who coincidentally realized he's into you at the exact same time? A guy you and I personally saw eat a worm at Tobey Steinman's thirteenth birthday party?"

Not one of Becks's finer moments.

"I know it's hard to believe, but yes."

Catching my eyes, she narrowed her own. "Or is this recent development not so recent? Have you been holding out on me, harboring a secret crush on him all these years, afraid to speak your true feelings for fear of rejection?"

I swallowed just as the crowd groaned. The other team had scored, but we were still up by one. Looking away from Hooker, I made a big show of straightening the plaid blanket thrown across our legs. The night breeze was chill, but it did nothing to cool the blood rushing to my face.

"What's the big deal?" I muttered. "Becks and I are going out. He's my boyfriend now. It's not that complicated."

Hooker stared at me a moment then sat back and crossed her arms.

"Say it as many times as you want, Spitz. I'm not buying it."

Stubborn, I thought, and entirely too perceptive.

From the beginning, she saw right through me and The Plan. I didn't know how, but she knew Becks and I weren't really together. Hooker wasn't like everyone else, swayed by a few lousy rumors. She was too smart for that—and she knew me too well. As much as I'd tried to lie and lie well, ever since that scene in the storeroom, she'd stubbornly refused to buy into the boyfriend ruse.

"Hey, Zane."

I sighed. Here we go again.

"Uh, that's not my name," said a deep, heavily accented voice.

"Great," Hooker said and as I opened my eyes I watched her reel Not-Zane in. It always started like this. "So, what is it then?"

"Julian."

And he'd passed test number one. Hooker hated guys named Zane, Blaine or Buddy on principle. She shot him a mega-watt smile. "Do you have a girlfriend, Julian?"

He shook his head. Test two, I thought. If he didn't have a girl, to Hooker, that meant he was fair game.

"Excellent, I'm Lillian, and this is my friend Sally," she said, patting the seat between us, which he fell into with a dopey grin. "Sally was just telling me how hot she thinks you are."

"Hooker," I hissed, but she shrugged.

"Sally's always been into foreign men."

Julian didn't glance my way. "And what do you like, Lillian?"

She waved him off. "Me? Who cares what I like? As I was saying, my girl Sally, here, is fluent in a second language. I bet you speak Spanish, don't you, Julian?"

"If you asked—" He raised her hand to his lips, placed a kiss on her knuckles. "—I would speak Spanish to you every night, *mi amor.*"

Hooker glanced over his shoulder wide-eyed, and I shook my head. What did she expect? It always went down this way: 1) Hooker hooks boy. 2) She tries to push boy my way. 3) Boy, already completely smitten with Hooker, doesn't even notice I exist.

"You don't go to Chariot, do you?" Hooker laughed, pulling her hand away.

"I graduated from Southside last year with honors."

Hooker hummed in approval. "I prefer my men dumb. The dumber the better I always say. But Sally's the Salutatorian of our senior class."

"Really?" For the first time, Julian's gaze shifted to me.

"She has a thing for smart guys."

I shot her a scowl. The girl really was impossible.

"I have a thing for smart girls as well," Julian said, assessing me with his deep brown eyes. Yeah, okay, so the guy was hot. His accent made him even hotter, but Hooker was the one who loved foreign men not me. "*Muy caliente.*"

"Okay," I squeaked, jumping to my feet as Julian pressed his thigh to mine. Sheesh. "I'm going to talk to Becks...my boyfriend."

"Boyfriend?" Julian repeated, but by that point I was already half-way down the bleachers. I had to give it to her. Hooker was talented. I hadn't said a word, and yet she'd convinced Julian he was interested. My bestie was a little scary at times.

What was the use, I wondered now, in having an F.B.F. if Hooker didn't believe me? I looked back over my shoulder. Her mulish expression, the determined look in her eyes was unmistakable. Julian was still there, trying to chat her up, but she wasn't paying attention. I could almost see her flipping through a catalogue of her rejects in her mind, comparing my likes and dislikes with theirs, almost like some jacked-up version of eHarmony. It was unacceptable. I'd have to find some way to convince her, but so far things weren't looking good.

At half-time, I made my way to the sidelines, hoping Becks would have some ideas.

He was busy talking with Rick Smythe and Coach Crenshaw by the time I got there, so I stood off to the side to wait.

"Sally Spitz is that you? Damn, girl, you've grown up. I'm telling you if I was a few years younger..."

"You'd what?" I said, turning to find Clayton Kent, assistant soccer coach and Becks's older brother, eyes twinkling.

"I'd tell you how torn up I was to hear my brother got to you first." He feigned hurt, but the twinkle remained. "How could you, Sally? In a couple years when I'm an old man of twenty-eight, you'd still be a pretty young thing, and we'd be perfect for each other. I was counting on you to keep me spry."

I tried not to smile but failed. "You look plenty spry to me, old-timer."

"Why thank you, Miss Spitz." Walking toward me, Clayton had all the self-assurance of his younger brother plus a healthy dose of Southern charm that hadn't deserted him, even after he'd come back with a Sport Management degree from U Mass. He was my favorite of Becks's siblings, mainly because when I was a kid he always used to buy me scratch-offs and let me drive his jeep around the cul-de-sac when no one was looking. "So, what's the story?"

I looked up as he stopped at my side. "What do you mean?"

"You and Becks," he laughed, meeting my eyes. "After all this time, you two just up and got it together? You didn't actually think I'd believe that."

"Why not?" I said defensively. That was one too many non-believers for me to stomach. "Why is that so hard to believe? Am I not good enough or something?"

"Now hang on there a minute," he said, pulling me into a one-armed hug. "That's not it, and you know it. If anyone's too good, it's you, Sally. Becks and you, you and Becks? It's just a little sudden that's all."

Jeez, now he sounded just like Hooker.

Becks sauntered over and propped his hands on his hips.

With a nod to the arm across my shoulders, he said, "Putting the moves on my girlfriend already? Moving a little fast there aren't you brother?"

I wanted to laugh but caught myself. "Jealous" Becks was immensely entertaining.

Clayton stepped back, hands held high like he'd committed a crime. "Sorry, Becks, didn't think you'd mind."

"Well, I do." Becks smiled, sidling up next to me. "Sal wouldn't go for you anyway."

"Why not?" Clayton said dryly. "I'm older, wiser."

"Yeah, this close to geriatric."

"Plus, I'm like ten times hotter than you, Baldwin Eugene."

I could've argued that, but it was way more fun listening to them banter.

"Clayton," Becks sighed. "If I thought you were serious, we might have a problem. I'd have to go all Hulk on your ass, and then what? I'd be green, left in nothing but a pair of shredded soccer shorts, and Sal would freak."

Clayton faked a yawn.

"And anyway," Becks pointed out, "you treat her like a kid sister."

"Yeah, but that was before she got to looking so fine."

I laughed as Clayton waggled his eyebrows at me, but Becks frowned.

"Say that again, and I'll kick your ass."

"Alright, alright, I get it. See you two love birds later." Chuckling, he threw a few parting words over his shoulder. "And if Mom had seen that look you just gave me, she'd skin your hide, Becks. Possessive people never prosper. Don't let him boss you around, Sally."

Becks waited until Clayton was out of earshot and then turned to me.

"How was that?" he asked, his face full of mischief.

Honestly, besides being momentarily speechless, I was amazed. He'd really sounded jealous, especially near the end there.

"Great," I said, glancing at the bleachers. Hooker was staring down at us like a hawk, slumped back in the same spot where I'd left her. Meeting my eyes, she lifted a brow in challenge. That small movement said it all. "But I'm not sure it was enough."

"What?"

"Becks, we seem to have a problem." Seeing his confusion, I explained, "Hooker doesn't believe you and me are actually a couple. She's not buying it, and neither was Clayton until about five seconds ago. I'm still not sure he's fully converted."

"So, what should we do?"

"I don't know," I said at a loss. "It's not like I really thought this through beforehand. The situation just sort of dropped into my lap, perfectly packaged with a little bow on top." Becks's lips pulled into a half-smile, and I rolled my eyes. "Oh, you know what I mean. Most everyone who heard that rumor accepted the fact that we're together, end of story. Hannah Thackeray even said it was inevitable. But it's the people who've known us forever that are questioning it, and those are exactly the ones we've got to win over—"

"Sal..."

"—It can't be that hard. I just need to think of a way—"

"Sal," Becks said more forcefully, stopping me midrant. "Just leave it to me."

I frowned. "But Becks, we need to talk about—"

"No more talk," he said, leaning closer. "Lillian still watching?"

With a gulp, I peered around him. "Yes."

"Good."

My heart beat triple-time as Becks leaned even closer, eyes on mine. I started slightly at the feel of his hand on my jaw, struggling for breath as it slid to my cheek, fingers finally coming to rest at the base of my neck. Ducking, he placed a lingering kiss on the spot right below my ear. The move made my hand shoot out to grip his jersey. Becks laughed silently, little puffs of air hitting my neck, as I shivered.

I could hear the grin in his voice as he said, "You know, Sal, you can't jump every time I touch you. What will people think?"

It took me two tries, but I eventually managed a breathless, "S-sorry."

"Practice at my house tomorrow. Ten sharp," he said as the whistle blew.

"Practice?" I said still dazed. "What—"

"*Becks*," Crenshaw bellowed from the other side of the bench, "stop making eyes at your girlfriend, and get your butt back in the game."

"Ten," Becks said again, running backwards. "Don't be late."

I tried to snap out of it, giving my head a shake. All that did was muddle my thoughts even further. When I looked up at Hooker, she gave an exaggerated yawn, like the kiss had been nothing at all. Unimpressive, her eyes said, and when I got back to my seat, her words echoed the sentiment.

"It's going to take a lot more than some dry peck to convince me," she grumbled.

I gaped at her. Dry peck? What was she talking about? Granted, I wasn't an expert—that kiss had been the extent of my romantic experience—but it'd turned my insides to mush. My skin still felt unnaturally hot where Becks's mouth had been. I couldn't forget the feel of his breath against my skin. Hooker was a lot more experienced than me, but that didn't mean she was blind. Couldn't she see how affected I was?

Glancing over at me, she shrugged. "Okay, okay. It was kind of hot, but Spitz, how *can* it be with Becks? You guys have been friends forever. It's almost like if me and you started going out."

"Hooker, no offense or anything," I said, "but you're not my type."

"None taken," she said back. "But really, you know everything about him. He knows everything about you. There's no mystery."

I flushed. "He doesn't know everything about me."

"Oh yeah? Name one thing he doesn't know about you?"

The same thing you don't, I thought but kept my mouth firmly shut.

"Exactly," she said like she'd proven her point, and we sat back to watch the second half.

I tried to take good notes, recorded the plays as best I could, cross-referencing my list of terms, but it was useless. The butterflies in my stomach were relentless. No matter how much I tried to squash them, the darn things just wouldn't die. Instead of watching the game, I kept replaying the kiss over and over. My hand would wander to the spot under my ear when I wasn't looking, and I'd have to jerk it away before Hooker saw what a loser I was. The Trojans ended up winning five to two, with Becks scoring three out of the five goals and assisting Ash Stryker with the last goal, an at the buzzer header. I didn't even need my cheat sheet for that one.

As the team headed for the lockers, I followed, trying not to feel awkward.

Becks and I had never been weird around each other before. Not even after I'd told him about my secret life-long crush on Lucius Malfoy from the *Harry Potter* series. That hair, the voice, that whole uptight baddie/aristocrat thing... It was embarrassing, but the guy was just yum. This couldn't be any bigger than that, could it?

Yeah, right, I thought, hanging back. This was so much bigger than my Lucius confession. This wasn't some fantasy; it was real life. The butterflies running amok in my insides could attest to that fact.

"You catch that last one, Spitz, or were you too busy staring at Mr. Wonderful?"

Grateful for the distraction, I pulled out my inner Southern Belle. "Well, goodness gracious sakes alive. Is *the* Ash Stryker, aka The Whip, speaking to little ol' me?"

"Funny," Ash said. "So did you see it or what?"

"Yeah, I saw. I always knew you had a hard head, Ash. Thanks for the proof."

He scoffed.

We were getting closer and closer to Becks, so I decided to quit teasing. "Can I get a comment? That was a pretty sweet play."

He came to a sudden stop. "*Pretty* sweet?"

"Alright," I said, turning back around, "it was awesome, tremendous, truly masterful. That better?"

"Much." Ash's lips curved up in an almost smile. "Here's a comment for you, Spitz. Becks needs to keep his head in the game. That's the only way we're going to win state again this year. Everyone's gunning for us."

"My head's always in the game, Stryker."

I jumped at the sound of Becks's voice then felt like an idiot.

"Didn't look that way at half-time," Ash said.

"Whatever, man." Becks came up beside me. "Why don't you hit the showers? Sal and I need to talk."

Ash shrugged then walked off.

"I really don't like that guy," Becks said, staring after him.

"He's okay," I said. Becks looked at me like I'd gone mental, which brought back the fluttering. Great, now I couldn't even look him in the eye. I cleared my throat. "What's this about Saturday? I can't come at ten. You know I've got to work until noon."

"Oh," Becks said, leaning back, "Make it one then. I thought we could work on a few things. I mean, if we want people to take the boyfriend thing seriously, we need to make it as authentic as possible, right?"

"What things?"

He smiled at my nervousness. "You'll see."

His cryptic reply annoyed me enough to kill a few of the chest insects dead, but the smile brought them back to life full force. By the time I got them under control and met Hooker at the car, she was looking pretty ticked.

"It took you that long to get a couple of lame quotes?" was the first thing she said as we got in the car.

"I was talking to Becks," I retorted.

"Becks," she repeated as if she'd never heard the name. "Becks, your boyfriend?"

I gritted my teeth. Her absolute refusal to believe my perfectly good lie was starting to get to me. "That's the one."

"You know what Spitz, there's this guy named Alex. He's a tattoo artist. I think you guys'd really hit it off."

"Thanks, but I'm good."

"Or if you're into athletes, there's John Poole. He goes to school with Will, pitcher for the Tarheels. Great guy, real smart. I could introduce—"

"Hooker," I interrupted, "I appreciate the offer, but I have a boyfriend. Becks is pretty laid back, but I'm not sure he'd be too happy about me dating other guys."

Hooker sniffed and reached between us to turn on the radio.

Whatever Becks had planned had better be good, I thought. It was clear Hooker wasn't going to hang up her matchmaking gloves without a fight. When we pulled up in front of her house, she shifted to face me instead of getting out immediately.

I killed the engine. Going by her thoughtful expression, we were going to be here for a bit.

"But it's just so weird," she said finally.

"What is?" I asked.

"You and Becks."

"And why is that weird? We hang out all the time. We've been friends forever. There's no one I trust more, except maybe you and Mom."

"That's my point." She grimaced. "It's almost incestuous, like he's your brother or something."

I snorted. "Becks is *so* not my brother."

"Yeah, but he acts like he is." Hooker's tone turned philosophical. "This is what comes from watching too many episodes of *Star Trek*. It's just not healthy. Next thing you know you'll be wearing doughnuts over your ears and calling yourself Princess Spitz."

"Firstly," I said, "that's *Star Wars*, not *Star Trek*." Hooker wasn't a big fan of The Force. "And secondly, Leia and Luke were never romantically involved. It's a common misconception. Skywalker wasn't her guy. For Leia, it was always Han Solo, nobody else."

She shook her head, lip curled in faint disgust. "You watch way too many movies, you know that?"

"And you don't watch enough to make that kind of comparison," I countered.

"Alright," she said, "I'll concede that. But…Becks? Really?"

I nodded.

"Not in an 'I like him' kind of way…in the 'I love him' way?" She was studying my face a little too close-ly, and I began to sweat. "That's what you're saying, isn't it Spitz? You're in love with the guy? Becks is your Han Solo?"

My throat closed up tight, holding back the words, but I knew this might be the only thing that would make Hooker believe.

"Yeah," I said, voice hoarse, looking her dead in the eye. "He is."

A moment went by in which Hooker continued to stare, presumably weighing my words, and I continued to sweat. Then, out of nowhere, she laughed.

"God, Spitz," she said. "You are such a liar." Getting out of the car, she waved goodbye. "I'll call you later."

I waved back, nearly overwhelmed by the relief. Of course, I wanted Hooker to believe my little lies. Stopping the epidemic of blind dates was the point of this plan and fooling her was integral to its success. But when I'd concocted the F.B.F. idea, I hadn't been thinking clearly. Everything had happened so fast, that I hadn't had a moment to consider the catch, the huge snag I'd missed when I'd so carelessly asked Becks to be my F.B.F. It hadn't even crossed my mind that I'd be revealing any of my secrets.

Hooker had called me a liar, and I'd told enough lies in the past few hours that it was basically true. Funny thing was I hadn't been lying at the time. It was my deepest, most well-kept, I-would-just-die-if-this-ever-got-out secret. One I hadn't revealed to a single soul.

Becks was totally my Han Solo.

Even if he didn't know it.

I'd been in love with him since we were kids, and I was only now realizing all the ways that the plan could backfire. I could only hope Mom would be an easier sell.

CHAPTER 6

She cleared her throat then fired off her first bomb.

Casually—too casually—she said, "How?"

"What do you mean?" I mumbled, though I thought I knew.

"Did he ask you or did you ask him? Where did it happen? Does Lillian know? What does she think?"

So much for an easy sell.

Pouring the milk slowly, careful not to spill a drop, I walked over, replaced the carton, and lowered myself into the seat across from The Interrogator. She was wearing one of the bridal tiaras she'd brought home, a white veil attached to the back. Her fingers were beating a lazy rhythm on the wooden table top, but the beady eyes remained.

"I asked him, Mom," I said, reaching across to grab an apple, saying the words like they were the easiest thing in the world. "In the storeroom, after first period."

"Did you?" Mom raised an eyebrow, drumming a constant five-count, pinky to thumb, pinky to thumb.

The sound was unnerving.

"Yes." I downed a big gulp of milk, quickly wiping away the excess on my top lip. "And yes, Hooker knows...but she doesn't believe me."

"Why not?" she asked.

"I don't know," I said, thinking back. "She says it's weird, that Becks and I know each other too well and there's no mystery." I laughed. "She actually said we're like siblings. What I really think is she can't believe Becks would go out with someone like me. I mean, he's my best friend, but he's still Becks."

The finger tapping stopped abruptly. "That's ridiculous."

I shrugged. In this at least, I was on sure footing. "That's what I said. Seriously, Mom, me and Becks related? He's too freaking pretty for that." Though as I said it, I noticed how beautiful my mom looked now, even as she frowned. I guessed good looks sometimes skip a generation.

"That's not what I meant at all." Her eyes were slits, never a good sign. Before I could figure it out, she went on. "And when was this?"

"Yesterday."

The seconds ticked by, each marked by her once again drumming fingers and the erratic beat of my heart. I'd just told her about me and Becks, and this was her response: a question-and-answer session sure to trip me up if I wasn't on my guard. Luckily, after Hooker, I'd been expecting it.

After a time, she sighed. "Why didn't you just tell me?" I looked up, shocked to see the sheen of tears in her eyes. "I would've been fine with you dating Becks so long as he treats you well—which I have no doubt he does. 'Yesterday'? You actually thought I'd buy that?"

I was floored. Was she actually saying...

"You don't have to lie," she continued. "This has obviously been going on for some time. But you didn't have to keep it a secret, Sally. I would've understood."

I couldn't believe it. Her quick acceptance was so unlike Hooker's flat-out refusal I had a hard time forming a reply.

"Sorry," I said after a beat. "I wasn't sure how you'd take it."

"Oh God," she said suddenly, raising a hand to her lips, "I feel so stupid now about helping Lillian with all those blind dates."

This was going much better than I'd expected. "Ah, don't feel *too* bad, Mom."

She sniffled. "I just can't believe you never told me. I mean, I've always thought of myself as a cool mom. You know, a friend as well as a parent, hip to the ways of the young crowd."

I leaned over to place a hand on her shoulder. "You are, by far, the hippest mom I've ever met," I said, looking her in the eye.

"Yeah, right."

"Mom, it's true."

"You're just saying that to make me feel better, but I love you for it." She took my hand in hers, a smile playing on her lips. "So, why didn't you just wait for Becks to ask you? Was he really dragging his feet that much?"

I shook my head at the idea. Becks ask me out? That was a laugh. "Becks would've never asked me first."

She looked confused. "Why not?"

Because, I answered mentally, even if Becks was the one who'd needed a fake girlfriend, he wouldn't have had to ask me. Girls would line up for a chance at him, fake or no. There were just too many other options, and besides, I was completely off his radar.

What I said was "Because he just wouldn't." Shrugging, I stood up, stretched and went to get my wand and cloak off the counter. "The kids will be arriving in about twenty minutes. I should get going."

"Why not, Sally?" Mom stepped in front of me, arms crossed, tiara sparkling, and I realized I had made a mistake.

Trying to laugh it off, with a flourish, I swirled the cloak around my shoulders and said, "Well because for all his strengths, Becks has never appreciated my flair for the dramatic." The pinky to thumb thing started again, soundless this time because it was on her arm. Dropping the act, I decided to get real. "Come on, Mom. You're not seriously asking me this. With every other girl vying for his attention, why the heck would he notice a bookworm like me?"

And then I stopped, suddenly realizing I was wrong. Becks *had* noticed me. Out of everyone else, he'd picked me, Sally Spitz, as his best friend. For once, I was happy to be wrong.

"Sally, you're gorgeous," Mom said, arms falling to her sides.

"Yeah, o-kay," I said, moving around her. A bit of sarcasm leaked through despite my best efforts. When I got to the door, she stopped me again, planting herself in front so I couldn't leave. "Mom, I really need to go. They can't start without me."

"Okay, okay." Lowering her chin, she narrowed her eyes. "But I'm serious, Sally Sue Spitz. You are my child, my baby, and nobody calls my baby ugly. Nobody. Not even you."

I couldn't help but roll my eyes. "Now Mom, gorgeous is a bit of stretch don't you think?"

"*Gorgeous*," she repeated firmly, slipping the top button of my cloak into place. "Now, go on before you're late. Those kids are probably tearing the place apart. When will you be home?"

"Not sure," I said and then added the cherry on top. "I'm going over to Becks's house after."

A light lit in her eyes. "Oh, okay. Good. Have fun."

Turning, I smiled to myself, knowing she was totally sold. One down, I thought, one to go. Look out, Hooker, I'm coming for you next.

"Oh, and Sally?"

As I got to my car, I looked back.

"Not *too* much fun, alright? Becks is a good boy, but...he *is* a boy. Tell him I said to keep it in his pants, okay? No babies for my baby, get me?"

I couldn't get away fast enough.

"Love you," she called as I drove off. "Say hi to Becks for me."

Through the embarrassment, I felt a sweet buzz of triumph steal up my spine. The F.B.F. train was rolling now. There were really only two train seats that needed filling, and Hooker's butt was about to be planted into one of those seats—whether she liked it or not.

It might've sounded strange, but my job always put me in a good mood. I know, I know, teenagers are supposed to be all "I hate my job. The pay sucks, the hours suck, the customers suck, my boss is out to get me." But none of those things applied to me. I must've gotten lucky because my job at the library was completely kick-ass.

Reading to the kids, seeing their faces rapt with attention, eager to hear what happens next, hearing them laugh out loud or gasp in surprise, it actually made minimum wage sound good. Seriously, I should've been paying them. The kids were so much fun—cooler than a lot of my so-called peers—and even if it was just on weekends, I loved sharing my favorite childhood books with them. Plus, sometimes they made me presents.

Like today, I'd received my very own pirate hat, completely blinged out with fake rhinestones and pink skull and crossbones. The thing barely fit on my head, but that was probably because of the braids. The gift and the Pippi Longstocking-esque hairdo were compliments of Gwendolyn Glick, one of my favorites. She wore red glasses two sizes too big for her face, spoke with a slight lisp and always had on the same t-shirt at story time, a faded black number featuring the Starship Enterprise and the saying "I Trek. Do you?"

What can I say? The kid and I were kindred spirits.

Even if I felt like an idiot, I jammed the hat on my head and wore it throughout the day along with my long black cloak. Those kids loved that cloak; the ones who knew the series said it reminded them of the professors at Hogwarts. I must've looked pretty silly—a cross between Severus Snape and Jack Sparrow—but Gwen's happy expression made it all worth it.

It was only after I'd knocked on Becks's door that I wished I'd remembered to take it off.

Clayton answered and nearly had a conniption. He was hooting and carrying on and looked like he was this close to passing out from lack of oxygen.

"Oooh," he said, gasping, face redder than his shirt.

He had the top three buttons undone, and the sight made me blush. Apparently Becks wasn't the only fit one in the family.

"Oh Sally—" He wiped tears of laughter from his eyes. "—girl, you keep coming 'round dressed like that one of these days I'm going to die laughing."

"Why wait?" I asked sweetly.

Becks came into view at that moment, his mouth spreading into a wide grin as he looked me over.

I shot him a warning glare, but that didn't stop him from saying, "Hey, Sal. That a new hat?" which, of course, set Clayton off again.

"Funny," I told him, tossing him *his* present. "Here, Gwen made you one, too."

"Well, that was sweet of her," he said, propping the thing on his head. "But why?"

I frowned, noticing how the pirate headgear didn't look half as ridiculous on Becks as I was sure it did on me. Dang it, he actually looked kind of cute. I couldn't help thinking that in that hat, with his perfect five o-clock shadow, Becks'd give Johnny Depp a run for his money.

"I think she's got a crush on you."

"Smart girl," he said, lifting the hat off easily. "Why don't we go to my room?"

"O-okay." The word came out unsteady. Considering I'd been to Becks's bedroom a ton of times, spent almost as much time there as I did in my own over the years, I shouldn't have been nervous. But as Clayton sauntered off making kissy noises and Becks placed his hand on my lower back, I was jumpier than a jackrabbit on speed. My heart was a wild thing in my chest. It was beating so fiercely and so fast that by the time we reached the top of the stairs I felt like I'd run a marathon.

As I entered Becks's room and heard the door click shut behind us, I took a deep breath before turning to face him.

"So," I said, backing up, removing the hat and cloak, voice higher than usual. Realizing I had nothing left to say, like an idiot, I repeated myself. "So..."

Becks shook his head. "Alright Sal, what's up?"

"What do you mean?" I asked, trying to play it cool.

"Exactly what I said." He crossed his arms. "What's with you? And don't try to say it's nothing. Since yesterday, you look like you're about to have a heart attack every time I lay a hand on you."

"I do not."

"Yes, Sal. You do."

My heart, so alive before, seemed to freeze in my chest.

"Sal, I'm not..." He flushed. Becks, unflappable, always self-assured Becks, actually flushed, while I stared in awe. "I wouldn't ever try anything on you. You know that, right?"

That's too bad, I thought, and even my mental voice sounded disappointed. "That's not it."

"Then, what is it?"

I stayed silent. If this conversation was going where I thought it was going, I was in big trouble.

"I know something's up," he said, locking eyes with me, "and I think I know what that something is."

I gulped. "You do?"

He couldn't know—could he?

"Yeah," he said, "But I really just wish you'd tell me. I won't be mad, you know."

I was glad to hear it, but Becks being mad at me for loving him wasn't necessarily my biggest fear. I was more afraid he'd laugh or hate me for ruining our friendship. I wasn't sure I could survive losing Becks as a friend. In fact, I was pretty sure I couldn't.

"We'll still be friends and everything." It was like he'd read my mind. Oh God, he didn't really know, did he? "Come on, Sal. Just tell me the truth about this whole fake boyfriend thing."

"The truth," I choked.

His next words confirmed, unquestionably, that we were *not* talking about the same thing.

"Just tell me who he is," Becks insisted.

"Who who is?" I asked, perplexed.

Becks was starting to look annoyed. "The guy."

"What guy?"

"Jeez, Sal." He ran a hand roughly through his hair. "The guy who you're crushing on so bad you had to hire a fake boyfriend to make him jealous."

I was shocked to say the least. Here I was thinking Becks had finally figured it out, figured *me* out, when he was really just as clueless as he'd ever been. That was a close one. After all that worry, my secret, my heart, was safe for now. Thank heaven for small favors.

Playing along, I said, "Well, why do you want to know?"

"I knew it," he exclaimed, pointing a finger at me. "I knew it. This was never just about the Lillian's setups. You're doing this for some guy you've got the hots for."

"You got me." I shrugged. Having him believe this lie was far better than telling him the life-altering, possibly friendship-wrecking truth. "How'd you figure it out?"

"Netflix," Becks replied. "So who is he?"

"Why should I tell you?"

The look he gave me was half-scathing, half-impressed. "I think I deserve to know, seeing as how you're using me. Is that all I am to you, Sal, arm candy?"

"Oh no." I was the one to cross my arms this time. I knew him too well to believe he was actually offended. "Don't pretend, Becks. Don't act like you're not totally loving this."

A slow grin started to form. "Well, I'm definitely not hating it."

I shook my head. "That is so wrong."

Becks rolled his eyes. "So, who is this guy anyway?" He took a seat in his desk chair and gestured for me to do the same. "He must be something for you to go to all this trouble."

Setting my hat and cloak on the floor, lowering myself slowly to the bed, straight-backed on the very edge, I forced myself not to look away. "He is," I said.

Becks made a weird noise in the back of his throat. "You could at least tell me the jerk's name."

"No."

"Aw, come on."

"No, Becks."

"Why not?"

Because you are *that jerk*, I thought, but just shook my head.

Becks furrowed his brow, deep in thought. Finally, he said, "Then can you just tell me about him? Is he athletic?"

Without meaning to, I took a glance at all the soccer trophies lining Becks's shelves. "Yes," I replied. "Very."

Becks nodded. "So, a jock, then. Must be pretty stupid, huh?"

Thinking of all the times he'd made honor roll, I shook my head. "He's actually really smart. Sounds like a great package, doesn't it?"

He made that noise again then said, "He's hideous, isn't he? Has a face only a mother could love, a mug that makes little kids cry on sight. Wonky ears, jacked-up teeth, a unibrow."

Picturing Becks with a unibrow, I laughed out loud, relaxed for the first time since I'd entered his room. "No way, he's totally beautiful."

"Beautiful?" Becks repeated dubiously. "Wait, is this guy one of those metro-sexuals or something? It's not that Beau LaFontaine from Physics is it? Ah, Sal, I thought you had better taste than that."

Still smiling, I let myself recline back a little on the bed. This was sort of fun. "No, that's not really my type. Besides, I don't think Beau's all that into sports."

Becks seemed to sag in relief.

"Why so interested?"

He suddenly righted himself, grinning, back to the confident Becks I'd always known. "No reason," he said. "Just wanted to know what we're dealing with. So, you ready to start lesson one?"

"Lesson?"

"Yeah, Sal." The twinkle in his eyes made me feel nervous and excited, scared and hopeful all at once.

"Like I said before, if we're going to make this believable, you're going to have to get used to us having more physical contact."

Physical contact? That sounded ominous.

He laughed. "Wouldn't want any future girlfriends getting the wrong impression, right? Your skittish reactions might put a damper on my rep. We need to practice here before we take it public"

"Go on," I said slowly.

Standing, he walked over and took a seat next to me on the bed. Angling his body toward mine, he said, "I thought we'd start easy, just a little touch exercise, since you seem so edgy."

Ignoring my thumping heart, I said, "I'm not edgy."

"Yes, you are."

"No, I'm not."

"Are to."

"No, I—"

Becks sighed, his hand suddenly on my thigh. The move jolted me so much I nearly fell off the bed.

"See?" he said, and I could tell he was trying not to smile.

He failed.

Throwing his hand away, all indignation, I jumped to my feet. "That wasn't fair! I wasn't ready."

Becks tugged me back down, looked me straight in the eye. "That's the point," he said. "Whenever we're walking down the hall, in class, wherever, you won't always know when I'm going to touch you, hug you, kiss you." At the thought of kissing Becks, my heart danced a jig in my chest, but Becks wasn't done. "You've got to be prepared, Sal. If you want to make this guy jealous, he has to believe we're a couple. He won't if you keep reacting that way. Hooker won't either."

He had a point.

Wearing my most serious face, I turned to him. "Alright, Mr. Miyagi, I'm ready to learn. Teach me all your skills."

Becks laughed. "Okay, Sally-san," he winked, "but we'll just stick to touch today. I wouldn't want to overwhelm you too fast."

I blushed, realizing how that must've sounded. But I'd be lying if I said there wasn't a part of me that wanted him to overwhelm me, as fast as he pleased.

Thankfully, Becks let it go.

Scooting closer, he lifted a hand. "I'm going to touch you now, okay?" he asked as if knowing it beforehand would make me less tense.

I jerked a nod. The knowing didn't help, kind of made it worse actually. Now that I knew what was coming—Becks, my Becks, touching his skin to my skin—my nerve endings were on full alert.

Gently, Becks placed his hand on top of mine.

I didn't jump this time, but my body was like a live wire, lit up from the inside.

"Jeez," Becks said quietly, running the tips of his fingers up and down my arm. "You're shaking, Sal."

Mortified, I looked down to see that he was right. Every time his fingers passed a certain place on my skin, gooseflesh appeared first followed by a tiny quiver.

"Sorry," I said, completely at a loss.

As much as I tried, I couldn't command myself to not react. Why was my body betraying me like this? Didn't it realize that if Becks saw how much I loved his touch, how much it moved me, he would *know*?

Just as I feared it might already be too late, he said, "This isn't working." Removing his hand, he sat back, shaking his head. "I don't know why I freak you out so much, but we need to try something different."

I was a lot of things, but "freaked out" was definitely not one of them.

"Here," he said, moving a bit closer. "You do me."

"What?"

"Well, if I can't touch you, you've got to touch me. Go ahead, Sal." He rolled his neck around, loosening up like he did sometimes before a game. "I promise I won't move a muscle."

I grimaced. As if I needed yet another reminder of how undesirable Becks found me. Here I was shaking like a leaf because of him, and there he was cool as a cucumber. Of course, he wouldn't move. Becks wasn't the one suffering from a severe case of Un-Requited Love Syndrome. Much as I wished he was, the only love-struck idiot here was me.

Determined to make him feel something, I leaned in. "Close your eyes," I said.

He did.

I took a second to study him, opening himself up to me, so vulnerable, and then started off the same way he had.

Resting my hand atop his, I looked for a reaction, any reaction, but he remained still, just as he'd promised. I glided my hand up the contours of his arm, feeling the dips and curves of every muscle, along the back of his forearm.

He laughed silently. "That tickles, Sal."

"Shhh," I said, "no talking."

Becks nodded then went back to motionless.

I hesitated only a moment before placing both hands on his shoulders. Moving my fingers to the back of his neck, I felt the muscles there tense. I used my thumbs to ease the tension, and then moved even closer. By this point, I was practically in his lap, but I'd wanted to do this for so long. Now that I'd finally gotten the chance, I wouldn't screw it up.

Bringing my right hand back around, I ghosted my fingertips along his jaw and up to his cheek, feeling the stubble rasp against my fingertips. "Oh," I breathed, "it's not so bad."

"Hmmm?"

"I thought it'd feel odd," I answered truthfully. "You know, I prefer you without facial hair."

Becks's voice was low, lower than it'd been a moment ago. His breathing had picked up too, I noticed. "Ah, you know you love it. Everyone does, Sal."

Feeling bold, I spoke softly right into his ear. "Not me."

His arms were around my waist in a blink, but I didn't move.

"I've always hated it."

"But why?" he asked, eyes still closed. "It's the reason I win so much."

I shook my head. "No, Becks." The frown on his face looked so adorable. I had the incredible urge to touch it, so I did. His eyes flipped open at the contact. "You're the reason you win so much."

Out of the blue, the door opened, and I heard Mrs. Kent's voice say, "Hey, honey, is Sally here? I thought I saw her car out front."

Without a thought, I reached up and plucked out one—or four—of Becks's eyelashes, causing him to curse.

I got to my feet smiling. "Eyelash," I said, holding it up for Mrs. Kent's inspection, praying she wouldn't see through the impromptu ruse. She was like a second mother, but if she knew I was up here working on "touch exercises" with her youngest, I didn't think she'd take it too well.

"It's so good to see you, Sally," she said, pulling me into a hug. There was nothing accusatory in her tone. Naturally, she didn't suspect a thing. Becks and I were just friends after all, always had been, always would be. "What're you two doing up here?"

Clayton popped his head in then. "Yes, Sally. What are you and Becks doing up here, all alone, completely unsupervised?"

"Calculus," Becks said, producing his book before I could say a word. "Sal was just helping me with some of the harder questions, isn't that right?" He looked to me.

I nodded a bit too vigorously. "Yep."

"Well, don't work too hard," Mrs. Kent said, shoving a grinning Clayton out the door. "And you," she said to him, "stop trying to cause trouble. They're just friends; you know that."

The door shut on that note, and Becks and I were left alone once again.

"So," he said, smiling, "I think lesson one was successful. What do you say we do some Calc homework?"

I smiled back, acting as if nothing had happened. It seemed so easy for Becks; why couldn't I do it, too? "I didn't bring my book."

"Oh, you can use mine," he said with a grin. "I won't be needing it."

As he handed me the thick text, I remembered the two demands he'd made when he'd agreed to be my F.B.F: Goobers and a month of Calc. "You were serious?"

"You know it."

The hour it took me to complete *our* homework was one of the longest of my life. Having Becks there, watching over my shoulder, pointing out mistakes every now and then, wasn't all that fun. Still, I couldn't keep the smile off my face.

At the door Becks stopped me and said, "So, what's the plan for Monday?"

"I guess we just act like boyfriend and girlfriend," I shrugged. "After today, it shouldn't be that hard, right?"

He nodded. "Okay, Sal, that might work for your guy and all. But you know Hooker's not going to be impressed by a little handholding. Just be prepared."

I agreed like it was a given. Hooker was a tough cookie, but lesson one had filled me with such a heady confidence; I was able to convince myself it'd be easy. I'd finally worked up the nerve to run my hand along Becks's lucky scruff, to whisper in his ear. Convince Hooker? Piece of cake compared to that. I'd never thought I would have the guts. Today, I was Superwoman, invincible. No one, not even Hooker, could touch me.

Even so, if I'd known what she was planning, I probably would've stayed home Monday.

CHAPTER 7

I managed to avoid Hooker over the weekend, but the true test didn't start for another seven minutes. The second-hand was like a countdown to detonation. I was watching it with such intense focus that I didn't even see Pisszilla approach.

Out of nowhere, fake French tips snapped an inch from my nose.

"And what do you call this?" she said, thrusting a copy of the week's newsletter at me.

I glanced at it before turning back to the clock. "The sports beat."

Pisszilla was in fine form this Monday morning. She slapped the paper down on the desk and growled,

"Twelve typos, Spitz. Twelve. It's only five-hundred words. What'd you do, type it blind?"

"No," I mumbled. My thoughts were simply pre-occupied. As I'd been writing, every time I ran across Becks's name in my notes, I had a flashback to our time spent in his room and got distracted. It wasn't my fault, though. Thoughts of Becks were already distracting. Add lesson one to the mix, and it was darn near impossible to concentrate on anything else. "It's not that bad, is it?"

"Not that bad?" she snapped. "You realize you referred to Southside's Coach Moorehouse in the masculine, eight times throughout the entire thing?"

I was confused. Did I add an extra "o" or something? "Isn't that his name?"

"*Her* name, Spitz. Coach Moorehouse is a woman."

"Huh," I said, "I had no idea." With that buzz cut, the deep voice, and those shoulders, who'd have thought?

Pisszilla wasn't done. "Doesn't matter," she said. "You should've checked. Spitz, if you think shoddy work like this is going to get you into Duke, you've got another thing coming."

Direct hit, I thought, recoiling as if I'd been slapped. Duke was the ultimate, the unattainable. It was my dream. Judging by the satisfied smile on Pisszilla's face, I got the feeling she knew it.

"What's the big deal? Man or woman, nobody from Southside's going to read that article anyway. I didn't even know Coach Moorehouse had lady parts."

I shot Ash a thankful look while Pisszilla swung her gaze to him.

"Your stupidity isn't the issue here, Ash." She pointed one of her talons at me. "Spitz is the one who made us all look like idiots. It was her responsibility to check."

Ash rolled his eyes. "Yeah, like you've never made a mistake."

Her nostrils flared. "I've never given someone a sex change in one of my articles if that's what you're saying."

I'd had about enough. "Alright, alright, Piss— umm, Priscilla, calm down." She glared, but I didn't let it stop me. "I'll try harder next time. Okay?"

She huffed out a few more insults but then left me in peace.

Unfortunately, the bell rang right on schedule. I knew Hooker would be waiting for me, on the lookout after the big brush-off this weekend, so I lagged behind. I'd felt prepared a few days ago, but now? Now, I realized there was no real way to prepare for Hooker. She wouldn't go down without a fight. Of that, I was certain.

"Priscilla seemed pretty pissed," Ash said.

Surprised, I looked up. "Yeah, I noticed."

"Don't worry about it. She's not as scary as she thinks."

I walked with him to the door. "She's not?" I asked. "Those nails looked pretty sharp to me."

He laughed. "You're right, she's terrifying."

I nodded. "Especially the claws."

Ash smiled then looked over my head. "Uh oh, looks like someone's jealous."

That was all the warning I got. A second later, Becks was next to me, arm wrapped around my waist like it was the most natural thing, like it belonged there.

"You shaved," I said in wonder, running my eyes over his face.

He rolled his shoulders, and I felt the movement. "'Course, I did," he said, grinning down at me. "The next game's not for another few days."

I was still staring like an idiot, inspecting his smooth, hairless jaw line as if it was the eighth wonder of the world. I hadn't seen it this way, this close in forever: Clean, strong, angular. Hands down it was the best jaw I'd ever laid eyes on.

"Hey, Sal," he said, catching my attention. "I missed you at your locker, so I brought your books. I was thinking maybe I could walk you to first?"

I swallowed. "Sure, Becks."

His eyes slid to Ash. "Stryker."

"Becks," Ash said back. To me, he said, "I'll see you around, Spitz."

"Bye," I said.

Becks rounded on me as soon as Ash turned the corner. "So, what's the deal with you and Ass Striker?"

"What?" I said, taken aback. The nickname wasn't a surprise. Becks had made that one up years ago, practically the instant he met Ash. What surprised me was his tone. Becks never sounded that serious about anything—except maybe soccer.

He must've realized it because his next words were teasing. "It's the second time I've caught you with him," he said. "You two-timing me, Sal? Got another F.B.F. on the side?"

"Becks," I warned.

"And why's he always giving you the hairy eyeball? If the guy looked at me like that, I'd kick his ass."

I smiled. "If Ash looked at you like that, he'd be gay."

"Whatever," Becks said, but he looked tense. "Just please tell me it's not him. It isn't, right?"

"What's not him?"

"Your crush."

"My what?"

Becks took a deep breath. It looked like he was counting to ten. "The guy you want to make jealous."

Oh, I thought. That. I really needed to start keeping track of all my lies.

"No," I replied, "it's not him."

"You're sure?" he said, squinting. "Because as much as I want to help you, Sal, I'm not too keen on the idea of you being Mrs. Ass Striker."

"Why not?" I asked as we stopped at Ms. Vega's classroom.

"I'm just not," he said, handing me my books. "He's not right for you, Sal."

"Oh really? And who is?"

My breath quickened as he brought a hand to my cheek, bending down to place a kiss in the same spot he had before, the skin below my left ear. The shiver came just as it had the first time.

"I don't know," he answered quietly. "But Lillian's watching, so we'd better make this look good."

Without turning, I knew that he was right. I could feel her eyes on my back as we stood there in the doorway.

I gave in to the impulse and placed a gentle kiss on Becks's jaw. It was the only thing I could reach since he'd stood back up, and besides, I'd wanted to do it since the moment I saw him. He stiffened at the contact.

"Thanks," I said, "I owe you one."

Becks slowly shook his head. "No, you don't. We had a deal remember?"

"That we do."

Looking over my shoulder, I caught Hooker's eye. I waved, and she gave a nod before turning to face front, her lips curved as Becks and I said our goodbyes. She looked awfully pleased about something. I wondered if she could read lips or if she had a superpower I didn't know about, like super-sonic hearing. As I walked into class and buried my head in German translations, I had the strangest feeling—like I should be worried, more worried than I already was. The flash I'd seen in those eyes meant trouble.

The first attack came half-way through the period.

"Sally, they need you in the office."

At the sound of Ms. Vega's voice, I looked up and saw Holden Wasserman, one of only two other members of the German Club besides myself, standing at the front of the room, staring at me expectantly. I'd been concentrating so hard, trying to ignore Hooker's expression; I hadn't even heard anyone come in.

"Okay," I said.

Holden held the door as I followed him out. Just as it swung shut, I glanced back, catching sight of Hooker's smirk. The entire way I couldn't shake the feeling I was walking into a trap.

"So, what's this about?" I asked as we reached the office.

"Your brother's on line one," he said and stepped up to the counter, gesturing to the office phone. "He says it's urgent."

"Brother?" I didn't have a brother. Holding up my hands, I said, "I think there's been a mistake."

"He specifically asked for you, says it's a family emergency." Holden held the receiver out to me. "Sure hope it's not your dad. That'd be tragic for everyone."

Considering the phone call was either a prank or meant for someone else, I wasn't too worried about dear old Dad. Perfect, I thought, a case of mistaken identity. I just hoped this guy, whoever he was, found his real sister soon.

Taking the cordless, I said, "Hello?"

"Hey," a male voice answered, "is this Sally Spitz?"

I frowned. If he was looking for his sister, how'd he get my name? "Yes, it is. But I think you've got the wrong person."

"Not if this is *the* Sally Spitz," he said, sounding far too cheery for someone in an emergency situation. "This is John Poole. I've been hearing a lot of great things about you."

"I'm sorry, who?" I recognized the name but couldn't place it.

"I go to UNC with Will. Lillian paid me twenty bucks to call and say I was your brother. She said you probably wouldn't talk to me otherwise."

"She did, did she?" As the memory hit, I was thinking of the effort this must've taken. Pulling me out of first period, paying this poor guy to lie, Hooker's methods were positively Machiavellian.

"Yes, she did," he said. "She also said you hate being called Spitz and blind dates. I figure I've only got about thirty seconds before you hang up, so here it goes. I'm a twenty-year-old Gemini with a love of all things baseball. My GPA's 3.8. I have a pit bull at home named Bruiser, and I've got no problem dating a high school girl, so long as she's not a fan of the Mets and isn't one of those European types who doesn't shave their underarms. Want to go out sometime?"

I stifled a laugh. Was this guy for real? He seemed nice and all, but this was just too awkward. When I got off this phone, Hooker was going to owe me a lifetime supply of Goobers.

"Did Hooker also mention I have a boyfriend?" I asked.

He cleared his throat. "Guess she forgot that one. I suppose it's a no then?"

"Yeah, I'm sorry, John. It was good talking to you. You seem great, but now I have to go strangle Hooker."

He laughed. "Good talking to you, too, Sally. Don't be too hard on her, okay? She really thought we'd hit it off."

Oh, I bet she did.

Class had already cleared out when I got back to German, but Hooker was there, watching for me.

"Sooo?" she said as I grabbed my books.

"So what?" I muttered.

"So, have you had any good convos lately, met anyone interesting? Oh, don't make me beg, Spitz. Were you into John or what? Was he totally lame? I told him not to be."

Listening to her confirmed what I already knew and lessened my annoyance a good deal. A lot of planning had gone into that phone call. Hooker looked so excited, like she expected a gold star or a pat on the back. She seemed so proud of herself; it was almost a shame to burst her bubble.

"John was...the least lame guy you've tried to set me up with," I admitted. "He was actually nice, but—"

"But what?" Hooker paused in her victory dance, arms dropping to her sides. "If he's not lame, and if you think he's 'nice,' what's the problem?"

"Hooker, I have a boyfriend."

"Oh yes, I forgot," she said. "Becks, your good buddy turned boyfriend, how's that working out?"

I didn't appreciate the sarcasm.

"It's working out fine, thanks."

"You know, John was the best I had," Hooker commented. "He's good looking, smart, nice voice. I thought you'd be a good match."

"And I thank you for thinking of me, but—"

"No." Hooker held up a hand. "I don't think you understand, Spitz." She looked me dead in the eye. "I *know* you're not really with Becks."

I fought to keep my expression neutral, wasn't sure I succeeded.

"If you were, you'd have told me sooner. Plus, you wouldn't be such a nervous wreck around him."

Shows what she knew.

Hooker raised an eyebrow. "So are you ready to fess up? Come clean, and I'll let you off the hook. We won't ever mention this again."

Yeah, and go back to blind dates every other night? No deal, *meine Freudin.*

I met her gaze and replied steadily, "In the immortal words of Darth Vader, I find your lack of faith disturbing. There's nothing to confess. I'm with Becks. End of story."

She sighed. "Alright, but it'll get worse before it gets better. Don't say I didn't warn you."

And it did get worse.

At lunch, Hooker launched her second attempt.

It came in the form of Buddy McCorkle, a sopho-more with a Mighty Mouse tee and the languid look of a stoner. He also had a thing about hands.

"Wow, your hands are so strong. They're like man hands," were the first words he said to me. Hooker made sure I couldn't escape, interrupting any time I tried to stop the conversation, blocking my exit with her body. Becks had a different lunch period, and she made the most of it. Ten minutes into lunch, Buddy had already measured, squeezed and even sniffed each of my fingers, remarking on the length and roundness of each.

But Buddy and his finger fetish was golden in com-parison to Terrell Feinberg's fascination with himself. The guy was gorgeous, silky brown hair, perfect teeth, rocking bod, and he knew it, too. Terrell didn't stop talking about himself, never asked me a single ques-tion, for an entire twenty minutes. Hooker was on guard duty again, so I had to sit and endure Terrell's thought-provoking argument over American versus European hair care products. His vote was for the lat-ter. I knew his last name meant "fine city" in German, but, in any language, Terrell Feinberg should've trans-lated: "big head."

Both guys backed off when I said Becks and I were a couple, but I was starting to feel put out. Why hadn't they *known* about us already? When I took a good look at them, I got it: a college guy, a stoner, and a guy who couldn't see past his own reflection.

Well played, Hooker. Well played.

In the halls, Becks walked me to each of my classes holding my hand—*my* hand!—but it didn't take long to see Hooker, as predicted, wasn't impressed. She watched us, tracked our movements like a bird of prey. Sometimes I'd see her head pop out of a classroom just to roll her eyes at me. Other times Becks and I would be passing, and she'd shake her head or sigh long and loud, making sure we heard.

I was waiting at Becks's locker, trying to think what else I could do, when Hooker stepped out from behind the line of lockers a few doors down. I scowled as she shrugged, but her entire stance said, "I warned you, didn't I?"

Becks sounded amused as he joined me. "What was that look about?"

"Nothing much," I said. "Hooker just threw three guys at me in an effort to disprove our fake relationship."

"Anyone interesting?" Becks asked.

"Very funny," I mumbled, wracking my brain.

Remembering Hooker, I snatched up Becks's hand. I wasn't close enough to tell, but it looked like she scoffed. Becks had been right. It was going to take more than handholding. The challenging tilt to Hooker's head made that perfectly clear. If Becks and I didn't convince her by the end of today, I was out of luck. It was time to up the ante.

"Becks," I said, turning to face him. Madness drove my mind to the one place I'd never allowed it to go, couldn't allow it to go. "Could you come here? I think this calls for drastic measures."

"Sure thing, Sal." He pushed off the lockers and came to stand in front of me. "What'd you have in mind?"

Courage or stupidity, I was going for broke. That is if my fiercely beating heart could hold on just a little longer. Were there always this many people in the hall between classes? I couldn't believe I was actually doing this.

Meeting his gaze, I forced out the words, "Ready to make it official?"

Becks grinned, and the sight of that familiar expression, the look in those eyes I'd loved forever, was enough to strengthen my resolve.

Reaching up, I gave myself no time to reconsider.

My lips were on his the next instant, meeting, feeling, rejoicing in this moment I'd never thought but always hoped would happen. I knew Becks was surprised, could feel it in the stiffness in his shoulders, the tight set to his mouth. But it didn't matter. I was *kissing* Becks, my best friend, my Han Solo, my one. This was the best moment of my life. I was certain it couldn't get any better.

But then Becks started kissing me back.

His arms wrapped around my waist, his lips guiding mine, as he went from passive passenger along for the ride to full-on conductor. I gasped as he bent me back over his arm, and felt him grin through the kiss. My toes just skimming the floor, supported almost entirely by Becks's strength, I was happy to let him lead. Becks wasn't just a great kisser. He was a master. Far as first kisses go, it was a showstopper.

What I'd remember most, though, wasn't how Vice Principal Matlock blew his whistle and broke us apart, giving Becks and I both after-school detention—to be served separately, of course. It wasn't even when Hooker came up after Becks had left, laid a hand on my shoulder, and said, "Guess you weren't kidding. I'll give it to you, Spitz. That kiss curled even my toes."

Even if he still just saw me as Sal, his friend who was a great girl but not girlfriend material, the thing I'd take with me, the feeling I'd bottle up and keep in my pocket if I could, was this: Becks kissed me like he meant it.

CHAPTER 8

Hugs.

Hands.

Kisses in what I now thought of as "Becks's spot."

The next few days were a whirlwind. By Friday, I was just trying to keep it together. The idea that Becks had an un-official "spot" on my body was enough to make my head spin. His five o'clock shadow was back, and there was a game tonight, so Becks was flying high. But me? Every time he touched me—Lord, every time he *looked* at me—I felt thrown. The way he'd been looking at me lately should've been criminal. It was much too easy for Becks to fake how he felt.

Intimate glances, soft caresses, secret smiles, if his soccer career tanked, there'd always be acting.

The more time I spent with my new F.B.F., the harder it was for me to tell fact from fiction.

Like right now.

He was walking with me to German, my hand tucked in his as if we'd walked this way for years. Schmuck that I was, I couldn't help thinking our hands fit just right.

Nowadays everyone, even Hooker, recognized us as a couple. I was still Spitz the dorky girl who cursed in German when she got really upset or angry. And he was still Becks the soccer phenom who pretended not to see girls throwing him inviting glances they thought I didn't see (which I did). But even those skeezy skeezes thought Becks and I were the real thing. They just didn't like it. It was like it was okay to flirt with him because, in their eyes, I was replaceable. Any day now Becks would realize his mistake and drop me. They thought they could break us up with a short skirt, a coy glance, a well-executed hair flip. It was frustrating.

First, could I get a little sisterly solidarity, please? And second, what the heck was wrong with everyone? The whole point of this plan had been to convince people, but I hadn't expected it to go this well. Didn't *anyone* get it? None of it was real. Becks was only going through the motions of being a boyfriend; it was all just a game.

More importantly: Didn't *I* get it?

As he faced me, lifted my hand and delivered a heart-stopping kiss to my knuckles, the answer was as embarrassing as it was telling.

God, I was such an idiot.

"I'll see you at assembly," he said, eyes growing concerned. "Don't worry, okay? He says anything offensive, cop or not, I'll give him five across the face."

The tingles shooting up my arm momentarily stole my hearing, so what he said didn't sink in until I walked into class (early for once), took a seat and found Hooker, the same concern written on her face.

"It'll be over before you know it," she said. "You two might not even have to speak. He'll be too busy getting his ass kissed by everyone else."

Before I could ask what she meant, a voice sounded over the intercom.

"Seniors please report to the auditorium for today's Crack Down on Crime assembly. We'll be calling juniors in the next few minutes, and then sophomores and freshmen subsequently."

I shut my eyes.

"What," Hooker said, "don't tell me you forgot? Spitz, you dread this day."

She was right. I usually planned ahead, arranged to be "sick" on CDOC day. My untimely forgetfulness showed how distracting Becks and the F.B.F. plan truly were. I considered telling Ms. Vega I was ill—my rolling stomach was a recent development, but it was real enough. She'd probably let me duck out of assembly, go to the nurse.

But then I would have let him scare me off.

That was something I couldn't—*wouldn't*—let happen. Taking a mental health day was one thing, but hiding in the nurse's station while he preened in front of my peers was plain out yellow-bellied.

There was only one thing to do.

"*Scheisse*," I cursed.

"*Scheisse*," Hooker agreed. "Your Dad's a total *scheisse* head full of *scheisse*. He's just one big piece of *scheisse* with a badge."

I forced a smile but couldn't make it stick.

Time to go watch Deputy Dad play the hero for a crowd of unsuspectings, I thought.

Dad was a good showman; I'd give him that. For the kids and most of the teachers, it was love at first sight. Him, the shiny black uniform, his stories of crime and capture, they bought it all. About thirty minutes in, a girl from my class leaned over and said, "Man, Spitz, your Dad is awesome." That was when he was demonstrating the different ways to take down an assailant on the run. The tackle had been impressive, I supposed, but not unexpected. The guy was half his size, and Dad, a former linebacker, had attacked from behind. Hardly fair, if you ask me.

Hearing this, stats teacher Mr. Woodruff spun around in his chair a row in front of us, stars in his eyes.

"Are you telling me that's your father up there?" Mr. Woodruff was obviously under Nick Spitz's spell.

"That's right," I said, trying not to sound bitter.

"You're one lucky girl," he remarked then turned back around.

I grimaced.

Dad and the other officers had moved on to the PowerPoint portion. There were multiple slides, one displaying a pie chart of casualty rates for the city, another with definitions for the different types of crime and prison sentences for each, a promo for the department, including traits they looked for in potential candidates, and the last outlining the ways citizens could help by upholding the law and cracking down on crime in their own neighborhoods. It ended with my dad spouting off some nonsense about how the youth was our future and could change the world.

When the never-ending PSA was over, everyone cheered. Hooker and I kept our hands planted in our laps. I was sure she did it more to support me than anything, but I appreciated the gesture.

Seniors got to stay behind and ask questions while the cops made their way down to the audience. Dad didn't look at me once. Not even when there was a question from the guy directly to my right, Everett Ponce, a total brownnoser. It was like I was invisible—which was fine with me so long as I got out of there without having to trade words with the jerk.

Classes started filing out. I thought I was in the clear when a familiar voice said, "Not even going to say hi to me, huh?"

I took a deep breath then pivoted around.

"Hey, Dad."

My voice sounded stiff, but it couldn't be helped. There he was, Deputy Nick Spitz, crime fighter, revered cop, award-winning officer and crap-tastic father of the decade. The last was my own personal award. He was a hero to everyone but me and for good reason.

"Hi there, Sally girl," he said like we chatted every day. "How's your mother?"

"Mom's fantastic." I hated when he called me that.

"Still working at that bridal place?"

"Yeah," I said, happy for the first time since I'd seen him. "She actually got a big promotion two months ago."

His smile widened. "Well, that's great. Not much farther she can go in that place, but that's just terrific. I'm glad to hear she's moving up in the world."

That's right, I thought. Moving up and doing fine without any help from you.

It'd taken a lot of courage for Mom to leave the great Nick Spitz when I was just five, but she'd gotten out of a bad relationship, raised me on her own, and was thriving in a job she loved. Despite Dad's insults and his constant put-downs, she was a fighter. It had to eat him up how successful Mom was in her job. I hoped it did.

"I see you're still wearing those odd clothes of yours." He gestured to my green "Yoda Knows Best" tee and shook his head. "Don't see how you're ever going attract a man wearing all that nonsense."

And suddenly Becks was there.

"Sal," he said, laying a gentle hand on my elbow, "you alright?"

"Fine," I said. This time his touch seemed to give me strength.

Hooker muttered, "Want me to give him five across the face?"

I shook my head, wondering when that expression had gotten so popular.

"Maybe I was mistaken," Dad said, giving Becks a long look. "You dating my daughter? Seems a little strange if you ask me."

"Yeah, I am," Becks said in a hard tone. "And nobody did ask you."

Dad held up his hands. "Easy there son, I was just stating facts."

Becks didn't fall for it. "I'm not your son."

"Okay, okay," Dad said, his smile a tight line. "No need to get angry. I'm just saying Sally girl isn't your typical Southern beauty. Has too much of her momma in her for that."

Alright, now even I wanted to give him five across the face, but before I could lift a hand, before I could form a fist, the Sheriff stepped in.

"How's it going over here, Nick?" His old eyes passed from one face to the other and stopped on me. "Well, I'll be," he said, looking from me to my Dad and back again. "I never knew you had a child."

"Yes, sir," Dad smiled as if he hadn't just told my F.B.F. I was ugly. "This is my Sally girl, the only one I've got."

Lucky me, I thought.

The Sherriff, hands on hips, puffed out his big barrel chest. "You must be pretty proud. I just cannot believe this. Nick here's prone to practical jokes. So tell me young woman, are you really Deputy Spitz's daughter?"

"No."

The word was out of my mouth before I could think. I didn't know what came over me...but it felt really good.

"Sally," Dad hissed, but I ignored him.

"No," I repeated, "I'm Martha Nicholls's daughter."

Brows contracted, the Sheriff asked, "But isn't Nick your father?"

I had a true *Star Wars* moment. The urge to scream "Nooooo!" at the top of my lungs, just as Luke had when Darth Vader revealed his parentage, was tempting. The possibility of seeing Dad's face was nearly too much to resist. Instead I decided to take the high road.

"I guess." I shrugged then looked over at my friends. They were both smiling. "We should get back to class."

"You're just like your mother," Dad said to my back.

Stopping, I turned. "You better believe it."

Hooker was so proud she called me Super Spitz the rest of the day; Becks couldn't stop grinning; and I was walking on air. Standing up to him, for my mom, for myself, it sent me on the best kind of power trip. I was free, liberated. For a second there I even considered burning my bra. Hours later adrenaline still coursed through my veins. There had to be some major endorphins going on there too because I was far too giddy for there not to be. What happened between fifth and sixth period was a result of this feeling—or at least, that's what I told myself.

It couldn't have been jealousy. No way, I was above all that, a rock of strength and conviction. My sense of justice was tested when I saw Twyla Cornish plastered all over Becks in the hall, her hands clinging to his right arm, body pressed to his side. Anger flared hot in my gut. I'd had about enough of women throwing themselves at my boyfriend—correction *fake* boyfriend...but the fake part wasn't common knowledge. This wasn't about the green-eyed monster, I assured myself as I strode directly to Becks and the bespectacled home wrecker, ripped her hands away and shoved Becks into the storeroom where we'd started this thing over a week ago. It was about self-respect.

As the bell rang, I glared at him. I was missing the first part of British Lit, my favorite class.

"Something wrong?" Becks asked.

Yeah, like he didn't know.

"Why're you looking at me like that, Sal?"

"Baldwin Eugene Charles Kent, *ich kann es nicht fassen,*" I huffed, letting my anger carry me away.

"*Wir hatten eine Abmachung, kannst Du Dich daran noch erinnern?*"

Becks looked confused. "What?"

"*Oh, hör auf, so zu tun. Du weisst genau, was ich meine.*"

"No, Sal, really," he said. "Yo no habla German. Remember?"

The innocent act didn't fool me. Full of indignation, I jabbed a finger at him, making sure to say it in English so he'd get it this time. "Now, I'm only going to say this once, so you better listen good." I enunciated each word, spelling it out clear as day. "I will not be cheated on, Becks, and I most certainly will not be cheated on with the likes of Twyla Cornish."

Stunned, he said, "How could I cheat? We're not even really going out."

I sniffed. "Still. I won't be made a fool of Becks. Not by you, not by anyone."

"Jeez, Sal, alright—" He rubbed the back of his neck. "—Let it go already."

"No, I want your word."

"My what?"

"Your word that you won't see anyone else for the duration of our agreement." Man, this power thing was addictive. I knew it was a lot to ask, and I also knew it was hard for Becks to say no to members of the female persuasion. But seeing Twyla glued to Becks's hip, watching her bat her eyelashes, pout her lips, had caused something inside me to snap.

There was a glint in Becks's eyes. He almost seemed pleased. "That wasn't part of the deal. A month's a long time to be tied down. There are girls who want to date me for real, you know."

I did know. I was one of them.

Crossing my arms, I waited. There was nothing I could do if he didn't agree, but I wouldn't let him see how nervous I was—or how desperate.

"Okay, Sal," he said finally, and I exhaled, "but I want something in return."

I was immediately on my guard. "What might that be?"

Becks shrugged. "Just a favor."

"Want to be a little more specific?"

"No can do," he said, grinning. "One day I'll ask for something. You won't know when or where or what that something's going to be, but you'll have to give it no questions asked."

"Been watching *The Godfather* recently?" I said.

Becks wouldn't be sidetracked. "Take it or leave it."

"I'll take it," I replied, holding out a hand. "But if this involves nudity in any way, I'm telling your mother."

We shook on it, and Becks's laughter was infectious. As we walked into the hall, the two of us were smiling like idiots.

"You've got to be kidding me."

The sharp female voice belonged to Roxy Culpepper. She was standing there, hip cocked to full capacity, short skirt riding high on her thighs, and a look of pure disdain on her face.

"This has to be a joke, right," she said again. "Becks, what is going on here?"

Becks was no longer smiling. "What do you mean?"

"I'm out a few days with Mono and come back to find you and Spitz are hooking up. I don't believe it." Roxy gestured in my direction. "You can't be serious, Becks. Look at her. She's not even pretty."

It was amazing how statements like that said by beautiful girls like Roxy could slice right through a person. I didn't even like the girl, and I still felt gutted.

"You're right," Becks said, bringing a hand to my cheek. My head snapped up in reflex. "She's not pretty."

He was speaking to her but looking at me. Though his words were insulting, the heat in his eyes made me flush and not from humiliation. How could he look at me like that in front of someone like Roxy? It defied logic.

"She's so much more than pretty," he breathed, running his thumb along my cheekbone before giving me another below-the-ear kiss.

I was vaguely aware of Roxy stomping away but wasn't sure of anything at the moment. Becks had done it again. His words were engraved in my mind. I would never forget what he said.

He was just acting, I reminded myself.

But he'd sounded sincere, my heart insisted. And that kiss...

Yeah, my brain responded, but it wasn't real.

But it felt real.

Yeah, but it wasn't.

This back and forth between heart and mind was so jarring; I felt completely off kilter.

"Why do you do that?" My voice was little more than a whisper.

He seemed to understand I was referring to the kiss.

"Because I can tell you like it." He paused, an odd look to his face, while I held my breath. "And you have a birthmark—" He brushed the place with the tip of his finger. "—right here."

Eyes wide, my hand flew up without my telling it to. "I do?"

He nodded. "You didn't know?"

I shook my head.

My heart was set to burst when he grinned and added, "Plus, girls have told me it's one of their favorite places to be kissed."

I let out a shaky breath. Naturally, Becks had kissed other girls that way before. I was stupid to have thought it was something special, something he did just for me.

Stepping back to put a little space between us, I said, "Well, it's very effective."

"You okay, Sal?"

I forced myself to look him in the eye, burying my emotions down deep. "'Course I am."

He studied me a moment. "Alright then," he said. "I'll see you same time this Saturday?"

"What for?" I asked.

"Lesson two," he smiled.

I gulped. "What's lesson two?"

"It's the next step in your training, Sally-san." Becks laughed. "Just be there, okay?"

I wanted to tell him there was no need. We'd already won everyone over, but instead I nodded incapable of speech. Oh Lord, I wasn't sure I was ready for lesson two. In fact, I knew I wasn't, but as Becks sauntered down the hall, I also knew I'd do just about anything for another one of those kisses.

I was a total schmuck.

CHAPTER 9

"What'd you call this again?" I gasped.

Becks lifted his head from my neck only an instant to mumble, "Nuzzling," and then was back on the attack.

"Oh."

If lesson one was hot, lesson two was freaking explosive. From this day forward I'd have to list nuzzling as one of my favorite pastimes. I was ready to burn up as Becks worked me over. His lips were hitting all the right spots, and whenever he found a particularly sensitive patch of skin, he'd mount a full-scale assault, kissing, nibbling, and stroking until I was a mushy heap of girl flesh at his mercy.

I think he knew it, too, because every time I gasped or stifled a moan, he'd double his efforts to make it happen again.

This was insane. I was insane for coming up with the F.B.F. idea, and Becks was insane for agreeing. It was impossible to separate my true emotions from the current situation. With every pass of his mouth, I became a little more his. Becks was already a part of me, but the reality of him was more than I'd ever hoped for. When a month's time was up, I wasn't sure I could go back to being just friends. I loved him so fiercely, had loved him before this, would continue to love him after. And all he'd ever feel for me was friendship.

This one, I thought sadly as Becks drew another gasp from my lips. This one could only end badly, and when it did, it was going to hurt.

A lot.

"How's it going up—Oh my!"

Becks froze like a stone, arms anchored to my waist and back, lips attached to my throat, while I tried (and failed) to will myself invisible.

When I finally got the courage to glance up, Mrs. Kent was immobile, straddling the threshold of Becks's room, one foot in one out, eyes staring at us on her son's bed, mouth gaping in pure, unadulterated shock.

We were pieces on a chessboard, each waiting for someone to make the first move.

Clayton sauntered in, saw us, saw his mom, and smiled.

"Guess the jig is up, Bally."

Mrs. Kent raised an eyebrow at that.

"Well," Clayton explained, "I could've gone with 'Secks,' but considering the current situation—"

"Everyone downstairs," Mrs. Kent ordered. "Time for a talk."

It turned out "everyone" meant me, Becks and Mrs. Kent. Clayton had to get back to CHS for the JV game, but he assured us he'd rather have stayed and watched the real action. His wise-guy humor did nothing to lighten the mood. Mrs. Kent seemed to have taken a page out of my mom's playbook. She was steely-eyed, pitched forward in her recliner as Becks and I sat side by side on the couch, but instead of finger-tapping, she sucked her teeth. It was a tossup which was worse.

"So you and Sally are a couple now," she said after a particularly long suck, and I was glad she'd asked him, not me.

I'd already lied to one parent, but that had been about self-preservation. I wasn't sure I could do it again, especially with the compromising position Mrs. Kent had found us in. Part of me wanted to deny it until I was blue in the face. *No way, Mrs. Kent. Your son's a girl-magnet equipped to give nuzzling lessons. He'd never be interested in someone like me.* Another part wanted any denial to be a lie, but I was too smart for that.

"Yes," Becks said.

"How long?" his mom volleyed back.

"Little over a week."

I shouldn't have been surprised. He'd demonstrated his acting chops from day one, but I'd never seen Becks lie to his mom. He did it with ease and confidence, like he did everything else. Even I almost believed him.

"And Sally—" Her eyes went to me, and I tried not to look too guilty. "—what were you two doing up there in Becks's room?"

"Well," I hesitated, unsure how to explain our lessons. "Well, Mrs. Kent…you see, we were just—"

"Doing what normal couples do," Becks said smoothly.

"Watch it, mister," Mrs. Kent warned. "You know you're not allowed to have girls in your room."

"Mom, Sal's been coming to my room since we were seven."

"Yes, but that was before…"she stuttered, searching for the right word. "Well, *before*."

"I don't see the difference."

I gaped at him. Oh boy, he was just asking for it.

"You're asking for it," Mrs. Kent echoed my thoughts exactly. "Baldwin Eugene Charles Kent, what do you have to say for yourself?"

In the face of his mother's accusing tone, Becks shrugged. "Sal and I have been friends a long time. It's only natural for us to want to take it to the next level. I thought you'd be happy for us, Mom. Sal's like a daughter to you, and here you are embarrassing her, trying to make her feel bad. To be completely honest, I'm a little disappointed in you."

She blinked.

I waited.

Becks sat back and watched his Mom absorb everything, a faint look of disapproval on his face.

The guy was unbelievable. Mrs. Kent would never buy it.

"I didn't mean it like that," she said. Her face fell as she looked at me. "I adore you Sally, I do. It's just finding you and Becks in his room...it took me by surprise."

"Totally understandable," I said.

"But I am so happy," she said, a smile forming, "over the moon, really, that you and Becks are finally together. I didn't mean to embarrass you, honey. I was trying to embarrass my son, but apparently he inherited his father's shamelessness."

"Talking about me again, dear?" Mr. Kent stepped into the room and dropped a kiss on his wife's head. Clayton had more of his dad in him than his mom, but Becks was a perfect marriage of the two. As Mr. Kent looked at us, I saw a matching set of Becks's eyes looking back at me. "Hi, Sally. I miss anything good?"

"Just Becks and his new girlfriend getting better acquainted in his bedroom," Mrs. Kent said, which finally—*finally*—made Becks blush. I'd been red as I could be since before she'd discovered us, so her comment really had no effect on my coloring.

"Really?" Mr. Kent was all smiles. "Well, isn't that something." Mrs. Kent shot him a look, and he quickly amended, "I mean, Becks how dare you take our innocent Sally here up to your room. Do we need to have a talk about the correct way to treat a lady?"

Mrs. Kent nodded her approval, but said, "That won't be necessary. The three of us already talked, and there will be no more hanging out in Becks's room with the door closed. Isn't that right you two?"

Becks and I nodded.

Guess this would be the end of our lessons. Too bad, I was looking forward to what lesson three might be.

As I was leaving, Mrs. Kent made sure to invite me and my mom to the Kent Family Cookout. It was late October; the last game of normal season play would be

this week before they announced the area/region quali-
fiers. Chariot was sure to make the sectionals, and it
was the perfect time to bring the family together, a
two birds situation. They all got to eat great food and
see Becks play (and most likely win).

I said I would come—what else could I do? Having
three Kents, two with Becks's persuasive eyes, staring
back at me I couldn't say no, didn't want to.

But when Monday rolled around, I was rethinking
my answer.

Again.

I'd changed my mind and changed it back too
many times to count. The smart thing would be not to
go. There'd be too many people, my mom, the Kents,
Becks's brothers. They knew me and Becks better than
anyone. The cookout was a minefield. One slip, that's
all it would take. Mom had yet to see us together after
the big announcement, and though Becks's parents
were on board now, none of them had watched the two
of us together for any length of time. The odds of dis-
covery had never been higher.

School was out today because of a state-wide
teacher's conference, so I couldn't use German Club or
having to stay after as my excuse to avoid the cookout. The library was closed for electrical repairs. My
options weren't looking good.

Cleaning the gutters was supposed to help clear my head. There were layers and layers of build up. I didn't think they'd been cleaned once the entire twelve years we'd owned the place. Mom hadn't done it. We hadn't hired anyone. I sure as heck hadn't climbed my butt up here to do it. But today, with the cookout fast approaching and no way out in sight, I'd needed something. The ladder I was using was a rusted out old heap that came with the house. I'd been at it nearly two hours; my mind was supposed to be a million miles away. The dirt and grime, the dead leaves, the pure grossness of the task should've diverted my attention...but it didn't.

"Crap," I said, suddenly dislodging a huge clump of gunk, "there's nothing I can do."

"Hey!"

The exclamation caught me by surprise, and I lost my footing. My arms were what saved me. They shot out completely on reflex, latched on to one of the gutters and didn't let go. The ladder was long gone, laying somewhere in the grass below. The oversize workman's gloves didn't help me now. It was next to impossible to get a good grip.

"A little warning next time would be nice, Sal."

Without looking I knew that voice.

"Becks," I said calm as possible—which wasn't calm at all. My hands were already slipping. "Could you get the ladder?"

"So you can what," he scoffed, "pull a Catwoman and spring onto the thing? Sal, just drop. I'll catch you."

I vigorously shook my head.

"Just get the ladder, please."

"Sal, I'm standing right beneath you. I'll catch you."

"No, you won't."

"Yes, I—God, Sal, stop being so stubborn and just drop."

I whimpered, fingers slipping another inch.

"I'll catch you. I promise."

"You better," I said then let go.

I couldn't control my girlish shriek, but Becks made no sound as I fell gracelessly into his arms. He caught me like he did this every day, as if girls dangling from rain gutters were his specialty. Who knew? Maybe they were.

Raising my head, I asked, "Have you done this before?"

"Never," he said, eyes smiling.

"You sure?"

"Positive." He gave me a pointed look. "But you know, unlike some people, when I say I'll catch someone, I actually do it."

I sighed. Of course, he would bring *that* up. "You're never going to let it go, are you?"

"Nope," he said and readjusted his hold. Surprised, I gripped his neck with both hands. "Some things are hard to forget."

"I said I was sorry about a million times."

"I know."

"And I was the one who got hurt, not you."

"I know, Sal."

"Then why do you always bring it up?" I muttered.

"Best day of my life." Becks shrugged, jostling me again, and I narrowed my eyes. Of all the times I'd asked him that exact question, he never gave a straight answer.

Mom came out of the house toting five food trays and smiled when she saw us.

"Hi, Becks," she said, as I scrambled to my feet, cheeks flaming. "Dare I ask?"

"Hey there, Mrs. Nicholls." He grinned. "I walked up and saw Sal stuck, hanging from one of the gutters. Naturally, I saved the day."

I cut him a glance. Nice how he forgot to mention he was the reason I'd been stuck in the first place.

"Sounds like history repeating itself," Mom said.

"Yeah," he replied, "except no one got injured this time."

I rolled my eyes. "It was second grade. You were bigger than me. What'd you expect?"

Becks raised a brow. "You *said* you'd catch me."

"Whatever, I didn't see anyone else volunteering." I'd tried to save him, too. I just hadn't been as successful. "If I hadn't come along and talked you down, you might've been trapped on those monkey bars for hours."

"You said—"

"*And*," I added, "I ended up with a broken arm after you nearly squashed me."

"You know I've always felt bad about that," Becks mumbled.

"Well, there you go," I nodded. "I've always felt bad about breaking your fall instead of catching you like I said I would. We're even."

"Even," Becks agreed, stuffing his hands into his pockets.

Mom, who'd been watching the exchange, sighed.

Becks and I looked at her.

"What, it's a great story," Mom said, wearing a dreamy expression. "You meet when you're young, become best friends, and then fall in love? I'm telling you it doesn't get much better than that. I hope you'll take care of my girl, Becks."

"Mom," I muttered, embarrassed.

"Don't worry, Mrs. Nicholls." Becks reached for my hand, and I gave it without a thought. Gazing lovingly into my eyes, he said, "I will."

Man, he was *good*.

I would've applauded the Oscar-worthy performance, but instead I smiled as he winked. We'd get through the cookout just fine so long as Becks kept that up.

Mom had called Mrs. Kent to have Becks drive us over (I swear, she had to be the one I got all my sneakiness from). The entire Kent Clan was there when we arrived, and the three oldest boys met us at the door.

Let the games begin, I thought, holding tight to Becks's hand.

He squeezed mine back.

"Martha," Clayton fairly squealed as he saw my mother. He reached out to take one of the trays, flipped back the foil and put a hand to his heart. "Macadamia Nut, my favorite. Tell me, would ever consider dating a younger man?"

Leonard Kent, the oldest, stepped in. "Stop hogging her," he said, flashing a winning smile. "Hey Martha, how's it going?"

Mom laughed. "It's going just fine. Oh and Leo, there's something for you, Ollie and Thad here, too."

At the sound of his name, Oliver poked his head out, smiled at Mom and grabbed his tray of peanut butter cookies. "Thanks, Martha. You're the best."

Every single one of the Kent brothers was in love with my mother.

This should've bothered me, but it didn't.

"Sally Spitz," Leo said squinting, "I think you're even prettier than when last I saw you. What the heck are you dating this guy for?"

Becks grunted.

Ollie spoke through a mouthful of cookie. "Yeah, Sally, what's the deal? I thought you and young Baldwin were strictly hands off. When'd you guys decide to become kissing buddies?"

And that was only the start.

The jabs kept coming.

The brothers surrounded us as we sat on the loveseat in the living room. Becks wore a tight-lipped grin, and I was left to field the questions. By that point Mom had made her way into the kitchen with Mrs. Kent, for which I was thankful. There were some things I just didn't want her to hear—like question one.

Leo: "I hear you and Becks got caught necking in his room. He any good?"

Me (flushed): "He's magnificent."

Ollie: "Oh yeah? So, when's the honeymoon gonna be?"

Me: "Undecided."

Clayton: "You'll name one of your kids after me, right?"

Me: "You wish."

Clayton: "Ah, come on Sally."

Me: "No."

Thad: "What about me? Thaddeus the Fifth sounds pretty darn good."

Me: "Not on your life."

No way was I naming my child Thaddeus. All of the Kent brothers were named after uncles; it was tradition, and both Mr. and Mrs. Kent had a long line of siblings to choose from. That's how Becks got saddled with his tongue twister. They knew he was going to be their last, and so every name that hadn't already been assigned got dropped on him.

Becks was looking more and more tense, enduring every snicker, every skeptical look, until he finally jumped up and said, "Who's up for a game?"

Nothing could distract the Kent brothers like a challenge.

We played every year, and to make it more fair, the game was touch football. Everyone knew if Becks got hold of a soccer ball, there was no contest. The brothers had learned the hard way, and male testosterone was alive and well in the Kent household. They hated to lose, especially to each other.

It was a serious competition.

"I can almost taste a victory," Clayton said, doing a couple lunges to warm up. "Can you taste it, Sally? That sweet budding taste of V-I-C-T-O-R-Y?"

"Yeah," I smiled, "tastes good."

I played to even up the teams, and once everything was settled here was the line-up: Me, Ollie, and Clayton versus Becks, Leo and Thad. I might not have had the upper body strength, but I had the quickness to compete with the boys. Plus, I'd grown up with these particular boys, so I knew their weaknesses.

"We got this," Ollie said, jogging in place. "We so got this."

"You got nothing." Leo smacked Ollie on the shoulder, laughing as he walked past.

"You won't be smiling when we annihilate you," Ollie said, glaring at Leo's back as if he saw a bull's-eye. They had a bit of sibling rivalry going on, being the two oldest. Leo was bigger, but Ollie had the better throwing arm. They usually focused on each other, so I wouldn't need to worry too much about Leo. "You ready to get that Troll, Sally?"

My eyes narrowed on the competition. "Heck, yeah."

The Golden Troll, a prize like no other, coveted, highly sought after, much beloved and a total piece of crap. The thing was butt ugly. The doll sported crazy red eyes, was missing most of its hair, had been spray-painted gold and nailed crooked onto a wooden base to complete the horrific appearance. Looks weren't important, though. If your team took the Troll, you earned a year's worth of bragging rights. It was all about the win.

Taking Leo out of the equation, I concentrated on Becks and Thad. Becks was difficult to pin down. He had weaknesses I was sure, but none I could easily spot. I usually tried to stay away from him. He knew I wasn't made of glass, and I knew he'd take me down if he could. Last year, in the mud, sweat and heat, it hadn't been pretty.

Thad was the weak link, my number one target. He had a soft spot for girls, all girls, so even if I was running right by him, he hardly made an effort, afraid he'd push too hard and I'd get hurt. Our strategy was simple. Get Thad on our side, effectively knocking him out of the game and taking Becks's team down to two players.

In the huddle, Ollie laid out the game plan then said, "Everyone understand?"

Clayton and I nodded.

Ollie looked to me. "You ready? This whole thing depends on you, Sally, so you've got to be willing to lie, cheat, steal, whatever it takes to get the Troll."

"Whatever it takes," I said.

Clayton raised an eyebrow. "Even if it means taking your boyfriend down a notch?"

Before I could say a word, Becks called out from across the yard. "Hey Sal, you want to hurry it up? Team Becks is getting impatient over here, waiting to claim our prize."

"That Troll is ours," Clayton shot back.

"Not this year," Leo said smugly. "Not last year either."

"That was a fluke," Ollie retorted. "Nothing but a fluke."

"Yeah," I said, "the sun got in my eyes."

"Sorry Sal—" Becks shook his head. "—but girlfriend or not, your team's going down. Don't worry sweetheart, I'll go easy on you."

It was the "sweetheart" that did it.

Turning back around, baring my teeth, I said, "He'll never see it coming. Let's do this."

And do it we did. The whole thing went off without a hitch. On the third play, I saw my opening and took it. Ollie had just thrown a perfect spiral, delivering the ball into my arms without the slightest wobble. I'd cradled it to my chest like a newborn babe and made a mad dash for the goal line, but Becks was there to intercept me less than five yards away. He tagged me with two hands to my side, a gentle pat, the lightest of touches, but I made the most of it, throwing my body to the side, taking a nosedive into the grass, groaning pitifully as I fell.

Becks was at my side in an instant, kneeling, checking me for injuries. "Sal?" he said, face stricken. I buried my head further into my shoulder, trying not to laugh. "Sal, are you hurt? I didn't mean to...I mean, I barely...Sal, say something, you're scaring me here."

At that, I looked up, eyes bright. "Aw, don't be scared Baldwin, I'm alright." Looking past him, I said, "But you better watch your back. Thad doesn't look happy."

"Huh?" was all Becks got out, and then he was wrenched away.

Thad was in a state. "What the heck's the matter with you, Becks? She's a girl for God's sake." I groaned again for good measure, letting him pull me to my feet. Gently, Thad said, "Sally, are you okay? Did he hurt you?"

"No, I'm fine," I said, shooting Becks a grin when no one was looking. "I guess Becks just doesn't know his own strength."

Becks's mouth dropped open.

Thad glared at him and Leo said, "Not cool man. Not cool."

After that the game was a cakewalk. Our strategy worked better than expected, getting not only Thad on our side but Leo as well. With their half-hearted showing, Becks was basically playing by himself. By game's end, Clayton and Ollie were having a victory toast, taunting the others for their abysmal performance, and I was in possession of the Golden Troll. Becks strolled up as I pretended to give it a polish.

"That was some dirty trick," he remarked. "Faking like that, making us think you were seriously injured, I didn't know you had it in you."

"You're just mad you didn't think of it first," I said, hugging the Troll to my chest. "Besides, it was Ollie's idea, not mine."

His eyes narrowed. "You really had me for a minute there."

"Becks, you barely touched me."

"Yeah, but it scared me just the same."

I studied his face, saw he was serious. "Sorry, I didn't mean to worry you."

"Nope."

"No, what?"

"Sorry's not going to cut it, Sal." Becks stood hands on hips, shaking his head. "I nearly died from the guilt. My nerves are still shot. It's gonna take something more, something valuable, something...golden."

"No way," I said, walking backward.

"You cheated," he said, matching me step for step.

"We won fair and square."

"I think you'd agree that's a stretch."

I did but stayed silent.

"Hand over the troll, Sal."

"Never." He had me trapped, pressed up against a tree in the Kent's backyard, but still I clutched the trophy tighter. "Goldie's mine this year. You can't have her, Becks. I won't let you."

Becks's eyes widened. "You named it?"

"Yes," I said, "a few years ago, so what?" I figured if it was so important, ugly or no, why not give the troll a name? Goldie wasn't much to look at, but this year she was going home with me. It was only the second time my team had won. He wouldn't get her without a fight. "I'm not giving her up, Becks. There's nothing you can say or do to make me change my mind."

He grinned. "I believe you owe me a favor."

Except that, I thought.

"Give her here," he said, holding out a hand.

Frowning, I took one last look at Goldie, smoothed out her thinning hair, then shoved the doll into his chest. "You're a poor loser, Baldwin Eugene. Anybody ever tell you that?"

He laughed breathlessly. I was glad to see I'd managed to wind him. "You guys play dirty, but I play dirtier. Cheaters never win, you should know that."

"Whatever," I mumbled, pushing past him.

"Sal," he called, but I just kept walking. Even though I loved him, sometimes Becks really got on my nerves.

Becks was only seconds behind as I took a seat at the table, and wouldn't you know it? They'd saved us two seats, side by side. Great.

"Don't be mad," Becks said, placing a hand on mine, setting Goldie on the floor between us. I took one look at her, met his eyes and looked away. "Aw, come on, Sal."

"Hey," Clayton said, pointing, "what're you doing with that? We gave the Troll to Sally for a job well done. She earned it."

Becks sighed, giving up. I was mad about the troll, and he'd just have to wait it out. "She gave it to me because she felt bad about tricking us."

"That true, Sally?" Ollie asked, taking a sip of Coke. "I thought it might've been 'cause you two are so in love."

I snorted, ignoring Becks's injured look.

"Who's in love?" Leo walked out of the kitchen, plate piled high. "Oh," he said, eyes landing on our hands. "You know, I knew about Becks, but I never suspected you, Sally. The crush he had was a big one that's for sure."

I felt my brow contract. What was Leo talking about?

"Yeah," Ollie laughed. "He was a goner practically from day one."

"Shut up," Becks said to no one in particular.

"Did he ever read you that poem?" Clayton asked, smiling.

"Yeah," Ollie said, "classic."

"What poem?" I asked curious. I had no idea what they were going on about, but it definitely sounded interesting. Plus, it was making Becks pink in the cheeks and, being mad at him, I wasn't above some well-deserved payback.

The answer came, but not from Becks.

As the parents and Thad joined us, setting food on the table, Mrs. Kent took the seat on my other side and laid a book out in front of me. It was thick with a flowery cover, and Becks sat back removing his hand from mind, running it through his hair instead.

"Jeez, Mom," he said, "is this really necessary?"

Mrs. Kent shot him a look but smiled at me. "I just wanted to show Martha and Sally some pictures." To my mother who was leaning toward us, she said, "I've been keeping this since they first met."

"Oh," Mom said happily, "we have a few shots at home but not a whole album. I'd love to get copies."

"I'll make you some," Mrs. Kent promised and opened the cover.

It was like traveling back in time. Pictures of me and Becks on our first day of high school, the two of us dressed up at Halloween, a prince and princess one year, Trekkies the next, complete with pointy ears and Spock eyebrows. The next page showed us at a Valentine's Day dance in middle school, me cheering in the stands at one of Becks's soccer games, a candid of Becks giving me a noogie. Becks pushing me on the swings. Me hugging Becks at the amusement park where he got sick after eating a bad corndog. The two of us at the aquarium, a parade, the movies. There were enough memories in this one little book to make me want to forget about Goldie and forgive Becks for being a jerk. But it wasn't until the last page that my anger changed to something else entirely.

"Oh," I said, reaching out to touch the final picture.

"Yes," Mrs. Kent said, "that's my favorite, too."

There we were, Becks at seven years old, me just barely turned. It was taken on the playground by the monkey bars where Becks had gotten stuck and I'd

talked him down. My arm was already in a bright pink
cast, so it must've been at least a week or two afterward, but Becks looked just as he had that first day.
Wavy black hair hanging low into his eyes, same boy-
ish grin he wore to this day. We were both looking at
each other, but I was laughing, tears streaming from
my eyes as I gazed back at Becks.

I loved him even then.

"Oh, I've got to have that one, Carole," Mom said.
"Just look at how he's looking at her."

Mrs. Kent nodded in agreement, but I couldn't see
that Becks was looking at me in any particular way.
Sure, his eyes were smiling like they did sometimes.
But he always looked at me like that.

"And here's the best part," Mrs. Kent smiled, slipping something from behind the photo and holding it
up. "It's to Sally, from Becks, but he never got around
to giving it to her."

"Mom," Becks exclaimed. He made a grab for the
paper but was too slow. Clayton had it in his hands,
unfolded, and was clearing his throat to read aloud as
Becks sank back into his chair, face red. I'd never seen
him look so embarrassed.

"To Sal, from Becks," Clayton read aloud. "Listen
up, Sally, you're not going to want to miss this."

Becks closed his eyes.

Okay, so now I was really curious—and confused. What could possibly make Becks act this way?

Clayton cleared his throat a second time then repeated, "To Sal, From Becks. There is a girl I like. She rides a yellow bike. Her hair is long. Her eyes are round. Her voice is nice. I like the sound."

Thad leaned toward Becks and said, "That's good, man, real good."

I saw Becks wave him off out of my peripheral but couldn't take my eyes away from Clayton.

"I broke her arm when we met. She was nice; I signed her cast." Clayton took a time-out to say, "You could've done better than that. 'Met' and 'cast' don't exactly rhyme, but I guess you were young."

"Here's where it gets good," Leo said to me.

With that Clayton read the last three lines. "She is my friend. Her name is Sal. I hope one day she'll be my gal." A lot of oohing and aahing followed. Clayton refolded the paper and handed it back to his mother. "Guess you got your wish, didn't you brother?"

It was just a poem, but it meant so much more. I wasn't alone. At one time, even if we'd only been kids, Becks had loved me back.

Turning to him, I could feel tears filling my eyes.

"You wrote that?" I asked.

Becks wouldn't look at me. "Yep."

"For me?"

He nodded, but still wouldn't meet my eyes.

Leaning in, I kissed his cheek. "Thank you," I murmured.

Becks looked at me then, surprised. "What's that for?"

"It's the sweetest thing I've ever heard." Catching myself, I lowered my voice so only he could hear. "Plus, our parents are watching, remember?"

"Sure," he said, lifting my hand for a kiss, but there was something strange in his tone. "You coming to the game? It's the last one before sectionals."

"Of course," I smiled. "I want to see you kick Boulder High's butt as much as anyone." Raising my voice again, I added, "Besides, what kind of girlfriend would I be if I didn't?"

His face seemed to close off, but I put that down to embarrassment. Before I left, I pulled Mrs. Kent aside and asked for the poem. She said it was mine anyway and gave it up without question. By the time I went to sleep that night, I'd read it thirteen times.

I hope one day she'll be my gal.

Ah Becks, I thought on the verge of sleep. I always have been.

CHAPTER 10

Guilt. It was eating me up from the inside out, and all I could do was sit there and rot while Becks made his third goal of the night. The crowd cheered, he pumped his fist, the fans on Boulder's side groaned. The boy was on fire. Girls were giving him the eye, catcalls flying left and right, the loudest coming from a pretty brunette about two rows down, holding a sign that read, "Becks, will you marry me?" encased in a big, glittery pink heart.

"You gonna let her get away with that?" Hooker asked at my side.

"What can I do about it?" I mumbled. "She's not hurting anyone."

Hooker frowned at me. "I tell you what I'd do. If Becks was my man, I'd rip that sign right up and throw it back in her face, teach her what's what."

"I can't do that."

"It'd serve her right."

I was a bad person, a full-on hypocrite, because that's what I'd been itching to do ever since I spotted the poster. The urge came on extra-strong when the girl tried to flash Becks as he turned around at halftime, scanning the stands.

"Hey, Becks," Ollie shouted, "I don't think the guys from Penn saw that one. You want to make it an even four?"

"Yeah," Thad said. "UCLA was looking, though. Maybe they want you more."

"My vote's Michigan," Clayton called from the bench.

"UNC," someone hollered and was greeted by a round of cheers.

"Indiana!"

"Gotta be Louisville!"

"No way, Ohio!"

"So, what's it gonna be, son?"

Becks shrugged as the crowd called out more schools, and the recruiters tried to look unruffled. They were doing a poor job of it. Every single one of them was on the edge of their seats, straight-back, tense, waiting to hear Becks's answer. It was due any day now. They'd been waiting for months. Apart from scoring three, Becks had already made five steals, two assists and blocked a couple goals. It was one of the main reasons they wanted him. He was just as strong on defense as he was on offense.

"Becks, you're so *hot*!" The brunette's voice was loud and high like a siren. The sound made the hairs on my neck stand up. "Come to my party this Saturday?"

"No, come home with me," this from a fiery redhead a few seats away. "I'll show you a good time."

I decided then and there I disliked the color red.

"Hey," the brunette shrieked. "He's mine!"

Red flipped her hair. "Keep dreamin' honey."

"Hey." Hooker stood, glaring at the two of them until they turned. "Becks is the property of Sally Sue Spitz. This girl—" She pointed at me, and I cringed. "—He's her boyfriend, you got that? Leave him be."

"Yeah, lay off," Leo added. A couple more "yeahs" came from the surrounding area, people I didn't even know. I sank further into my seat.

The girls scoffed, but stopped arguing.

"Good." Hooker eased back down, satisfied.

Locking eyes with me, Becks smiled and held up his palms as if to say, "They love me. What're you going to do?" before Crenshaw dragged him back to the group.

"It's alright." Leo patted my shoulder. "Becks would never go for them anyway."

"Got that right," Thad agreed. "He's all yours, Sally."

"Even if the redhead was pretty hot," Ollie added, which earned him a slap on the head from Mr. Kent. "Holy cow, I was just saying he's loyal. That's all."

This seemed to satisfy the parents, and Mrs. Kent went back to talking with my mom, who shot me a wink and gave Hooker an approving nod.

My return smile was part grimace.

Sitting there in my Gryffindor jersey, I felt like the lowest of the low, a fraud, a scoundrel.

A Slytherin.

After all, only a Slytherin would tell lies for their own gain. Only a Slytherin would take advantage of a friend and ask them to do something so dishonest. And nobody but a Slytherin would keep this thing going simply because they were too scared, too much of a coward, to call it off. Even when it meant keeping her friend from doing what he wanted, seeing who he wanted.

Like the hot redhead who'd just given him an open invitation.

I wasn't sure why this was hitting me now. Becks and I had been lying for weeks. We'd convinced everyone that we were a couple, soul mates, made for each other. With Becks doing such a spectacular job on the F.B.F. front and me falling for him more each day, it hadn't been hard. But here in the stands, watching Becks singlehandedly knock out the competition, hearing an endless supply of girls call his name, listening to Hooker claim Becks as mine, I couldn't stand myself.

It was that poem, had to be. The words, beautiful and heartfelt, were also guilt-inducing. If I really loved Becks, how could I do this to him? Wouldn't the right thing be to let him go?

The attack on my conscience was so great it made me want to confess everything. I could do it. It'd make a lot of people mad, and I'd probably be condemning myself to a lifetime of matchmaking hell, but I could do it. Becks would be angry at first, but he'd get over it. Like he'd said, there were girls who wanted to date him for real. I was holding him back. Maybe it'd be best to come clean before he started to resent me—or worse, before I did something stupid and gave myself away. I didn't want him feeling sorry for me. Becks was my best friend and I loved him, but I'd jump off a skyscraper before I let him tie himself to me out of pity.

I've got to do it, I thought. Confess everything, fess up for Becks's sake. For mine.

It was what any good Gryffindor would do.

Taking a deep breath, I opened my mouth and...

"Sally?"

The interruption startled me, the words trapped in my throat.

"I think that boy's calling you," Mrs. Kent whispered.

Oh my God.

A whistle blew. The game restarted.

My throat closed up tight. Sense returned with a vengeance, piercing my flimsy shield of courage and replacing it with dread. All the reasons why I shouldn't confess slapped me in the face, one after the other, leaving me dazed. Lord, what was I thinking?

"Sally Spitz?"

"Slytherin," I muttered under my breath.

"What was that?" Hooker asked, but I stayed quiet.

Forget Gryffindor. My middle name wasn't Sue; it was Chicken. My favorite color wasn't blue but green. I was nothing but a big old, shaking-in-my-boots snake in the grass. I sighed. When in the world had I become such a first-class coward?

"Sally?" The voice was much closer now.

"Uh oh," Hooker said, "it's Mr. Sexy Surfer in his Chinos. Want me to get rid of him?"

I followed her gaze and saw Austin Harris, Mr. Sexy Surfer as Hooker called him, standing at the end of our row, smiling at me. Our first (and only) date had been short but memorable. It's not every day you see a guy declare his undying love to a girl. Especially when you're the girl. And the guy's only known you for three hours. I fondly remembered Austin as a wackadoo with a heart. That night seemed like it happened ages ago, to someone else.

"Hey," he said, "I thought it was you. Love the shirt by the way."

"Thanks," I said, making my way over. I tried not to feel like too much of an impostor. When I reached him, I gestured to his chest. "Where's your tie?"

"Left it at home," he said. "So, how are you?"

Was that a trick question? "I'm good, and you?"

"Oh, I'm great. Actually I—"

Just then, the crowd erupted.

Thad jumped up, thrusting his hand out to encompass the field. "Are you blind? That was a flagrant. Call something ref!"

"Do your damn job," Ollie yelled.

This time Mrs. Kent tagged him with a hard pinch to the ear. Judging by the sounds he was making, that had to hurt.

Austin tilted his head toward the game. "Is that your boyfriend down there? He's killing us."

"You mean, Becks," I swallowed, feeling the lie stick in my throat. "Yeah, I guess so."

"Man." Austin shook his head as play resumed, and Becks made a breakaway. "It's probably a good thing it didn't work out between us," he sighed dramatically. "I could've never competed with that."

I laughed. No one could compete with Becks, at least in my view. "Not a big soccer fan?"

He grinned. "No, I'm more into role playing. Final Fantasy, World of Warcraft, that kind of thing. Actually that's where I met my girlfriend. She's right down there, front row, toward the middle."

I saw where he was pointing and did a double take. The girl was gorgeous, almost as gorgeous as Austin, and that was saying something. Flashing the two of us a grin, she blew him a kiss, and he pretended to catch and tuck it into his pocket.

"Isn't she great?" he said.

"Great," I repeated then got serious. "But I thought you said you loved me?"

He blushed, rocked back on his heels. "Well...about that, I—"

"I'm just kidding," I said, punching him in the shoulder. "I'm glad you found someone. She's beautiful."

"Oh, good," he said, capturing my hand. The twinkle in his eyes was unmistakable as he bent forward. "But you know you'll always be my first, Sally." Bowing low, he dropped a quick kiss to my hand and looked up through his lashes, causing us both to laugh.

Someone cleared their throat. Loudly.

Glancing over, I saw Hooker, her boyfriend Will, my mom, Becks's parents, and all the brothers watching us. Actually, the boys were giving Austin looks that ranged anywhere from dirty to threatening. I guess we'd taken their attention away from the game. Yippee.

I blushed as Austin released my hand and stood upright.

"Guess I'll see you around," he said, throwing nervous glances at the Kents.

I felt their stares shift to me. "Okay, I'll—"

A thousand gasps seemed to ripple through the stadium at once.

I turned my head, heard Mrs. Kent scream as the others rushed by me to get to the stairs—but I couldn't move. Couldn't breathe.

"Sally?"

"Spitz, you okay?"

Austin and Hooker were calling my name, but I couldn't focus. All my attention was on the chilling scene below.

Becks was on his back, clutching his right leg to his chest, face contorted in agony, as Clayton tried to get him to straighten out.

"No, no, no..."

Was that my voice?

Tripping over my own feet, I was vaguely aware of the hands steadying me down the stairs.

"He'll be okay." Hooker's voice at my ear. "Don't worry, Spitz. He'll be fine."

I barely heard her as two medics jogged onto the field and went to work. Each one of Becks's groans was amplified to a sonic boom in my ears, loud, deafening.

This can't be happening, I thought, finally making it to ground level. Becks couldn't be hurt. He just couldn't be. Soccer was his passion, what he was made to do. God wouldn't take that away from him, not now, not ever. It would be too cruel.

Please, don't take this away from him, I prayed silently.

Eyes stinging, I watched them carry Becks off the field on a stretcher. It was one of those things I'd have nightmares about long after this day.

"Spitz." I looked to the side and saw Hooker. Guess she'd been there the whole time. "He'll be fine," she said with certainty. But how could she know?

"Sally, I'm going to take Mrs. Kent and the boys home," Mom said, holding Mrs. Kent's hand, the rest of the boys following close behind. They looked destroyed. "Can Hooker or Clayton take you home?"

"No problem," Hooker said and led me to the locker room.

My heart sank further as I spotted my dad, blocking the door. Deputy Spitz must've gotten called in to work security for the game. He was in uniform and watched impassively as we approached.

"Can we go in?" Hooker asked.

Dad shook his head. "Family and team members only."

But Becks is *my family*, I wanted to scream, but my voice had gone mute the minute I saw Becks laid out on that stretcher.

Hooker didn't seem to have that problem.

"You're kidding me, right?" she said, eyes narrowed. "You can't seriously be that heartless to your own daughter. Can't you see she's upset?"

Upset didn't even begin to cover it. Honestly, it was like I was suffocating, dying a little more with every second I was away from Becks. But I was glad Hooker was there. I'd need her strength if I was going to get through this next part.

Swallowing hard, I did the one thing I'd promised myself I would never do. Something I'd sworn off over a decade ago.

I asked my father for a favor.

"Please," I said, voice shaking, from despair or disgust I wasn't sure. "Let me in. I...I need to see him, Dad. To make sure he's okay, to see if Becks needs me. I need to know he's alright, so just...please."

His eyes moved slowly over my face, his expression unreadable. I wasn't sure what he saw, but I felt like I was going to dry heave right there on the concrete. I'd never asked him for anything after he'd cheated on Mom. Not once. There were no weekly visitations. There were no yearly birthday cards with cash in them. If I overlooked the fact that we lived in the same town, I could practically pretend he didn't exist. I'd never cared that he wasn't around, preferred it that way. But I needed to see Becks, needed it like air in my lungs.

If my father was the key to getting to him, I'd do whatever it took.

Dad met my eyes a moment later, and I knew even before he spoke what his answer would be.

"Sorry, Sally girl," he said with a shrug. "It's the policy. There's nothing I can do."

Hooker's mouth hung open like she couldn't believe it—but I could.

I'd given up on him a long time ago. Somehow, though, he still managed to disappoint me.

Hooker shook her head then said, "You really are a bastard, aren't you?"

"You watch your mouth." Dad frowned, tugging up his belt and holding a hand out to me. "She's just overreacting like her mother always did. She'll get over it."

"No," I said, and they turned to me. "It's fine, Hooker, I'll just wait."

"But—"

I shook my head. "No," I repeated. No, I wouldn't get over it. And no, I wouldn't ask again. "I'll wait."

I sent Hooker home with Will about an hour later when the game ended. I could tell my pacing was getting to her, but I couldn't help myself. I pretended like my dad wasn't there, and he did the same. We didn't speak again. The fans ambled past, some throwing me pitying looks. One even told me Boulder had come back strong in the second half, but because of Becks we'd still outscored them by a goal, and wasn't I happy my boyfriend had at least taken them to the first round of sectionals undefeated?

That person was lucky I was so focused on Becks. Otherwise, I'd have coldcocked him and directed my next round of paces over his stupid, too-happy face.

What was taking so long? Was Becks really that hurt? I didn't know what I'd do if he was.

I watched as player after player exited the dressing room until the last one left.

Still no Becks. No Clayton either, I noticed.

God, what were they doing to him in there?

"Waiting on your boyfriend?" I stopped as Ash joined me. "He and his dad left about thirty minutes ago."

"What?" I said, confused.

"Becks," he said, hefting a large duffle bag onto his shoulder. "He left. Weren't you waiting for him?"

That made absolutely no sense. "But I've been standing here the whole time," I said. "I didn't see him leave."

"They went out the side door around back." Ash pointed to my face. "There's no need for that. It was just a sprain, wouldn't have even happened if you hadn't distracted him. He'll be alright."

"What?" I reached up. He was right; my cheeks were damp. I must've been crying the whole time, but I hadn't felt a thing. "Did you say a sprain? That's it?"

Ash nodded, and I sighed in relief. A sprain was nothing. Becks had had so many of those he'd probably be back on the field in a week. Then something else struck me.

"Wait, what do you mean *I* distracted him?" Becks was going to be fine. He was okay, so what was Ash talking about? "How could I do that? We were in the top row; he could barely even see me."

"Trust me, he saw," Ash said. "He saw you and that blond guy getting friendly, and it messed with his head. I was standing right there when a player from the other team blindsided him. He wasn't even paying attention."

"You mean, Austin?" I scoffed. "He's just a friend."

"Yeah, didn't look that way."

I stared but got distracted when Clayton stepped out of the dressing room. He didn't look any better than I felt. Guess he'd been worried about his baby brother, too.

"Well, Sally," he said, stopping in front of me. "I think our boy's going to make it through just fine, but you think you could tone down the flirting? Becks'll be useless to us if you distract him like that in the finals."

I couldn't believe what I was hearing.

"Told you," Ash said.

My mouth opened and closed a few times, no sound coming out.

"You ready to go?" Clayton asked. "Your Mom called to make sure you had a ride home."

Drawing in some air, trying to sound firm and not snippy, I said, "Sure, Clayton, I'm ready. And by the way you're both wrong." I looked at them coolly. "Becks doesn't get distracted, especially not by something like that."

Ash and Clayton exchanged a look, and though they didn't say it, I knew they were making fun of me. I stalked to Clayton's truck in a huff and refused to speak to him the entire ride—which seemed fine by him. We both had a lot to think over.

Later on, I dialed Becks to give him a piece of my mind. I'd been waiting and waiting for him to call, but he never did. One sprained ankle didn't mean he couldn't pick up the phone.

He answered on the fourth ring. "Hey, Sal."

Hey, Sal? I'd reached my limit. "Hey, Sal," I repeated, "that's all you have to say? No, 'I'm sorry I didn't call. I feel just horrible about it. I'm a complete jerk off for making you worry.'"

"You were worried?" He sounded far too pleased.

"Only a little," I lied.

"You know, I can tell when you're lying, Sal."

Blast.

"Well, I shouldn't have been," I said. "You seem completely fine. Fine enough to tease me, fine enough not to call. I guess I shouldn't have waited outside that locker room with my crappy father for hours. Guess I shouldn't have been worried at all."

Becks paused then said, "Your dad was there?"

"Yeah, he wouldn't let me in the locker room to see you."

"That was a real jerk move."

"I know," I said, "seems to be a lot of that going around lately."

He sighed. "You're mad."

"And you're a genius," I retorted, flipping on the TV. Maybe some mindless entertainment would divert my attention. Why hadn't he called?

"I'm sorry," he said finally.

"For what?"

"For being a jerk."

"And?"

"And for not calling, I just figured someone would've told you."

"Well, they didn't."

"Sorry," he said again.

"Stop saying that," I said, feeling a bit of my anger subside. "How are you anyway? I heard it was just a sprain."

"Well, my foot hurts like a mother and Clayton's none too happy about my lack of concentration. Other than that I'm just terrific."

I pressed back into the pillows. "Yeah, what happened out there? I missed it. Are you going to sit out any games?"

There was rustling at the other end of the line, and I imagined Becks getting more comfortable as well.

Skipping the first question, Becks said, "Yeah, only the next one. I should be better if we make it to the third round."

"*When*," I said, "when you make it."

"When," he agreed. There was silence for a beat and then, "So, who's the Ken lookalike? He the one you have your eye on?"

It took me a second to understand.

Hesitantly, I asked, "Are you talking about Austin Harris?"

"If Austin Harris was that guy putting the moves on you, then yes."

"He was *not* putting the moves on me."

"He was kissing you," Becks said flatly.

"Yeah, on the hand," I said back. Could Clayton and Ash have been right? Was Becks actually distracted by me talking to some other guy? Was he jealous? I knew the answer and mentally laughed at myself. Yeah, right. Like that would ever happen.

"So, is it him? Is Austin Harris the guy that sets your heart pounding? The one you're trying to impress with a fake boyfriend?"

His tone was light, his words teasing, but he seemed to be waiting for an answer.

"No," I said, "it's not Austin."

"Oh," Becks said, and, in my mind, I saw him grin.

"The guy I like is much hotter." I heard Becks stutter and nearly cracked up. "Almost too hot for his own good."

"Nobody's that hot" Becks mumbled.

If you only knew, I thought. "But Austin was impressed," I added.

"With what?"

"You."

"Who wouldn't be?"

I laughed at his cocky tone, looked up at the TV and laughed some more. "You aren't going to believe this," I said.

"What?" he asked.

"You're on TV, channel six."

"What?" he said then groaned. "Oh God, this is so embarrassing."

"No, it's not, Becks. You're a movie star."

Becks cursed, but I paid no mind. I was listening to the interview. The main subject seemed to be where Becks would play college ball. I was waiting for the answer to that one myself.

Erica Pinkerton, former Miss North Carolina, current anchorwoman at large, smiled. "Welcome, Becks Kent to our program. It's great to have you."

"Great to be here," the TV Becks said.

"Awww," I crooned, "aren't you just the cutest thing?"

Becks grumbled something unintelligible, but the newscaster seemed to agree.

"You're sweet," she said, smile widening, "and talented. You've already led your team to one undefeated season, and the Chariot Trojans seem on track for another. That's never been done, Becks. How do you feel going into the qualifying rounds? Confident? Nervous?"

"A little of both actually," he laughed. "We are confident, but we're just going to have to wait and see how everything plays out. Our team's well-conditioned. We've got a deep bench and solid coaching. I'm hoping we'll make it to the end."

"And so is the rest of Chariot." She winked to camera then turned back to Becks. "So Becks, where's it going to be? We've heard reports all over town. All the top schools have offered. Naturally, most of us want you to stay right here in North Carolina, but for a successful athlete like you, the choices are limitless."

She held the microphone out to him and licked her lips, making sure to brush him with her arm. Very subtle.

"Well, I don't know," Becks said, gifting her with one of his killer grins. "There are a lot of great schools out there."

"You're a real sweetheart," Pinkerton said. "Any of those schools would be lucky to have you, of course. But what our viewers want to know is how will you choose? With so many offers on the table, what's it going to take to set that school apart, make it the one?"

Again she brushed him with her arm, and again I gritted my teeth. The woman had to be at least forty. The cougar was out of her cage and preying on my Becks. It was just wrong.

"We'll just have to wait and see," Becks said cryptically.

"Ah, come on, Becks." The woman would not be denied. "The two favorites seem to be Penn State and Ohio. Couldn't you at least tell us the one you're leaning toward?"

The thought of Becks going so far away made me feel sick—and then mad about feeling that way. Even if Becks decided on Penn—a great distance from Duke no matter how you spun it—as his friend, as his *best* friend, I should support him, right? Right?

The Becks on TV shook his head. "They both have great teams and coaching. Every school I've heard from does. All I can say is this: I'm looking for something extraordinary. That one special spark that no other school has. That'll be what makes my decision."

"Well, there you go, ladies and gentlemen." Pinkerton took the ball and ran, seeing he wouldn't give her anymore details. "It's going to take that special spark to get Becks Kent through the door. We'll have the answer to which school has it in a couple of weeks."

As they went to commercial, I turned off the screen.

Trying to sound carefree, feeling anything but, I repeated Pinkerton's words. "So Becks," I said to the silence on the other end, "where's it going to be?"

"We talked about this, Sal." I couldn't see it, but I knew he was shaking his head.

"But Becks—"

"You'll find out when everyone else does."

"But I'm your best friend," I protested.

"Yeah," Becks said, "and you promised you wouldn't nag me about this."

"I just don't see why I have to wait," I said. "At least tell me this. Have you made your decision?"

"I have an idea," Becks said, which told me nothing. "Have you gotten your letter from Duke, yet?"

"Way to change the subject, and no. I haven't heard."

"You'll get in."

I forced a laugh. "Don't be so sure." It would take a miracle. Mom was a middle-income single-parent, and I'd need a scholarship to fit the bill. I'd worked on my writing samples for months in advance, editing, perfecting, until everything was spit-shined. Problem was I wasn't the only Salutatorian applying to major in creative writing with nothing but a few clubs, good grades and a dream to her name.

"You will," Becks said. "I know you will. You'll get in and write a freaking bestseller your first time out."

I played along. "And you'll be on a soccer pitch somewhere, winning your third World Cup."

"And we'll still be friends," Becks added. "Through everything, no matter where we are, no matter what happens, we'll always be friends, right Sal?"

I thought of how I'd kissed him, how he'd kissed me back. I thought of how he'd held my hand, been there whenever I needed him, the poem I'd never known he'd written until just a few days ago.

"Right?" Becks insisted.

"Right," I choked. "Becks, I've gotta go, okay?"

"Okay. Night, Sal."

"Night."

I hung up, utterly defeated. It'd been less than three weeks, but I couldn't keep doing this. The F.B.F. plan was good in theory, but in practice it was more trouble than I could handle. The havoc it was wreaking on my heart was too much. Something had to be done and fast. Becks would understand. He'd probably be relieved, might even thank me for it.

Tomorrow, I decided. Slytherin or not, I would do it tomorrow. What I needed to figure out was how best to do the deed.

CHAPTER 11

Becks wasn't happy.

"What the hell, Sal?"

Correction, Becks was *pissed*.

As I approached, he stayed locked in his position against my locker, stiff-legged, an unfamiliar scowl on his face. I only ever saw it those rare times when he failed a test (hardly ever) or lost a game. The expression had been safely tucked away for over a year, but it was clearly on display today.

I decided to play dumb.

"How's it going, Becks?" I asked. "Your ankle any better?"

"My ankle's fine," he said tightly, "and I was too until about ten minutes ago."

"Really?" I was eyes down, giving every spare bit of attention to my combination. With Becks breathing down my neck, I'd already screwed it up twice.

"Umm, you know why?"

Third time did the trick, and I scrambled to get my books in and out as fast as I could.

"No idea, huh?" Becks leaned closer, his voice whisper-soft. "Well, now let's see. My girlfriend just broke up with me, and you know what? She didn't even have the guts to do it to my face. Pretty messed up, right?"

"Pretend," I said, slamming my locker closed. In a voice just as quiet, I faced him and said, "*Pretend* girl-friend, Becks. We were going to end this in a couple of weeks anyway. What's the big deal?"

He stared at me, and then held up his phone. "A text, Sal?"

I flinched.

"'F.B.F. plan not working. Want 2 break early. It's me, not U.'" Becks recited the message like I might've forgotten.

As if.

I glared at my hands. They'd shaken for an entire minute after I pushed send.

"So?" His tone, his eyes demanded an explanation.

I didn't have one—or at least not one I was ready to tell him—so instead I said, "I just don't want to hold you back."

"What?"

"Like you said, there are plenty of girls out there." I shrugged and started walking. "At the game, I realized just how many. School's going to end soon. It's not right for me to take advantage of you like this."

"But you knew that from the start," he said, trying to keep pace. I adjusted my stride to his—taking into account his bad ankle—though all I really wanted to do was run. "And I let you take advantage. What changed?"

Hmm, let's see: I realized I was a bad friend, a manipulator, and a Slytherin. We lied to our parents. You wrote that poem. We kissed. A lot of things had changed, but I couldn't say any of that to Becks.

"Hey Bally," Rick Smythe said, giving Becks a high five as we passed. "I'm all for UCLA my friend. Go Bruins!"

Becks nodded, but his eyes were on me.

"Bally," someone shouted, "Ohio's the way to go, man!"

"Yo, Bally." Trent Zuckerman gave Becks's cheeks a two-handed rub down, smiled at me then went on his way.

"What's that they're calling you?" I muttered. We were almost to Ms. Vega's door. If I could just hold him off until then, maybe he'd let it rest.

"Us," he said. "Not me, us. Don't you remember Clayton's couple name?"

"Don't tell me," I groaned.

"Apparently Bally is catching on." He tugged on my arm as we reached the door. "Sal, I need you to tell me what happened. Is something wrong?"

The concern in his face undid me.

Pulling him a little ways down the hall, I took a deep breath, not knowing what I was going to say exactly, but before I could speak Becks asked the most ridiculous question.

"Was it something I did?" he asked. "Something I said?"

"What, no." I was taken aback. "You didn't do anything. It was just time."

"Is it him? Did your guy finally wise up?"

"I'm not following."

"Jeez, do I have to say it? Sal, are you dumping me for the competition or what?"

Ah, I thought with sudden clarity. My made-up crush.

I would've laugh at his sullen expression if I didn't feel like a total jerk for putting it there. Well, that explained the bitterness—which was actually pretty ironic because the only competition Becks had was himself.

"Listen." I took his face between my hands, much gentler than I'd seen Zuckerman do, and looked him in the eye. I owed him this much. "It's not that at all. There's no competition, Becks. I don't even think I like him that much anymore."

Liar, liar, pants on fire. My mind said it over and over, but since when was that news? These days it felt like I was born to lie.

"I've just been feeling so guilty lately," I continued. "That's really all it was." For the most part.

"But Sal," he said, using the same reasonable tone, "the deal was a month. You said so yourself, it's not going to be as believable otherwise. Plus, do you really think people are going to buy it? That we broke up, just like that, for no good reason? Because I don't. We've done our job too well. People love us together."

As if to reinforce his words, the pretty brunette from Tuesday's game sauntered up and handed Becks a pink envelope.

Smiling bright, she said to me, "No hard feelings, okay? Man, are you lucky."

The smile I gave back must've really made an impression because the girl took a step back. Good, I thought. Like Hooker said, serves her right for first proposing to Becks then trying to flash him in the middle of a game. I mean, who does that?

"Yeah, I am." I dropped my hands, but stayed close. I didn't want to give her too much room. She might try and get her shirt over her head, hoping Becks'll dump me for nice teeth and an overly perky bust line. Yeah, not today, sweetheart. "And I'm not a man."

"Oh, I know that," she laughed nervously. "I just wanted to make sure you guys had your invite. The party's next Saturday at my house, to celebrate after the first round. Later, Bally. Hope you guys can make it."

With that, she turned on her heels and scurried away. It was a nice touch, adding our couple name, but there was no mistaking who the invitation and the flirtatious glance she threw over her shoulder were for.

"You're really good at that."

Startled, I looked back at Becks. "Good at what?"

"Playing the jealous girlfriend," he said, eyes narrowed. "If I didn't know better, I'd say you were really jealous."

I forced a smile. "Well, technically, you are still my boyfriend as far as she knows."

He studied my face, and I was afraid I might've given myself away.

I tried not to fidget.

Finally, Becks ran a hand through his hair and said, "Sal, this isn't going to work."

"What's not?" I asked.

"I don't see why we couldn't just keep it going. That would only be a couple more weeks, not even. If Mercedes is asking us to come to one of her parties, it's—"

"Wait," I said, "her name is *Mercedes*? Like the car?"

Becks nodded. "Yeah, she's a senior, too, just transferred this year. She's promised to throw a party for every win we get in sectionals."

"How generous." It bothered me how much Becks knew about her.

The warning bell sounded.

"Listen, Sal," Becks said. "We've got to do it big and public. That's the only way anyone will believe our break-up. Let's just keep it going until Mercedes's party."

"But—"

He touched my hand, and I watched him shake his head. "It'll be the perfect place. Trust me. Plus, this'll give us more time to ease people into it."

"But what if you want to—"

"Let's talk about it later, okay?" He dipped his head to look me in the eye. "No more break-up texts, alright?"

Reluctantly, I nodded. Guess Becks didn't like getting dumped by phone, even by fake girlfriends. "Alright, but we will talk. Like I said, Becks, I don't want to hold you back."

"You're not." He smiled, squeezed my hand then jogged away.

Maybe he's right, I thought, walking to first. Springing this on people might not have been my best idea. The text had definitely been a mistake, but I'd been going for quick and painless.

"Trouble in paradise?"

Hooker was waiting for me at the door.

"No," I said, walking past her, and she followed. "Becks just got invited to some party."

"Oh." Hooker held up her own pink envelope. "You mean, this one? Mercedes was the one with the poster, right?"

"Yeah," I muttered, remembering the look she'd given Becks. That made at least one girl who'd enjoy our big break-up. She'd probably hit on him before he even left the party.

"You know what this means?"

I sighed and shook my head.

Hooker's smile widened. "It's been a while since we performed, Spitz. I'm thinking this would be the perfect opportunity to pull out the old Stetson."

My mood lifted. "You think so?"

"It's tradition." There was an odd twinkle in her eyes now. "Besides, it's senior year. We've got to do it."

I could feel my eyes twinkling, too. "Which scene?"

"You know which scene."

I did.

"Do you remember your lines?" I asked, grinning.

She rolled her eyes. "Do you?"

"I'm in," I said just as the bell rang and Ms. Vega called Hooker's name.

"Great," Hooker said, standing. "You better be ready, Spitz. Last time before graduation, we need to make it good."

The thought had me smiling throughout German.

As the days went on, though, even the idea of crashing Mercedes's party couldn't keep my spirits up. Everyone—even teachers—kept stopping Becks, telling him which school he should choose, where he should go. Most of them were so far away; it made me want to cry—or punch someone. When Mr. Pulaski suggested Becks play overseas, I'd seriously considered giving him five across the face.

If our plan was to ease people into the idea of us not being together, he was making it difficult. *Really* difficult. I couldn't understand it. Whenever I'd bring up the subject of our break-up, he'd just brush me off and say, "Like I said, big and public. We can talk about it more later."

But we never did.

Worse, after our talk, Becks had upped his F.B.F. game to the nth degree, more handholding, more beneath the ear kisses. He took me to the movies, to dinner, invited me to hang out at his house, came to watch TV at mine. None of this was new. We'd done all those things for years, but there was one huge difference.

He was always touching me in some way, my hand, my waist, my face. It wasn't that I didn't like it. There wasn't a nerve in my body that didn't respond to him. He had no idea what those small touches did to me—and that was the problem. It didn't mean the same thing to Becks. He was playing a part, and I was enjoying it all too much. A person could only endure so many of Becks's touches before their mind turned to the dark side. The idea of keeping Becks as my F.B.F. forever had already passed through my head. We needed to end it. Soon.

Hooker called me Saturday to get my head straight.

"Did you practice?"

"Didn't need to," I said, pulling the last roller out of my hair. I'd gone for the sexy hair again. If I was going to break up with Becks, I at least wanted to look good doing it.

She snorted. "Me either. Cicero's coming to pick me up in a few minutes, and then we're going to drive over. Mercedes isn't going to know what hit her."

I wrapped my holster around my waist and pulled on my black duster. "Okay. I'll see you there."

"Be ready," Hooker cautioned. "I don't want us to look stupid or anything."

Grabbing my Stetson, I couldn't help but smile at that one. "Don't worry. I'll be ready."

"Are you gonna wear the 'stache?"

"No, are you?"

"Of course. Afraid Becks might get turned off if he sees hair growing on top of your lip?"

"No," I said, taking a deep breath. Our act wasn't the only one I'd have to pull off tonight. "See you later, Hooker."

"I'll be waiting. And don't forget your pistol."

On that note, she hung up.

Mom stopped me in the kitchen. "What's that outfit about? Are you and Hooker...?"

"Yeah," I said. "It's our last time before graduation."

"You two have fun." She shook her head, looking me over. "Is Becks going, too?"

I swallowed. "He's coming."

"Does he know what you guys are planning?"

"Not yet."

"Well, tell him I said hey."

"Okay, Mom." She was still looking at me funny. God, I knew I shouldn't have applied that extra coat of mascara. "Do I look bad or something?"

"No." Mom shook her head, a small smile on her lips. "You look great. Just make sure Becks keeps his hands to himself. I don't care how old that hair makes you look. You're still my baby."

Mom was obviously not a fan of the sex hair.

"I'm not ready to be a Grandma yet," she added. "Even if Becks is such a nice boy."

"Love you, Mom." I waved as I walked out the door, feeling guilty. Hopefully, she'd still think Becks was a nice boy after we broke up.

We'd decided to meet at Becks's house and go to the party together. As I pulled into his driveway, I sat in the car a second after turning off the engine. I didn't know how I was going to break up with Becks, if he had a plan or not. But the day was here. After this party, Becks and I wouldn't be fake boyfriend and girlfriend. We'd just be friends again. Considering all the stress I'd been feeling, the thought should've made me happy, but it didn't.

Clayton met me at the door.

"Oh my God," he gasped, smiling, hand to his chest. His eyes were glued to my Stetson, the grin on his face stretched from ear to ear. "I think...I think I'm...having a...heart attack."

I raised my eyebrows, and he laughed some more.

"Sally, you've got to stop coming 'round here in those get-ups." Clayton's face was beet red as he tried to contain himself. "I'm loving that hair, though."

Becks stepped around Clayton. He got a good look at me and sighed. "That's because she's gorgeous, and you're a perv. Let's go, Sal."

I let him lead me to the car, hardly hearing Clayton's protests. Had Becks really just called me gorgeous? I'd have to start doing my hair like this more often.

We didn't talk much on the way to Mercedes's. Becks kept looking at my outfit and shaking his head, but I was still high off that last comment. When we finally got to her street, the house was unmistakable. She'd decorated it in green and white streamers, and the line of cars looped around the block. CHS had won, of course. Even with Becks out, they'd played well, and Ash had led them to a three to one victory.

"Lucky," Becks called it now, walking up the steps to the giant two-story. The door was gaping, so you could hear music all the way out here. "If Stryker had been paying attention, they would've never scored in the first place."

"I thought you said he did good."

"Good," he repeated. "Not great. Now, are you and Hooker really going to do this? Again?"

I stopped, turned to face him. "We haven't even done it for almost two years."

"I know, but why?"

"Why not?" I countered. Stepping back, I held out my arms. "How do I look?"

Grinning, he reached up and tugged the Stetson more securely onto my head. "You look great and you know it, Sal."

Compliment number two. This night was going a whole lot better than I'd predicted.

As we entered, Becks was greeted in the usual way. Everyone wanted to say hi and give him pats on the back. Though he'd had to sit out, everyone knew the team wouldn't have gotten where they were without Becks—and he'd be back in for the next game.

"Oh my gosh!" Mercedes appeared, long hair waving in an unseen breeze, wearing a tight green dress that looked painted on. "I'm so glad you guys could come. Having Bally here is going to make it so much more epic."

Having Bally call it quits, I corrected mentally.

Before I could get too down, the music cut off abruptly, and I heard a voice behind me.

"Well," she drawled, drawing the attention of everyone in the room. "I didn't think you had it in you."

Slowly, I turned, delivering the line like I said it every day.

"I'm your Huckleberry."

Hooker grimaced, eyes widening comically.

I grinned.

Her reaction was perfect. The dusty black coat, the red sash next to the gun at her hip, the mustache, her accent, everything was flawless. We were in the zone, both of us wanting to knock this last one out of the park. Mercedes had been wrong. Bally wasn't what was going to make this party epic. Doc Holliday and Johnny Ringo were here to have a duel to the death, and they were about to steal the show.

CHAPTER 12

Hooker had never died better.

As she went down choking and groaning, she made sure to fall at Mercedes's feet, nearly pulling the other girl down in the process. Our hostess looked as if she might faint. When it was done—after Johnny Ringo (Hooker) had taken his last breath, and Doc Holliday (Me) delivered that last line about him being "no daisy"—there was a moment of silence. Hooker and I didn't care. We took a bow, and half the room burst into applause, the other half still looking like "What the heck?" *Tombstone* was on TV all the time now, but most of them hadn't seen it.

"Man, I love *Tombstone*." Trent Zuckerman was one of the few who had. "It was like the best movie ever. You did great, Lillian."

"Thanks," Hooker said, pulling off her 'stache.

"I mean *really* great," Trent gushed then tried for a thick Southern accent. "'I am your Huckleberry.' Man, that's awesome. You two are like legends."

Hooker and I looked at each other. He'd sounded more like a Cali boy on crack, and he hadn't even gotten the line right.

"I've got to go find Cicero," Hooker laughed, turning to walk away. "Nice job, Doc."

I smiled. Cicero was Hooker's latest boy toy, a Greek transfer student. "You too, Ringo."

Trent moved to follow, calling, "Hey, Lil, hold up!"

It looked like Zuckerman had a crush. I wondered if it was the facial hair or Hooker's drawl that did it.

"What is it with that movie?" When I looked back, Becks was shaking his head, looking after Trent with a frown. "I don't get it."

I patted his shoulder. "That's okay. I don't hold that against you."

"Sal, I know you've got a thing for that Kilmer guy, but that movie sucked. That's why nobody's seen it."

"It did not," I argued, snatching my hand back. "And people haven't seen it because that's the definition of a cult classic. Val was freaking awesome as Doc Holliday, and the lines in the movie were amazing."

"But he's old," Becks complained.

"He's a great actor."

"Yeah, but he's like three times your age."

I shrugged. Val was Val.

"What is it with you and old guys?" He grinned. "First that Lucius guy, then Kilmer? I'm kind of seeing a pattern here, Sal."

My cheeks filled with heat. I knew I should've never told him about my Lucius crush. "It's not their age."

"Then what?" he asked.

I threw off my embarrassment and lifted my chin. "Maybe I just have a thing for guys with accents. Nobody does a sexy Southern drawl like Val."

"So it's the voice, huh?" Becks raised his eyebrows then grinned. In a pitch perfect imitation of Doc himself, he said, "I'm your Huckleberry."

I gaped at him.

"How was that?" When I didn't say anything, he titled his head. "Sal, you okay? It wasn't that bad was it?"

I was at a loss. He couldn't have known. It was one of the few things I'd never told anyone, not even him. My voice had disappeared the moment he spoke the words. It was my favorite line of the entire movie, and he'd done it so well, *too* well. Even though it wasn't used romantically in the movie, the sentiment had always sounded like a promise to my ears. *I'm your Huckleberry.* I'm the one you're looking for. I. Am. For. You. I'd always dreamed of someone saying it to me. If I hadn't been in love before, those words coming from his lips would've done me in.

"Sal?"

Forcing a laugh, heart in my throat, I said, "Perfect. That was...yeah, perfect."

"Glad you approve."

I was afraid if I stuck around he'd see just how much I approved. The glint in his eye said he already did. "I need a drink. You want one?"

I didn't wait for an answer.

Making a beeline for the snack table, I grabbed a water bottle and drank. Becks had outshined every other guy I'd met, and now he'd even beaten Val at his own game. It was a sad truth, but Doc Holliday had nothing on him. Now whenever I watched the movie, it'd be Becks's voice I heard, not Kilmer's. I took another swig of water.

When Pisszilla snuck up behind me, I nearly choked.

"Did he tell you yet?" I whirled to face her, eyes tearing. "We need that story, Spitz. If we can get the dirt first, it'll put our paper on the map."

"What?"

She rolled her eyes. "Becks, where's he going to college? You're his girlfriend, so he must've told you, right?"

I shook my head. "No, I asked, but he refused to say."

"Well, *make* him tell you."

"How?"

"Good God, Spitz, are you slow or something?" She poked me in the chest with one of her sharp talons. "Use your feminine wiles to get it out of him."

I blinked. "Feminine what?"

"Tell him you won't have sex with him unless he tells you."

"We don't...I mean, Becks and I have never...," I sputtered.

"Well now, that doesn't sound fair." Ash reached between us and grabbed a bottle of his own. Looking at my face, he added, "Spitz isn't the kind of girl to hold something like that over a guy's head."

"There's nothing to hold," I said through gritted teeth.

"In that case—" He turned to our evil editor. "—Priscilla, I think you're going to have to come up with a new plan. Sounds like she and Becks have yet to do the deed."

Cheeks hot, I glared at them both. "That's none of your business."

"I don't care how you do it," Priscilla sneered. "Just get the info. I want it before anyone else, got it?"

She flipped her blond mane over her shoulder and strutted away, heels clicking sharply against the hardwood floor.

"Sounds like she really wants that story," Ash said.

I looked at him. "Well, I do, too. Becks just won't tell me."

"Hasn't told any of us on the team either. I think Crenshaw might be pulling for Penn."

"Hmm," I said, noncommittally.

"Know where you're going to school?"

"No, not yet. You?"

Ash smiled. "I've still got another year to think it over."

"Oh yeah, I forgot," I said, grinning. "You're still a junior. Enjoy this time while you can, young one. You'll be a grown-up soon enough."

He shook his head, keeping his eyes on mine. "I'm not that young."

"Yeah right," I teased. "Compared to me, you're practically a baby."

"You know, I've always had a thing for older women."

It wasn't what he said, but the look he gave me that made me blush.

Ash just smiled. "You're so easy, Spitz."

I laughed at myself. Of course, he was just joking. Guys didn't see me like that, and the only one I wanted to was currently over on the other side of the room, sitting on the couch, getting his scruffy cheeks rubbed by a line of people that'd formed sometime after I'd left. It was like they were at a petting zoo, and Becks was the main attraction.

Ash followed my gaze. "Does he really think that works? The non-shaving thing?"

"Guess so." I shrugged as one guy took it a step farther and placed a passionate kiss on his cheek. If Becks swung that way, I might've been worried. He was a very pretty guy. As it was, I smiled as Becks tried not to look too uncomfortable. "He's a great player, but he's also superstitious. Three days before a game means no more shaving."

"That's just stupid."

I shifted my eyes to his. "You guys won yesterday, didn't you?"

"Yeah," Ash said, "because we're good, not because of some stupid lucky beard."

"I tried to tell him that."

"Guess you and me are the only ones who think that way." He gestured to where Becks sat. "Everyone else seems to buy it."

I looked over and saw Mercedes sitting in Becks's lap. She was running a hand through his hair and staring deeply into his eyes, pressing against his chest in her too-tight dress. The sight made me furious. Who did that skank think she was?

"Looks like someone's trying to steal your man, Spitz. Better run on over there, and claim what's yours."

The anger in my chest withered away, settling in my stomach like a dead weight. Becks wasn't mine, not really, just for pretend. At some point tonight, after our break up, he wouldn't even be that.

"He's not my man," I said sadly.

Ash looked unconvinced. "Isn't he?"

I shook my head.

"Well, he's looking at you like he is."

Snapping to attention, I saw Ash was right. Becks *was* staring at me from across the room, his face unreadable. As he went to stand, Mercedes caught his neck, and I made a break for it.

"Later, Ash," I said, speed walking through the crush of people and entering the first door I saw.

It was a bathroom, the perfect hiding place.

Flipping the lock, I took in my surroundings.

It looked like one of those fancy schmancy bathrooms you'd find in a high price restaurant. Seriously, there was a small chaise, two chairs, toilet, shower, jet tub, mints, perfumes, hand soaps, gels and lotions, anything you'd need. A person could live in Mercedes's bathroom, and I was going to do just that, at least for a while.

I'd already splashed my face, used some silky soft lotion, and eaten five mints when the first knock came at the door.

"It's occupied," I called, popping another mint into my mouth.

"Sal, it's me. Can I come in?"

Eyes wide, I spit the mint back out, dropped it in the trash. When I opened the door, Becks was standing there, leaning against the jamb.

"Yes?" I said.

"What were you doing in there?" Peering past me, Becks's eyes widened. "Whoa, that is one mighty fine bathroom."

I crossed my arms. "Did you want something? Towel, hand sanitizer, mint?"

He looked at me. "I just wanted to make sure you were okay. You rushed in here pretty quick."

"I'm fine," I said. "Where's Mercedes? Seems like she might want first crack at you after we've broken up."

"Yeah, no kidding," he said. "That girl is relentless, Sal."

"That's a nice way of putting it," I mumbled.

"Relentless," he repeated. "Are you mad at me or something?"

"What makes you say that?"

"You're glaring hard enough to burn a hole through my chest."

"Am I?"

"Yeah," Becks said, lifting my chin. "You are."

I tried to look indifferent but don't think I succeeded. The picture of Mercedes sitting on his lap was still right there, blazing bright in my head. I couldn't help but be mad at her for what she'd done and at Becks for what he didn't do.

"You know, it's not my fault Mercedes sat in my lap."

"Yeah, but you could've thrown her off."

"I did. You just ran off too fast to catch it."

"Not right away, though."

Becks shook his head, running a hand along his stubbly jaw. "I just didn't want to hurt her feelings, Sal. What can I do to make it up to you?"

I said nothing. It was probably true, but what a lame excuse.

"There's got to be something you want," he coaxed. "I'll do anything."

I watched him through narrowed eyes. "That's a big offer."

"I mean it, Sal, whatever you want." He held up his hands. "Just please, stop looking at me like that."

"Hey, you guys almost done? I really need to use the restroom."

Rick Smythe was doing what I liked to call the pee-pee dance, legs clenched standing behind Becks, hopping from one foot to the other. I knew right then what I wanted. Turning, I grabbed a towel and a couple of things from the counter then stepped out of the room.

"It's all yours," I said.

Rick said, "Thanks, Bally," slapped a hand to Becks's cheek and waddled inside, pulling the door closed after him.

"Decide what you want yet?" Becks asked.

I nodded, smiling wide. "Follow me to the kitchen, please."

"You sure you don't want to think on it some more?"

"Nope."

"That was fast," Becks muttered. "What's that razor for? Should I be nervous?"

"A little fear never hurt anyone," I threw back, making him suffer.

People were drifting in and out, but the kitchen was mostly empty. All the food for the party, the music, the dancing was in the living room, so nobody stuck around for long. The kitchen was like everything else in the house: huge, wide-open, and more than a bit obnoxious.

Looking around for a place to sit, there were only two options, the dining table or the countertop. I guessed Mercedes had cleared out all the chairs before the party. Since it would put me right next to the sink, I picked the counter. Becks was much taller, so it'd also help make up for the height difference.

"Sal, what are you doing?" Becks looked on as I tried to lever myself up. I was on my third attempt.

"What does it look like?" I huffed, jumping and sliding right back down. On second thought, maybe this hadn't been such a good idea. Stupid rich people and their stupid high counters.

He sighed, walked over and gripped my waist. I gasped as he lifted and placed me on the counter on the first try, as if I weighed nothing at all.

I'd been right. Height was no longer an issue. In fact, with Becks's hands still attached to my waist, I was only inches away from his beautiful eyes, staring straight into them, the ones that pulled me in. I caught myself leaning closer, and shifted back.

"Thanks," I said, looking away, grabbing for the shaving cream like a lifeline. "You said anything, right?"

Becks nodded. "I did."

"Okay. Then I want to shave it off."

"*What?*" He dropped his hands, looking horrified.

I nodded to his face. "Your scruff."

"Jeez," he said, shoulders drooping. "Don't scare me like that, Sal."

"What'd you think I meant?" I laughed. "Your head?"

He nodded. "You were looking pretty pissed."

"Nah, I love your hair too much for that." Becks looked up sharply, and I played it off with another laugh. "So, will you let me do it? Shave your sacred five o'clock shadow?"

"You really don't like it, do you?"

I waited.

"Sure." Becks shrugged. "Why not? There's not another game until next week. The luck'll still work if I don't shave again past Wednesday."

Pouring some cream into my hands, I got a good lather going and spread it gently across his cheeks. "It's got nothing to do with luck, Becks. You'd win even without this."

"But why chance it?"

I shook my head, rinsed my hands then filled a bowl with water, placing it at my side. "I just hate that you can't see how talented you are. Why won't you believe me?"

"I want to, Sal. Really, I do. It's just I'm not willing to take a chance on something so important and lose." He tried to catch my gaze. "If I was wrong, the fallout would be too painful. You know what I mean?"

I did. That was exactly how I felt about my love for Becks. I really wanted him to feel the same, but I'd never risk losing him as a friend. That wouldn't just be painful; it'd most likely kill me. How could I live without having Becks there with me, to talk to and laugh with? There was just too much at stake.

"I get it." Light gleamed off the razor's blade as I picked it up, tucking my right leg beneath me to get more comfortable. "I still disagree. You and I both know you'd win without this beard, but I understand what you're saying. You ready?"

"Yep," he said.

"You're going to have to come a little closer."

"Like this?" Becks moved so he was only a hairsbreadth away.

My throat went dry. "That's good."

I could make out his grin through the foam.

"Listen, I've never done this before, so you're going to have to stay still."

"No movement, got it." Just as I was about to put the razor to his cheek, he smiled. "Great song."

"Becks," I warned.

He stopped talking.

As I raised the blade to his skin, I realized he was right. This song was great, setting the mood perfectly, slow and lazy, filled with repressed emotion. The rasp of the singer's voice, Becks's closeness, the whole situation left me feeling raw, exposed. I'd never realized how intimate shaving could be.

My hand shook on the first stroke, leaving a long, untidy line of bare skin. I traced it with the tip of my finger, watching Becks's lids flutter. Silky smooth.

His reaction satisfied me in a way I couldn't explain.

The second pass of the razor revealed more skin, the next even more. A glimpse of cheekbone. A hint of jaw. I tried to keep my breathing steady, but Becks wasn't making it easy. Despite his promise, he did move. Barely—less than an inch—but it was enough. Becks swayed toward me every time I leaned in. It was like he couldn't help it.

Sort of like I couldn't help touching each patch of newly uncovered flesh.

I was close enough to count his eyelashes, to see the tiny scar in his eyebrow that he'd gotten falling off his bike in sixth grade. There was something powerful about the way his eyes followed my every move. After tonight, I wouldn't be able to touch him like this, so I took my time. I'd miss him being my F.B.F.

"So," I said about half-way through, "pick a college yet?"

Becks gave me a look.

"Okay, okay. It was worth a shot." Pisszilla was not going to be happy, but I had more immediate concerns. "How're we going to do this anyway? The break up. I know you said big and ·public. We want to do it in front of the most people possible, right?"

Becks couldn't say anything. I was being very cautious around his lips.

Dipping the shaver in the bowl, I shook off the excess foam then went back to work—and rambling.

"Are you going to break up with me? Or am I breaking up with you? Are we supposed to fight or not? We never really talked about it, Becks."

"Sal," he murmured.

Noticing a small area I'd missed, I titled his head and placed the blade gently against his jaw.

"Sal, I don't think we should break up."

I was so surprised my hand slipped, and he winced.

"Oh God," I said, grabbing the towel, dabbing at his cut. It was small, but those always hurt the most. "I'm so sorry, Becks. Are you alright?"

"It's fine." He covered my hand with his. "I cut myself shaving all the time."

"Sorry." Pulling my hand away, I let him wipe off the left-over cream. I couldn't have heard right. "What did you just say? Becks, you were the one who said this would be the perfect place."

"I know." He laid the cloth aside.

"We have to ease people into it. Those were your words."

"I remember."

"Well? What changed?"

Becks locked eyes with me. "Do you really love my hair?"

The question threw me. "It's not horrible."

"You're a terrible liar." Becks shook his head, gliding a hand across my cheek. "I don't think we should break up."

"You don't?"

"No."

My voice was paper thin. "Why?"

"Well, the fake boyfriend thing has worked out pretty good so far. Don't you think?"

I couldn't speak as he leaned even closer.

"And there are some advantages."

Before I could ask what those were, his lips were on mine. Becks's fingers threaded into my hair, the other hand at my waist, his mouth warm, caressing. I could feel the kiss down to my bones. It rippled through me, his passion, and my love for him rose up to meet it. Like waves crashing, we tangled together, mixing, melting into each other. It was the first time Becks had ever kissed me, *really* kissed me, and for a few seconds afterward, I couldn't speak. He'd stolen my breath.

"Becks," I gasped, eyes closed, his forehead pressed against mine. I was so happy; my voice shook.

"Hmm?"

"I can't believe you just did that."

He laughed roughly. "Me either."

As I opened my eyes, his were still shut, a small smile on his lips as he played with the ends of my hair. I turned my head and caught flash of bright green by the door. Mercedes.

"Oh." I pulled away, heart sinking. "I get it now."

"Get what?" Becks said.

"This was for her." As Becks followed my gaze, the girl jumped and hurried away. With each tap of her heels, I felt another pang go through me. "Good one, Becks. You were really convincing."

"Yeah," he said, back still to me, "convincing."

"That's what this was, wasn't it? What you said, that kiss, it was just you being a great fake boyfriend." In my mind, I begged him to say no. To tell me I was wrong. Please, please, let me be wrong. "This was all just part of the plan to convince her."

Becks studied my face. There was an odd little frown on his mouth, but it disappeared as he grinned. "Of course, it was. Jeez, Sal, don't look so worried. Was she watching the whole time?"

"Not sure," I said, smile wavering. My eyes felt wet, but I wouldn't let the tears fall. "You know, I didn't realize we had an audience."

Becks shrugged, his eyes watching me carefully. "Why else would I kiss you?"

That hit home.

Jumping from the counter, I rushed for the front door. I heard Becks call my name but didn't pause. Getting away was the only option. Otherwise, he'd see me cry, and that wasn't going to happen, not over this. I wasn't stupid. I'd known Becks didn't love me, but having it confirmed, having it said so plainly after that amazing kiss, I couldn't take it.

Becks caught my arm on the last step of the porch. "Sal, what's wrong?"

I didn't know if it was his touch or the stupid question, but something sparked a fire inside me.

Spinning around, I let it all out. My frustration, my anger, my love, the truth, the words poured from my lips like a waterfall. I told him how mad I was that he'd kissed me just for Mercedes's benefit, how I wanted him as my real boyfriend not a fake one, how I'd loved him all my life and what an idiot he was for not noticing. I told him everything I'd been afraid to tell him over the years.

And true to form, I said it all in German.

Whenever my blood was up, it became my native tongue. There was something freeing in saying everything out loud, and I did it without fear or restraint, knowing that neither Becks nor any of the bystanders looking would understand what I was saying. And there were plenty of those. Half the party seemed to have followed us onto the front lawn, watching as I ranted at Becks like a mad woman.

When I came to the end, I was breathing heavy, and Becks looked more shocked than I'd ever seen him.

"Sal…" He reached for me again, but I backed away.

"No, Becks." I was back to English. I wanted him to understand this time. "I can't do this anymore. Let's call it off, okay?"

"But Sal, I—"

"It's over." I shook my head. He'd wanted big and public, and the crowd around us was hanging on every word, silent enough you could hear crickets chirping. Guess he'd gotten his wish. "It's just…over."

As I turned to walk away, I ran straight into Ash Stryker. He was staring at me, wearing an odd expression. I supposed I'd better get used to people looking at me like that.

"Sorry," I muttered, stepping around him, making my way over to Hooker. Her mouth was hanging open, and she looked nearly as devastated as I felt. "Can you give me a lift?"

She immediately snapped to attention. Shooting a glare at Becks, she linked her arm through mine and said, "Sure thing, Spitz."

Hooker led me away from the crowd, and I was glad. At that point, her arm was the only thing keeping me on my feet.

The F.B.F. plan was officially null and void. I'd actually told Becks the truth, in a language he couldn't understand, but I'd done it. On Monday, everything would be back to normal, no more Bally, no more lies, just me and Becks as we'd always been, best friends. It was a good thing, a *great* thing, a relief.

But then why did I feel like I'd taken a wrecking ball to the chest?

CHAPTER 13

There was a light knock at the door.

I grunted, burrowing deeper under the covers. My bed was a safe place, my cocoon, and I wasn't leaving until someone forced me out.

I heard the door slowly open, footsteps on the carpet, felt my weight shift as someone sat down beside me.

"Sally, are you okay?" The voice was soft. "What's wrong honey?"

Oh nothing, Mom. My heart's like one big bruise, but other than that everything's peachy.

"Just tired," I mumbled.

"Did something happen last night?"

"Nmph." I flipped onto my side, giving her my back. The reminder of last night was like putting a chisel to that bruise and pressing down, hard. I didn't want her to see me crack under the pressure.

"Sally?" she said, laying a hand on my back. A few tears leaked out at the concern I heard there. "Sally, Becks is downstairs."

"*What?*" I threw the covers from my head in panic, whirling to face her. Why was he here? I couldn't let him see me like this. It would ruin everything. "You can't let him up here, Mom."

"Why not?" Her painful expression was knowing. Too late I remembered what I must look like, my eyes red and puffy from crying, cheeks tearstained.

"I don't—" My voice broke, then came back in a low rasp, throat clogged with tears. "I don't want to see him."

"Ah, honey." She gathered me up in a tight hug. "It's okay. Whatever happened you guys will get past this. You always do."

I shook my head, wrapping my arms around her.

"Whatever he did," she went on, "it can't be that bad, right? You and Becks are great together."

Nice of her to assume it was his fault, but the only thing Becks did was tell the truth.

Why else would I kiss you? Closing my eyes, my heart gave another painful kick. I'd never forget what he said. As much as it killed me, I needed to stop playing pretend and face facts.

"We're better off as friends." I hated the words as soon as they left my mouth.

"Are you sure?" Mom leaned back, keeping her hands on my shoulders. "Sally, maybe—"

"I'm sure." I tried to put force behind the words. "Me and Becks are done, Mom. It'll be better this way."

She smoothed my hair back. "But Sally, he was your first boyfriend, your first love."

One out of two wasn't bad. She didn't know that my first boyfriend was actually no boyfriend at all, just a guy helping out his desperate dork of a best friend. My chest tightened. "I'll get over it."

"That's right." Mom nodded encouragingly, changing tactics. "There'll be other boys. They'll be lining up; just you wait."

That jolted me. I'd ended all things F.B.F. less than twenty-four hours ago, and already she was back into matchmaking mode. The idea of dating anyone besides Becks—fake boyfriend or not—made me nauseated.

"I think I'm going to take it easy on the guy front, Mom. My heart's kind of fragile right now." *More like shattered.* "I need a little recovery time, you know?"

"Okay," she said grudgingly as she rose from the bed. At the door, she stopped and glanced over her shoulder. "What should I tell Becks?"

I shrugged, stiff-backed.

"Alright, I'll handle it." Just before pulling the door closed, her eyes soft, Mom added, "I meant what I said, honey. There will be other boys. Don't break your heart permanently over this first one, okay?"

I swallowed. "I'll try not to."

Once she was gone I flopped back onto the bed, gazing up at the ceiling. Mom really didn't understand. Becks wasn't just the first. He was first, last and all the others in between. I didn't want anyone else. Becks was it for me. As much as it hurt now, that was the way it'd always been, would always be. Yet no matter how I felt, we were destined to be nothing more or less than friends. I'd made peace with that fact before, and I'd do it again. I'd *have* to do it again. If it was the only way to have Becks in my life, then that was that.

I jumped as my phone buzzed on my nightstand.

Reaching over, I flipped it open and read the text from Becks.

"R U OK?" it said.

I took a deep breath then typed, "Of course I am :)"

Even with the emoticon, Becks didn't fall for it. "BS. Sal, why won't U see me??"

Closing my eyes, I decided: There was only one thing to do. This time I let my fingers do the lying for me.

"Just act for Mom. Have to make BrkUp look real, right?"

A few moments ticked by, and then Becks texted back. "Right... See U at school 2morrow?"

I sighed, glad he'd let it go. "U bet. Bye, Becks."

"Bye, Sal..."

I slid the phone shut, switching it from one hand to the other, hoping I would be as convincing in person.

The next day I'd showered, put on new, clean clothes, got to my zero period on time. My insides were still a mess, but I thought I'd managed to hide it pretty well.

"So," Pisszilla said, tapping her pen on the paper in front of her, "did you get it, Spitz?"

"Get what?" I asked.

She raised an eyebrow. "The college. Did you get the name before that embarrassing scene on Mercedes's lawn, or did Becks dump your sorry butt before you had a chance?"

I flushed. Naturally, Pisszilla would bring something like that up, right here in front of everyone on the paper, where it'd cause the most humiliation.

"Are you deaf?" Ash said, and her eyes shot to him. "Didn't you hear what happened? She broke up with him, not the other way around."

"Of course, I heard. Everyone did." Pisszilla pointed at me, her carefully made-up eyes filled with malicious glee. "She was speaking in tongues, making a fool out of herself, having a breakdown right there at the party."

"German," I mumbled.

"What?" she hissed.

I looked her square in the eye, sick of her crap. "I was speaking in German. And no, I didn't get the name of the college. Guess you'll just have to get it yourself."

"Fine, I will."

"Yeah, good luck with that."

She glared. "And what's that supposed to mean?"

"Becks and I are—" God, what were we now? I went with the one thing that'd never changed. "—best friends. If he didn't tell me, I'm sure he's not going to tell a cold-hearted, vicious spewing, too-much-make-up wearing, peroxide blond jerk like you."

She gasped, hands flying to her hair. "You bitch! This is all natural."

I raised an eyebrow of my own.

"Roots don't lie, Prissy."

She sputtered, glaring as snickers went up around the room.

Before Pisszilla could get another word in, the bell rang, and I walked out, feeling a bit lighter.

"Hey, Spitz."

I turned as Ash stepped up next to me. "What's up, Ash?"

"I need to talk to you," he said. "It's about something you said at the party..."

I was hardly listening. Becks was standing a little ways down the hall, Mercedes on one side, nearly spilling out of her top, Roxy on the other, hip cocked wide in a pair of short shorts. It was impossible to tell who was showing the most skin. They were both talking to him, speaking over each other, but he was scanning the hall. When he locked eyes with me, Becks shook them off in one fluid movement, heading my way with a determined look on his face.

That couldn't mean anything good.

"Ash, can we talk later?" I said, already moving for the bathroom.

"Okay," he said, "but Spitz—"

"Alright, bye." I rushed across the hall and made it inside as the warning bell sounded. I caught a glimpse of Ash and Becks, both wearing identical looks of surprise, but I didn't care. My heart had skipped a beat when I'd seen Becks. All I could think about was that kiss on Mercedes's countertop. A little more time, I decided. That's all I needed was a little more time. Then I'd be ready to face him.

Waiting for the bell to ring, I washed my hands, took my time examining the soap machine. I was going to be late for first, but Ms. Vega loved me, and German was my best subject. I didn't want to chance running into anyone on my way out.

The bell sounded, and I exhaled. Grabbing my books, I pulled open the door and stepped out into the empty hallway.

"That's the second time you've done that."

I gasped, spinning to find Becks leaning against the little strip of wall directly beside the bathroom.

"Becks, you scared me," I said, still trying to calm my frantic nerves.

"Sorry." He straightened and walked over, not stopping until we were face to face. "What's up with all this running into bathrooms whenever you see me?"

When in doubt, go for the gross-out factor. "Well, I ate some really bad fish last night and—"

He held up a hand, nose scrunched. "Yeah, okay. I don't want to know."

"Okay."

Looking down, he shoved his hands into his pockets. "Listen Sal...about what happened at the party, I—"

"It was great, wasn't it?" I chuckled, just like I'd practiced it at home, as his head shot up in surprise. "That was some of my best work."

"What are you talking about?"

"I don't think anyone had any doubts after that performance. Bally is *officially* over. It's such a relief, isn't it?"

"You're saying it was all an act?" His eyes narrowed in suspicion. "I didn't know you could cry on cue, Sal."

I waved him off dismissively. "The tears were a great touch, right? I think it added just the right amount of drama."

"So, when you were saying all that stuff... What did you say exactly?"

"Basically, a whole bunch of crap about how I couldn't keep doing this—," *Truth.* "—how you'd broken my heart—," *Truth.* "—and how I'd never forgive you—." *Lie.* "—That kind of stuff."

"And you did it in German because..." he trailed off, waiting for me to fill in the blanks.

"Well, because no one would understand it, of course. Again, it was all about upping the drama." I widened my eyes, reaching out to grab his arm. "You're not mad are you? Oh Becks, I tried my best to do it right. Was it too over the top? Do you think people might not have believed me?"

"I sure did," he muttered, running a hand through his hair. Why did he look so...upset? "So, we're okay?"

"'Course we are." I smiled so hard it hurt my cheeks. "Why wouldn't we be?"

"Sal, I want you to know—" He stopped suddenly, shook his head.

"What, Becks?"

"Nothing." He cleared his throat and then grinned. "Thanks for letting me be your fake boyfriend, Sal. I'm glad you asked me. It was fun."

"Yeah," I said, "I'm glad, too. Now that you're not chained to me, you can go out with whoever you want. I'm sure all the girls'll be happy to have you back."

"Hmm," he agreed, "and you can give it a go with that secret crush of yours."

The sound that escaped my lips was too strangled to be a laugh. I only hoped Becks didn't notice.

"I've got to go," he said, turning, "but I'll see you at practice after school, okay?"

"Sure."

As soon as he was gone, I slumped, the smile slipping from my face. At least he'd believed me, I thought. And now there was nothing holding him back anymore. Becks could get any girl he wanted. I wished I could've been happier for him, but with my own feelings so mixed up, there was just no way. The guilt was gone—that was a plus—but in its place there were all these new emotions.

Like whenever I saw him with another girl.

"Hey, Becks." A cheek rub. "Looking good."

"Wanna go out tonight, Becks?"

"God Becks, your arms are so *tight*. Come over to my house later?"

The flirting was old news, but the way it made me feel was what'd changed. Anger came first, hot and heavy, followed by jealousy and then the quick sting of self-loathing as I realized I had no right to either of those feelings

When Mercedes kissed his cheek, I finally blew.

"You're just going let her do that?" I said, voice angry, though it'd been her fault, not his.

"What?" Becks said. "The girl pounced. What was I supposed to do, hit her?"

I shook my head in disgust. "Don't you have any self-respect?"

"Calm down, Sal. It was just—"

"Save it." I hadn't talked to him for the rest of the day.

After that, I learned to turn off my emotions. I didn't want to be *that girl*. It was better to be a shell, empty. Go to school. Come home. Repeat. Over the next couple of days, I was pretty much unaware of anything.

When Mom let Hooker into the house, I didn't even look up from my book. Gilbert was about to ask Anne to marry him, and like an idiot, she was going to stomp all over his heart. Turning the page, I sighed. Nice people always got trampled by the ones they loved.

"Spitz, *what* are you wearing?"

"Oh, hey," I said, startled. Carefully, I slid my bookmark into place. "How's it going, Hooker?"

"So you can still form complete sentences. I was starting to get worried." She took a seat on the couch, and tugged on my fleece. "You didn't seriously pay money for this."

"What?" I looked down at myself. "Are you talking about my snuggie?"

"Your what-ee?"

"Snuggie," I repeated. "It's like a big, soft blanket you can wear as a robe."

"Spitz—" Her lip curled as she held up one corner. "—it's got that little green guy on it."

I tugged the material away, frowning. "That's Yoda."

"I know who it is."

"It's a *Star Wars* snuggie. Special edition."

Hooker sighed. "Spitz, are you kidding me with this?"

"What?"

"*This.*" She held out a hand, gesturing to me. "Are you really going to let Becks do this to you?"

"This isn't about Becks," I said, teeth clenched.

Hooker rolled her eyes. "Yeah, okay."

"It's not."

"You're not fooling anybody, Spitz." She shook her head. "Your mom's worried. I'm worried. You know, I even think Becks is worried. This isn't healthy."

Crossing my arms over my chest, I sniffed. "I have no idea what you're talking about."

"This is an intervention. Get up," she demanded, pulling on my arm. "We're having a Girls Night."

I blinked. "What?"

"You know, Girls Night, make-up, clothing, ice cream, popcorn and a movie, the works."

"Which movie?"

Sensing she was getting nowhere, she dropped my arm and said, "I was thinking maybe we'd watch one of those episodes you love so much."

"You mean..."

"Yes, yes, I mean the ones with Yoda and Skytalker and all those freaks."

I grinned. "It's Skywalker."

"Whatever."

"But you never agreed to watch them before—and you know how much I hate make-up."

"This is an emergency," Hooker said, looking me over. "It's all about give and take, Spitz. God, just look at that hair. I'm going to have to spend like an hour alone on that frizz."

Actually, it took more like thirty minutes.

Once I'd showered, I let Hooker do her thing. Hair came first, tackling what she called "the danger zone," then make-up, which took another thirty. She went a bit heavy on the eyeliner if you ask me, but I wasn't arguing. Hooker had never watched any of the episodes before. "Superheroes are one thing," she'd said. "Talking robots and a full-grown man in a Big Foot suit is another story." I'd told her a thousand times that Chewie was not in fact a relation of Big Foot, just a Wookiee slave turned smuggler, but she'd refused to listen. By the end of tonight, she'd understand.

Finding the right clothes took another hour and a half since Hooker said the choices were slim. "Hideous," was the word she used, but Hooker was one of those people who had no filter, so I let it slide.

"Phew," Hooker said, swiping a hand across her forehead. "You actually look human again. Just look at yourself, Spitz. You are one hot mama."

Looking in the mirror, I thought the skirt was a little short, the top too tight, the heels ridiculous and the make-up just silly, but I didn't say anything. Hooker had worked hard to make me look this slutty.

"Thanks, Hooker," I said instead. "You did great."

"Yeah, I know." She rested her chin on my shoulder, smiling at our reflection. "I'm a miracle worker. Let's go downstairs and show Martha."

Mom nearly dropped the cookies she was taking out of the oven when she saw us.

"Sally, where did you get those clothes?" *Me*, I corrected mentally. When she saw me. "That skirt is...it's..."

"It's hot, right?" Hooker said, nodding.

"It's...something," Mom said finally.

"Thanks?" I shook my head then turned to Hooker. "So where do you want to start? Technically, *Episode One: The Phantom Menace* is the beginning, but one through three was pretty much crap in comparison to four through six. I say we start with *Episode Four: A New Hope*. That's the best, original cast, first to hit theaters. What do you think?"

"I, ah..." Hooker looked to Mom.

"Oh yeah," I said. "Mom, you can watch, too, if you want. Hooker had this whole idea for a Girls Night, and we're going to watch *Star Wars*."

"Well..." Mom said, placing the last cookies onto the rack to cool. She refused to meet my eyes. "I've kind of got something..."

"What?" I asked just as the doorbell rang.

"I'll get it," Hooker and Mom said at the same time.

Slowly, I followed them to the door, suspicion gnawing at me.

As Mom opened the door, my fears were confirmed.

"Hello," Mom said, reaching out, "you must be Ash?"

"Yes, ma'am," Ash said as they shook hands. "And you must be Sally's mom. My dad told me you were beautiful." Looking over her shoulder, he waved. "Hey, Spitz."

Mom blushed and tittered while I pulled Hooker aside.

She looked so downright pleased with herself; I wanted to slap her.

"Hooker," I growled. "What is this?"

"I told you," she said coolly, "it's an intervention. Martha agrees with me. You've got to get back on that horse."

"I've never ridden a day in my life."

That got me an eye roll. "I mean dating. We've got to get you over Becks, and the only way it's going to happen is for you to find somebody new. "

"But it's only been a few days," I argued.

"And that's plenty of time to wallow in self-pity. We've got to snap you out of this funk," Hooker declared, then said again, "Your mom agrees."

"Mom?" I repeated, watching her and Ash out of the corner of my eye. It looked like they were old friends.

"She knows Ash's parents from high school." Hooker shrugged. "When she asked me about him, I said he was alright, good soccer player, great looks, decent car. We decided you two would make a good match."

I stared at her in horror. I'd had my suspicions, but this was my first time seeing them in action. Hooker and my mother, two matchmakers on a mission. My worst fears confirmed.

"I won't do it," I said, crossing my arms—or at least trying to. This shirt was so tight I couldn't even do that without ripping a seam. Instead I settled for fists on hips.

"Yes, you will," Hooker countered. "If you don't, you'll hurt Ash's feelings—and just look at how good he is with Martha."

When I looked over, Mom had her head thrown back, laughing at something Ash said like it was the funniest thing in the world.

"Fine," I said, snagging my fleece from the coat rack. "But I'm wearing the snuggie."

Hooker paled, opened her mouth, but then Mom said, "Come on, Lillian. Let's leave Sally and Ash to their date." When she winked at me, I tugged the snuggie over my shoulders in retaliation. Mom simply shrugged, stepping out onto the porch with Hooker bringing up the rear.

After they were gone, Ash stepped forward and nodded at my attire. "Yoda. Nice."

I rolled my eyes and led him into the living room.

Being alone with Ash wasn't really so bad. Not bad at all, actually. He told me he'd seen all the movies, didn't get mad when I quoted lines and didn't even comment on my singing along with the credits. He was pretty much silent throughout—which was how I liked it. That way we could pay attention to the movie. We talked some afterward, but he seemed to be a bit preoccupied. I pulled out all my tricks, talking about the nerdiest, most annoying tidbits I could think of ("Did you know Luke Skywalker used to be Luke Starkiller?" "Were you aware that Chewie's appearance was based off of an Alaskan Malamute?" "You know, John Williams also composed the scores for the first three Harry Potter films. My favorite was Hedwig's theme. It goes like this..."), but nothing seemed to put him off.

As I walked him out, Mom and Hooker pulled into the driveway. They didn't get out of the car, and I knew they were watching us. Ash seemed to know it, too.

"So," he said, glancing over his shoulder then back at me, "what do you think they expect us to do?"

"Don't know." I shrugged. "Why'd you agree to this anyway?"

"Like I said, Spitz, I'm into older women."

Just like before, I blushed, and he grinned.

"But besides that," Ash went on, "I had something to tell you."

"Why didn't you talk to me at school?" I asked.

"I tried, but it just seemed like you weren't all there."

"Oh."

"I'm sorry about what went down with Becks."

"That's nice of you to say," I said, forcing a smile.

"Yeah, well..." A small breeze fluttered the ends of his dirty blond hair as he nodded to himself. "A kiss should satisfy them, I think."

"What do you—?"

Before I could finish, Ash had leaned down to my cheek, placing a soft kiss just next to my temple and sliding something from his pocket into my hand.

"Thanks for tonight, Spitz." Then in a voice barely audible, he added, "If you want to do something about Becks, let me know."

With that, he pulled back and walked away.

I was frozen in place.

"*Oooh*, that was so cute," Hooker said, gliding up to me. "The temple kiss, classic gentlemanly behavior. One point, Ash. What'd he give you anyway?"

With stiff fingers, I opened the note, staring as I realized I hadn't imagined what I'd heard.

Hooker frowned. "What's it say, Spitz? You know I can't read German."

My voice sounded as if it came from a distance. "It says, 'Meet me outside Chem Lab, tomorrow at six o'clock.'"

"Demanding," she said with a nod. "I like it." When I didn't respond, she looked at my face. "You okay, Spitz?"

I honestly didn't know.

What I'd heard Ash say before, what he *had* said, wasn't exactly, "If you want to do something about Becks, let me know." That was the English translation.

What he'd said was: "*Wenn ich mich um Becks kümmern soll, sag Bescheid.*"

CHAPTER 14

At the party, I'd never once stopped to consider. My emotions had swept me away on a wind of disappointment, anger and finally exhaustion. The ten other people who took German had trouble stringing two sentences together, and besides, they weren't even there (besides Hooker). It'd been a relief to tell my secret, and *not* tell it at the same time.

There was just one problem: Someone at the party had understood every word.

And he had absolutely no reason to keep quiet.

Where was he?

Pacing the width of the hall, I looked right and left. Ash's note had said to be here at six—an ungodly hour, especially since I'd gotten next to no sleep last night. My nerves had kept me awake, tossing and turning, until I just gave up. The bad thing was that gave me plenty of time to think up all the ways this meeting could go sour. When I got to one hundred, I stopped counting.

I re-checked the note then looked at my cell.

Great. He was already five minutes late.

My footsteps echoed off the tile in the empty place. I'd never been inside Chariot High when it was this deserted. It was a little eerie. When I'd driven up, there were seriously only three other cars in the lot. Probably janitorial staff.

I checked the time again. 6:07a.m.

Fantastic. Ash was blowing me off. He'd probably decided it wasn't worth it to drag his butt out of bed, even though he's the one who set the time. Serves me right for putting my faith in a guy whose name was one letter away from ass.

At that moment, a hand reached out and grabbed my shirt, jerking me backward.

The space was dark, cramped. I couldn't see three inches in front of me but knew I wasn't alone. I was about to start screaming to high heaven, had drawn in a breath, when the light clicked on.

"Morning, Spitz," Ash said with a grin. "Sleep well last night?"

I frowned, taking in my surroundings. My sleep-deprived mind took a second to recognize where I was, but once I did, I nearly let lose a string of hysterical laughter. It was the same storeroom I'd pulled Becks into, where I'd asked and he'd agreed to be my F.B.F. Now Ash was looking at my face with the power to expose me, his eyes far too assessing. It didn't get much more ironical than that.

"So," I said, leaning back, playing it cool, "you speak German."

"*Ja,*" he said, taking up the same position on the opposite wall. "My grandma and grandpa are from the old country, spent every summer there since I was two. 'Stryker' is German, you know."

Mentally, I cursed. We'd gone over German surnames back in sophomore year. Why hadn't I paid better attention? It might've saved me from this whole sticky situation.

I met his gaze straight on, switching easily to the other language. "*Du hast also...*"

"*...alles verstanden,*" he replied. "*Jedes einzelne Wort.* Honestly, I speak German better than I do English."

My heart sank. I was good, but Ash didn't even have to pause. He articulated both with spot-on diction and pronunciation, barely taking a second to change from one to the other. I'd known he understood, but having him say so was like getting blind-sided a second time.

"I know that you and Becks were never really going out," he continued airily. "I know that you guys had some kind of messed-up relationship that was supposed to be fake—but it wasn't for you. How could it have been? You're in love with the guy."

I slowly crossed my arms, using the time to get my voice back. The truth was a bitter pill to swallow.

"And what do you plan to do with the information?" I said.

"That depends." Ash had a gleam in his eyes.

"On what?"

"On you." He raised an eyebrow. "Listen, Spitz. Even if Becks didn't have the balls to ask you out for real, I do. I know you're not over him yet, but I'm not afraid of a challenge."

I was totally thrown. What was he talking about? "I don't understand."

"Don't you?" Ash was shaking his head at me, like it was obvious. "I'm telling you I'm interested. Have been for a while."

"What?"

"Were you always this dense, or is this a new development?" Ash pushed off the wall, running a hand through his hair in frustration.

I glared at that.

"I'm saying I want to be your boyfriend." His eyes widened comically.

The words hung there suspended as my jaw hit the floor. I wasn't sure who looked more surprised, me or Ash.

He cleared his throat. "You're a little out there, but I like that."

I shot him a questioning look. He couldn't possibly mean what I thought he meant.

Ash sighed, shoving a hand though his hair once again. "I like you," he said baldly. "I know you're still into Becks, but I'm willing to give it a go if you are. Even if it doesn't work out, at least we could show Becks what he's missing. Right?"

"It won't work," I said automatically.

"Why not?"

With a heavy sigh, I dropped my arms. Ash Stryker asking me out was unbelievable, but even more mind-boggling was his offer to help me with Becks. Unfortunately, even if he did, it wouldn't do any good.

"Becks doesn't like me that way." I shrugged. "I guess you missed that part. He's always just seen me as Sal, not a guy but not really a girl either. He doesn't want me."

"Are you serious?" I looked up at his incredulous tone. "Spitz, he wants you. Trust me. What guy in his right mind wouldn't?"

"Thanks," I mumbled. "But you're wrong."

He crossed the space between us and took my hands, forcing me to look at him. "You don't get it. You don't understand how guys like Becks operate. Spitz, you've got to show him that you're desirable, that you won't wait around forever."

Ash made it sound so easy. Like all I'd have to do is parade some guy in front of Becks, and *Poof!* Ta-dah, he'd realize he loves me and we'd live happily ever after.

"Who knows? You might even like me better."

I smiled. That sounded more like the Ash I knew.

"Come on, Spitz," Ash said. "Say yes. You know you want to; I can see it in your eyes. Go out with me. What have you got to lose?"

Nothing, I thought. Becks wasn't any closer to being my boyfriend now then he was before the F.B.F. disaster. Why not give Ash a shot? There was just one thing I didn't get.

Brow furrowed, I asked, "Why me? If you know I'm still hung up on Becks, why would you want to date me?"

"You mean, besides morbid curiosity?"

I waited.

"Well, apart from the fact that I'd really like to get to know you better—" He wore a shit-eating grin. "—

you've starred in basically every erotic dream I've had since freshman year."

"Ew." My nose scrunched. Definitely too much information. "And I thought you were such a nice guy," I muttered. Could I really do this? Why was I even considering it?

"I am a nice guy," Ash said, stepping closer. "The nicest."

Rolling my eyes, I pushed him back.

"Alright," I said suddenly, thinking what's the worst that could happen? Why not go out with a guy who's interested in me? In my heart, the answer to that question was simple—I was in love with someone else—but I didn't want to hurt Ash's feelings. He'd really put himself out there, which I still hadn't managed to do after all these years.

"Great." Ash smiled. "This should be fun."

I smiled back.

Ash held the door and followed me out. There were lots of people in the hall now, lockers slamming, people talking as they walked to class. Zero period was canceled for today, which was a good thing since this "meeting" had taken longer than I'd thought. Ash and I stood side by side, watching everyone hurry past.

"You sure you want to do this?"

Turning to face me, he said, "Absolutely. You?"

"Sure," I said, trying not to blush. "Thanks, Ash."

"Anything for you, Spitz." His eyes widened, one corner of his lips turned up as he looked over my head. "And so it begins."

Before I could wonder what he meant, a familiar voice called, "Sal."

Becks sounded annoyed, and when he reached us his expression matched his tone.

"Becks," Ash said easily, looping an arm around my shoulders. I nearly gasped in surprise but managed to hold it in. "How's it going man? You ready to take on Myers Park today?"

"I'm always ready." His voice was icy, but his eyes burned, tracking the movements of that arm with a scowl on his face. "Sal, what's going on?"

"Nothing," I said.

"Oh don't lie to him, Spitz." I did gasp this time as Ash nuzzled my hair. What was he doing? "He's a big boy. He can take it."

"Take what?" Becks said, looking right at me.

"Well, we...I mean, we're..." I'd never been too good at lying to Becks, and now with him looking so intense, staring right through me, it was next to impossible. I didn't know why, but I didn't want to admit that Ash and I were going out.

Luckily, Ash didn't have that problem.

"Spitz just agreed to go out with me," he said.

I stared at him slack-jawed. Ash had put it right out there.

If Becks's eyes could shoot fire, Ash would've been dust. Without looking at me, he gritted out, "Sal, can I see you for a sec?"

He didn't wait for an answer, simply tugged me a few feet away and started his tirade.

"What was that?" he said, head lowered, voice angry. "I asked you before what was going on with you and Ass Striker, and you said nothing. You aren't seriously interested in that jerk?"

"Well, I—"

"He's just playing you, Sal." Becks shook his head, looking at me with pity. "And you're letting him do it. I thought you were smarter than this."

I set my chin, remembering how Ash had just admitted his feelings. No fear, no hesitation. I had to admire that.

"I like him," I said.

"And you honestly think he likes you?" Becks laughed, but it wasn't a funny sound. "How could he, Sal? He barely knows you."

"Yeah, but he wants to," I retorted.

"Yeah, he wants something," Becks muttered.

"What?"

"You heard me."

"Why are you getting so upset?" I asked, eyeing the hard planes of his face. "It's not like you haven't gone out with a ton of girls."

"That's different." His tone was pleading. "You don't know Ash. I do. We've played on the same team for years. He's a complete ass."

I took a step back. "Well, what if I want to get to know *him* better? He's always been nice to me, Becks."

Becks searched my face. "It's him, isn't it? I was right."

"Right about what?"

"God, why didn't I see it before," he said, throwing up his hands. "Your crush, athletic, smart, good-looking. Sal, you're kidding me, right? Ass Striker? You really think *he's* attractive?"

Looking over, Ash winked, nodding, encouraging me. Our relationship was already off and running, and I'd barely had time to blink, let alone get used to the idea.

Wanting to see how Becks would react, I tested the waters.

"Sure," I said, checking Ash out with a grin. "He's funny, nice and has a great body. Not as good as yours, of course, Becks, but he is a year younger."

Becks stepped back as if I'd struck him. "Sal..."

"Hmm?" I tried hard not to notice the look of hurt that flashed across his face.

"He doesn't want you. Not really."

The fact that Becks didn't think any guy could want me wasn't a surprise. The words still cut to the bone.

"Why not, Becks?" I refused to cry. "Because you don't?"

"That's not—"

"Enough talk," Ash said, arm sliding around me once again. "Want me to walk you to class?"

Looking away from Becks, trying to smile, I said, "No, that's okay. I think I can manage."

Ash sighed loudly. "Well, alright, if you're going to play hard to get." Then to Becks, "I'm glad you let her go, man. Otherwise, I might've suffered in silence, burying my feelings down deep forever. It's crazy how much I love her already."

He was such a bull-shitter, it made me smile for real.

"Bye, Spitz," he said, voice low, intimate. "I'll see you later."

Grinning at Becks, Ash lowered his head and then did the unthinkable. He placed a kiss, the briefest brush of lips on skin, just behind my ear. *Becks's spot.* He'd just put his mouth directly over Becks's spot.

I was wide-eyed as he straightened, looking carefree as a clam. Becks wore an expression similar to mine. Completely gobsmacked.

"Thanks again, man." Ash lifted his chin. "Sal's a great girl."

I wasn't sure if it was the kiss or the 'Sal' that did it, but between one blink and the next Ash and Becks were on the floor, rolling around like a pair of angry cats. Becks had the upper hand. I could tell that much. Ash wasn't much smaller than him, but Becks looked like he had the most rage. Coach Crenshaw was actually the one who broke them up. As he tugged them to his office, I heard him saying, "What is wrong with you two idiots? Don't you know we've got a game? Save that aggression for the field."

I didn't know what to feel. Two guys fighting over little old me. It was every girl's dream, right? I wanted that zing of happiness to overtake me, but there was too much worry for that. I was nervous for Becks and Ash; I was pretty sure Crenshaw wouldn't bench them—they were the best he had. But I didn't want either of them getting into trouble, least of all on my account.

Hooker found me at lunch, nearly buzzing with excitement. She was sprinting as fast as she could, bouncing a little more than usual, making the male population in the cafeteria stare.

"Is it true?" she asked, out of breath as she collapsed into the chair next to mine. "Did Becks seriously try to stab Ash? Did Stryker kick him in the balls? Tell me, Spitz. Hurry up, I'm dying over here."

For a second, I couldn't speak. What she'd said was that out there.

"Spitz, *tell me.*"

"Hooker, *none* of that is true." I couldn't help but laugh at her disappointed expression. "They just had a disagreement. That's all."

"A disagreement?" she deadpanned.

"Yeah."

"One that ended with them duking it out on the ground?" I didn't answer. "What were they fighting over anyway?"

"Well..." I blushed, coming up short. There was no way I could tell her what Ash had done—or how Becks had reacted. No. Way.

"No," Hooker said, eyes widening, a crooked smile sitting on her face. "No freaking way."

Was she a mind reader or something? I shifted uncomfortably in my seat. "What?"

"Spitz!" She slapped me on the arm, sharp and unapologetic. "You're with Ash now, aren't you? I can't believe you're trying to keep it a secret. Have you forgotten that me and Martha were the ones who set this whole thing in motion?"

"Yeah, congratulations," I mumbled, rubbing my abused biceps. If this thing with Ash bombed, at least

I had two other people to blame. Besides my stupid self that is.

"Ah, don't be like that." Hooker was still smiling. "So...who's the better kisser?"

"Hooker."

"What?" she asked, all innocent. "I can't tell just from looking. Ash has better lips, but Becks looks like he has skills." Her gaze turned pensive as she rested her chin on her hand. "Actually, they both look like they could make a girl happy. Real happy."

"Jeez," I said, hand over my eyes. "Stop, Hooker. Please, you're freaking me out."

"Huh, why? It's perfectly natural to compare kisses."

Yeah, well, I couldn't exactly do that since I'd only kissed Becks. But what freaked me out more was how much thought Hooker had obviously given to how good a kisser Becks would be. It was just wrong. And there was no way Ash had better lips than Becks.

"Okay, then who was your best kiss?" I asked.

She didn't even hesitate. "Wade Weathersbee, seventh grade, behind the gym. Weathersbee had a lot of enthusiasm and could do this really cool rolling thing with his tongue. Naturally gifted." Hooker waggled her eyebrows. "If you know what I mean."

I didn't—but it sounded really interesting.

As I was working up the nerve to ask her about it, someone said, "Sally, you busy?"

I looked up, straight into the eyes of Clayton Kent. He was wearing his usual assistant coach uniform, but the seriousness in his expression was so out of place, it made me uneasy.

"Oh hey, Clayton," I said, trying to act natural.

"Would you mind stepping over here so we can talk?"

"Got something you can't say in front of me, Coach Kent?" Hooker pouted. "And I thought you were a Southern gentleman."

He gave her a patronizing smile then faced me. "Sally?"

"Sure." Following him to the next table over, empty on one end—the one closest to us—I steeled myself.

Clayton didn't beat around the bush. "Sally, did you really dump Becks?"

I gulped. God, he looked mad. "Yeah, I guess."

"What'd he do?"

"Huh?" I said, dumbly.

"What'd he say? Was he a jerk?" His eyes flashed, and I didn't think I'd ever seen him look so hostile. "Did he hurt you? I'll kill him if he did, Sally. I swear it. You just tell me now, and I'll take care of it."

The threat was good, but the look on his face was better. I couldn't contain myself. The laughter started low in my chest and bubbled out of my mouth, long and loud.

"Oh," I gasped. "Clayton, I can't believe you just said that." Wiping tears from my eyes, I laid my hand on his arm. "Becks would never hurt me. He wouldn't hurt any girl, and you know it."

"Yeah," Clayton agreed, reluctantly. "I was just hoping for a reason. You know, he'd get a whooping from each of us. Leo, Thad, Ollie and me wouldn't stand for him making you cry. He didn't, did he?"

"No," I said quickly. His eyes got all squinty, but I smiled. "It's sweet of you to offer, though. You know you're my favorite, right, Clayton?"

"Of course," he said, pulling me into a one-armed hug. "So you and The Whip are dating now?"

I shrugged. "That's what they say."

Clayton set me away from him, his hand resting on my shoulder. "You working your way through my bench or what? First Becks, now Ash. Next you'll be going after Rick Smythe. He's got a great block, nice set of calves."

"Please." I rolled my eyes. "How'd you know about me and Ash?"

"Heard it straight from the horse's mouth as he and Becks were getting reamed by Crenshaw. The coach didn't look too happy."

That didn't sound good. "They won't get in trouble, will they?"

"Nah." Clayton waved it off. "They'll be fine. A little scuffed up, but fine. So...my Sally and Ash Stryker, huh? 'Sash,'" he said to himself. "That's not bad."

"Yep," I said, ducking my head. It was strange how he seemed to accept me and Ash easier than me and Becks. It'd taken him less than an hour to link our names together.

Sash. Good grief.

"Hey." Clayton waited until I met his eyes, then said, "Make him suffer."

"What?" I asked.

"Becks," he grinned. His crystal clear eyes seemed to see too much. "My brother needs to be smacked over the head sometimes. Don't you dare let him off easy, Sally. You just be sure you make him work a little before giving in."

"But Clayton..." I stammered as he walked away.

"Make him suffer, Sally," he tossed over his shoulder, leaving me dumbfounded.

Clayton was a terrible big brother for saying that, but he was a good friend to me, and I appreciated the support. I didn't want to hurt Becks, but it would be sweet to make him a little jealous—to know that he *could get* jealous over me, like a guy gets over a girl, a man over a woman. Time would tell, but in the meantime, I had to get back to Hooker and find out more about this tongue rolling thing.

CHAPTER 15

They won (of course). Chariot breezed past the second round of sectionals and the quarterfinals as well. Becks was playing better than ever. Like I'd heard Crenshaw say, it was as if someone had put gasoline on his already lit fire. He was unstoppable on the field, a one-man army of soccer devastation. The coach made the most out of Becks's and Ash's new feud, always putting them in together, never letting one sit out when the other was in action.

Not like they'd let him.

The two seemed to be in an all-out battle to see who could do the best, score the most. It was amazing to watch Ash try and rise up to Becks's level. The

Whip had already been a force to be reckoned with, but this was something else. Becks ended up outscoring him in the second round but not the third—which I could tell disturbed him greatly.

The day after it happened, Becks came up to me and said, "Did you go to the movies with Ass Striker?"

I shut my locker, doing a mental eye roll at the name. "Yeah, how'd you know?"

"The jerk tweeted it," he said in disgust.

"He did?" I couldn't hide my surprise. "What did he say?"

Becks held his phone out to me, and I scanned the screen.

The account was for @AshTheWhip24/7, and it said: "Scream Deluxe, popcorn, and a hot older woman at my side. Doesn't get better than that."

I laughed. Ash was such a goober.

"Sal, we were supposed to go see that one together."

It was true. Becks was a huge fan of horror, but Ash had asked me first, and like he said, I couldn't wait around forever. I wouldn't. Becks's puppy dog eyes had always worked on me in the past, but now I was a rock. Stone cold, hard, impassive. I just wished he didn't look so disappointed in me.

I shrugged. "We can go see it again if you want, but I might have to check and see if I'm doing anything with Ash."

"What's up with that?" he said in exasperation. "Is he your babysitter now? Sal, you hate Twitter. Just last year you called the people who do it 'online attention seekers with no life.' What happened?"

You, I thought. You happened, and now I'm on this stupid mission to make you see me as a girl and to give someone who actually likes me a shot, and it'll probably go nowhere, but I'm going to try my best anyway. Call me what you like, but Sally Spitz was no quitter.

"So Ash tweets," I said. "It's not that big a deal. I accept him for who he is, and he accepts me for who I am."

"Hmph," Becks said and then stalked off without a backward glance.

Later on, the coach was drilling them hard. This would be the last practice before the semis, and he wanted his team both mentally and physically prepared. They'd been at it a full hour and a half before he let them have their first break.

Ash jogged up to me, hair plastered to his head with sweat, muscles shifting beneath his skin, his shirt long gone.

"Hey," he said, pulling me into a very warm, very wet hug.

"Ugh," I laughed, then whispered, "when I agreed to go out with you, I don't think sweaty hugs were part of the deal."

"They totally were." He released me with a tug on my ponytail. "Fine print, Spitz. Never forget to read it. You'll be sorry if you do."

"I heard about your tweet."

"Who'd you hear that from, I wonder?" Ash looked pleased. "Tell me, was he crying when he told you? Did he get down on one knee right there, sweep you into his arms, and ask you to forgive him for being such a loser?"

"Hey," I said, "no calling Becks a loser. We talked about this."

"Alright, alright," he said. "I'm working on it."

"He's my best friend, Ash. And if we're going to be friends, you need to work harder."

"I said okay." Ash crossed his arms. "So I assume this means you're still in love with—"

"Shhh!" I hissed, clapping a hand over his mouth. "He might hear you."

Ash stared at me balefully until I removed my hand. "I'll take that as a yes," he mumbled.

A second later Becks was there at my side, drawing me into my second sticky hug of the day. Despite the sweat, I closed my eyes, couldn't bring myself to pull away, sinking into him like home. It'd been a while since Becks touched me.

"Hey, Sal," Becks murmured, tightening his hold.

"Becks," I sighed. He really did give the best hugs.

Who knows how long I might've stayed there (probably forever) if Ash hadn't chosen that moment to grunt, a loud and piercing sound that cut through my Becks haze.

Shaking myself out of his embrace, I tried to stop the blush from stealing up my cheeks. From Becks's smile and Ash's faint look of disapproval, I could tell I was unsuccessful.

"Mount Tabor doesn't stand a chance," I said to fill the awkward silence. "You guys look really great out there."

"Why thank you, Spitz." Ash smiled. "You're looking good yourself."

"I-I didn't—"

"No need to stutter." Looking down at himself, he flexed which brought even more heat to my face. "Many a woman has admired my physique."

Becks snorted, crossing his arms, his own muscles contracting with the movement.

The cheerleaders threw catcalls our way; a couple nearly swooned and I couldn't even blame them. I was about to pass out myself. I kept switching from Becks to Ash, Ash to Becks, chest to chest, but no matter where I looked there was more skin. With that much excellent male flesh on display, what's a girl to do?

Ash was smirking at me, and Becks didn't seem too thrilled about it.

Looking between us, one eyebrow cocked, Becks said, "You two are pretty close then, huh?"

He'd addressed the question to me, so I answered, "Yeah, we're getting there."

"Very close," Ash agreed, coming up beside me, placing a hand on my back. He dropped a quick kiss to my hair, and Becks winced.

"How's that going?" was Becks's next question.

"Great." I gulped. No need to tell him Ash was turning out to be more of a friend than a boyfriend. There was absolutely no need to tell Becks there was no spark. Not like I'd felt with him.

"Great," he repeated, staring me down. "It's strange don't you think? How quick you two came together."

"Sometimes you just know," Ash said.

Becks grunted.

I was still having hallucinations from all the nakedness, so I was glad Ash was on top of things.

"Spitz has everything I'm looking for," Ash went on. "She's way too smart for me, but I love her quirky sense of humor. It doesn't hurt that she's beautiful."

Stupidly, I felt flattered. Sure, it was a bunch of crap, but crap or not, Ash was good at flattery.

"So I assume she's shown you her CWC."

"Becks," I hissed. Nothing could've snapped me to attention quicker.

"Her what?" Becks grinned at Ash's confused expression. "Spitz, what's a CWC?"

"Go ahead," Becks prompted. "Show him, Sal."

Oh, he was *so* dead. I was fairly sure steam was coming out of my ears, and it had nothing to do with the midday heat.

"What's wrong, Sal? You said you two were close." He shrugged, shooting me that same infuriating smile. "Just thought he'd like to see some of your hidden talents."

"Hidden talents?" Ash asked. "Is CWC slang for something—" He ran his fingers down my spine, and I jumped up in shock. "—'cause if it is, I'd be happy to see whatever you've got to show me."

"You disgust me," Becks spat.

"And you bug the hell out of me," Ash replied. "We're even. By the way, that lucky beard is stupid."

"And so are you. I guess we're even there, too."

"A real soccer player wouldn't need to rely on tricks to win a game. Some of us get by on natural talent."

"Shut up, Stryker." Becks's eyes flashed. "You don't know anything about it."

"I know we don't need some dumb fairytale to help us win State," he said and before Becks could say anything else, "Spitz? You gonna show me or what?"

They were both looking at me expectantly.

"C'mon," Becks said, his frown dissolving into a slow smile. "We worked on it for weeks in fifth grade, remember?"

"What?" Ash said in shock. "Fifth grade? That's pretty young isn't it?"

"Fine," I sighed.

It'd be better to just get it over with, and someone had to get Ash's mind out of the gutter. Drawing in a deep breath, rolling my eyes at Becks's grin, I titled my head up and released a sound somewhere between bird mating call and dying dog. It lasted all of ten seconds before I ran out of air.

"Wow," Becks said, sounding like he meant it. "That was great, Sal."

"I know, right?" I smiled. Instead of feeling the waves of embarrassment I expected, I was proud of myself. That was one of the best Wookiee calls I'd ever done.

"What'd you think, Ash?" Seeing his perplexed expression, I said, "CWC stands for Chewbacca's Wookiee Call. Becks and I learned how to do it off this online tutorial." I smirked at Becks, "But he couldn't even get the first note right."

"Hey," Becks said indignant, "I could outdo your Vader any day." And then he proceeded to demonstrate the fact, grinning afterward as I gave a silent round of applause. He was a good Darth—raspy voice, low and menacing—but he couldn't do Chewie to save his life.

"I thought it was 'Luke, I am your father,'" Ash said.

"Amateur." Becks switched his focus to Ash, a challenge in his eyes. "What can you do, Stryker?"

If I didn't like him more than anything, I'd have said Becks was being a real jerk to Ash. But The Whip refused to be intimidated. Ash pursed his lips, looking around a moment. Walking a few steps, he grabbed up a lacrosse stick and waited until he had our full attention.

Lifting that stick high in the air, he scowled at nothing then gripped it between both hands and bellowed, "*You shall not pass!*" He drove the stick into the ground with all his might, arms quivering with the force of impact.

After a moment, I said, "I didn't know you do Gandalf. That's one of my favorites."

Ash chucked the stick back to where it'd come from, sauntering over with a grin. "It's nothing."

"No, that was awesome. Wasn't it Becks?" I turned but Becks wasn't there anymore. He'd rejoined the team on the field. The whistle blew and the coach called the stragglers back to practice.

"Don't worry about it," Ash said, but I did. I couldn't help it.

Mount Tabor went down fighting, but between Becks and Ash, there was no contest. I'd waited until after school to approach Becks and congratulate him. He'd been surrounded all day. It was Becks's senior year, and he was in a good way to get State MVP and win yet another championship. Some athletes crumbled beneath the pressure but not my Becks. I was so proud of him; I could barely see straight.

After Roxy finally left (she'd been talking his ear off, flashing him her cleavage for about fifteen minutes), I walked over to Becks, finding him in one of those rare moments that he was alone.

He'd zipped his bag, and I'd opened my mouth, wearing a smile just for him, when he said, "If this is about Stryker, I don't want to hear it."

I recoiled. "I just came over to say great job," I said. "You did it, Becks. CHS has a chance at State, third year in a row."

"Thanks, I know," he said. "Was there something else?"

"No." Again, I was taken aback. Who was this cold person, and what had they done with my Becks? "I'm...I'm proud of you. That's all."

Becks looked at me for a long moment.

"Ash said you guys are likely to win if you can——"

"If you're going to talk about Ash, don't talk to me."

"Becks..."

"See ya," he said, turning away. No Sal, no grin, nothing.

Ash came up behind me and laid a hand on my shoulder. "Hey, Spitz, want to go to a party tonight?"

I was too numb to speak, so instead I listened to Ash as he invited me to another one of Mercedes's parties. It was supposed to be bigger and better than any of the others so far, a real celebration since Chariot had made it to the final round. He said that everyone was going. I must've agreed, though I definitely didn't remember doing so.

Hooker had come to my house to fix my hair and make-up, and Ash drove us to Mercedes's house. We got there late, the party already half-over when we arrived. That was mostly my doing. I'd taken a lot of time getting ready, so I wouldn't have to stay long. Ash hadn't minded. "Just an appearance," he'd said. "We'll just make an appearance then leave." I was still wary. My last visit to Mercedes's house had ended in heartbreak, tears, and a lot of German swearing. I was determined not to let that happen again.

But the first thing I saw when I walked inside was Becks sitting slumped between two girls I'd never met before. They were both smiling, happy as all get out to be that close to the man that was going to lead Chariot to its next victory.

The sight made my anger rise—not at them, but at myself.

Becks looked horrible. His eyes were downcast, his beard looked a little rougher than usual, and his head drooped on his shoulders. Was this what having a boyfriend meant? Leaving all my other friends behind? I didn't even know what was bothering him. Seeing him in that state made me hate myself a little.

"I'm going to go get myself something to drink," Ash said into my ear, "you want anything?"

I shook my head.

"Be right back." He dashed off without another word.

As if he'd been waiting for Ash to leave, Becks lifted his head, his eyes going straight to mine. What had put that sadness there? I wondered as he rose and walked up to me.

"Sal," he said, voice soft.

"Becks."

"You want to dance?"

"Sure," I said, taking his hand. The contact still sent tingles running through me.

We made our way to the center of the living room where other couples were already dancing. I hardly noticed. After Becks put his hands on my waist, my arms reaching up to twine around his neck, I was gone. It was just him and me. Nothing else mattered.

"Sorry about earlier," he said.

"That's okay." I rested my cheek against his chest and felt the strong beat of his heart, steady, sure. "I'm sorry you're so sad," I said quietly.

Becks sighed, pulling me closer. "I'm not sad, Sal."

"You're not?"

After a moment, Becks whispered, "I miss you."

I swallowed heavily as he rested his cheek against my hair. "Me, too."

We didn't say anything else, didn't have to. Mercedes must've had a party playlist or something because the song we were dancing to now was the same one that'd been playing when I'd given Becks his shave. The soundtrack to the first (and only) kiss he'd ever given me. I'd never forget that song.

As the final notes died away, Becks and I separated.

"Can I cut in?" Ash said.

Becks looked at him, at me, then turned around and walked back to his seat.

Another ballad started, and Ash and I assumed the position, his arms holding me closer than necessary. Leaning down, he spoke quietly so only I could hear, "What's with him?"

"I don't know," I answered as he melded our two bodies further. There was no space between Ash and me now, and those sad eyes, the ones I loved, were locked on us, looking tired.

"Forget about it, Spitz," Ash said, nuzzling my neck. "He'll get over it."

No, I thought. He looks miserable. Becks looked completely, utterly miserable. He needed his best friend. He needed me. If having a boyfriend was taking up too much of my time, there was only one thing to do.

CHAPTER 16

"You want to break up?" Ash repeated.

I nodded. "I think it's for the best."

We were sitting outside, on one of the benches in front of the library. I'd forced him to meet me here extra early (6:30 a.m. on a Saturday) in retribution. Hey, if he could call a meeting at the crack of dawn so could I. Though, really I'd done it because I had to be here anyway for my kids. Reading Corner didn't start for another hour or so, but I liked to be early whenever I could.

My cape fluttered at my ankles. There was a nice breeze today.

"You're serious," he said and then pointed at me. "And you're gonna break up with me wearing that?"

"You have something against wizard-wear?" I asked.

Ash shook his head. "Spitz, this is so embarrassing. Couldn't we go inside, where no one can see us? I can't believe you're out in public dressed like this."

"We can't go inside. They're not officially open yet." I watched his face closely. "Does it really bother you?"

"No," he said. "What bothers me is the lightning bolt on your forehead. And what do you mean, you want to break up?"

I sighed. I'd known this wouldn't go well.

"Ash, when we first started this thing, I honestly thought you'd get sick of me after one date."

Ash scoffed, throwing his arm over the back of the bench, making a "Go on" gesture with his other hand.

"Then I thought, maybe you could help me get over Becks like you offered," I continued. "I did end up liking you, just like you said. It's been great hanging out with you this past week."

"So, what's the problem?" He sat up. "You like hanging out with me. I like hanging out with you. Even if you were using me to make Becks jealous, I wouldn't care. His face when we danced was like—"

"That wasn't jealousy," I cut in. "It was misery."

Ash shrugged. "Same thing."

"No, it's really not." Reaching out, I laid my hand over the top of his. He'd treated me so well, and I really did like talking with him. If nothing else, I'd gained a friend. "I don't want to make Becks unhappy. That was never what I wanted."

"Well..."

"I know, I know, you don't like Becks—" I shook my head, lifted my shoulders helplessly, "—but I do. Even if he doesn't feel the same about me, I'm still his friend. I can't stand to see him so sad."

"Spitz, the guy makes you sad whenever he's around another girl. What's he done to save your feelings?"

I flushed. He had a point, but it didn't change anything.

"You're incredible," Ash said, looking at my expression. "Becks is blind for not seeing what's in front of him, but you, Spitz. I've never met someone like you before."

"What's that mean?"

"It means you're a freak of nature." I made to pull away, but Ash wasn't having it. He captured my fingers, his other hand joining the first. "After all he's put your through, most girls would want to tear Becks's throat out, but not you."

I felt the need to set the record straight. "He didn't mean to. Becks has no idea about my feelings, so it's not really his fault."

Ash pointed at me. "That's it. That's what I'm talking about."

"What?"

"Did you hear yourself just then? You defended him. He's the one who's put your heart in a grinder, and here you are sticking up for him." Ash's eyebrows lowered; in a strange voice he said, "You really love the guy, don't you?"

"I do," I said. Odd how easy it was to say that to Ash. I'd never thought I could admit that to anyone, let alone The Whip, but there it was.

He looked away, released my hand slowly, passing his fingertips through his hair.

"Guess I can't compete with that," he said under his breath.

"Thanks for everything, Ash." I smiled, meaning it. "Now that I know you—the *real* you—I can honestly say you're one of the nicest guys I've ever met."

Ash laughed. "You're just as bad as Becks, you know that?"

I frowned. Where did that come from?

"Spitz, I'm not a nice guy," he said flatly. "I don't want to be your friend."

"Huh?"

He rolled his eyes as he stood. "You smart girls are always the last to figure these things out. Why would a guy like me ask you out if all I wanted was friendship? You may be cute, but you're not too observant."

"Huh?" I said again. I understood the words coming out of his mouth, but the meaning behind them was a mystery. It was like he was intentionally trying to confuse me.

Leaning down, trapping me between his arms, he placed a hand on the bench on either side my head.

I gulped as he studied my face. His resulting smile was pure bad boy, no nice guy in there whatsoever.

"I told you before, I like you, Spitz," he said, and I drew in a breath. "I like you a lot."

While I sat there in shock, he smoothly closed the space between us, his lips moving over mine in a kiss like a match striking tinder. Heat shot up between the two of us. It burned for a few seconds and didn't immediately cool as he leaned back.

Hooker had been right. Ash was a great kisser. It was brash and unexpected, sort of like the man himself, but it went no deeper than that. As good as he was, as hot as the kiss had been—and it had been smokin', believe me—I hadn't felt anything like I did with Becks. When Becks kissed me, it'd been right, so completely perfect that I knew instantly. That was where I belonged.

"Ash, I like you, too, but..." I trailed off, not wanting to embarrass him. It wasn't that I hadn't liked kissing Ash. Any girl would've loved kissing him, but there was one problem: He wasn't Becks. How was I supposed to let him down easily?

The Whip shrugged as if he could read my mind. "Just wanted to let you know you have options. Maybe it's for the best, since neither of us will be in Chariot next year."

"You won't?" I asked, surprised. "Why?"

"Dad's got his eye on a Senate seat," he said sarcastically. "So guess that means I'm off to private school for senior year. Fun, fun."

We both knew it wouldn't be. For a senior with collegiate soccer aspirations, Chariot High was *the* place to be. It was a real shame his parents were taking him out before he could get scouted.

"I'm so sorry, Ash." Reaching out, I placed a hand on his arm in sympathy. "That sucks."

"It does." He caught my hand, eyes playful, as he ran his thumb along the back of my knuckles. "I'll miss you, Sally Spitz."

I laughed. "Miss you, too, Stryker."

"If things don't work out with Becks, let me know."

With one last grin and a gentle kiss to my temple, he walked off.

I stared after him for longer than I should have. Ash might as well have told me he was an alien from the planet Vulcan. It would've stunned me less if he had. A boy, not just any boy but Ash "The Whip" Styker, liked me, Sally Spitz, a first-class dork with a degree in geek. Not just liked, but *liked*. The news was about as believable as science fiction, but he'd been serious. And that kiss had definitely been real. My lips were still on fire.

Shaking my head, I went inside. Besides tossing me into a confusion spiral, and let's face it, upping my confidence as a woman, the talk with Ash made me realize one indisputable fact: Boys were strange.

I got further confirmation of that a little later as I was in the middle of reading Harry Potter. Ten of the twelve kids registered had shown up today. We were at a really good part, the one where Hagrid finds Harry and the Dursleys holed up in a shack surrounded by the sea. The kids were loving it. I'd been doing all the voices, and not one of them could resist the pull of Jo Rowling's writing.

Lowering my voice, I gave the kids a conspiratorial wink then said, affecting Hagrid's deep Cockney accent, "'Ah, go boil yer heads, both of yeh.'"

They giggled as I got shushed by my boss, Mrs. Carranza, librarian at large.

The young eyes around me were saucers, pitched forward as the announcement drew closer.

"'Harry—yer a...'"

I stopped mid-sentence, catching sight of Becks, standing at the edge of our circle, looking at me with a smile in his eyes.

"A what? A *what?*" Gwen Glick said, tugging at my arm.

"Shut up, Gwen. Let her finish." Vince Splotts pushed her hand away.

I looked at him sternly, trying to forget about Becks. "Now, Vince, you know we don't talk that way during Corner."

"I know, but—"

"Apologize, please," I said.

"But Miss Sally, she was being annoying. I was just saying—"

"I heard what you said." I crossed my arms and tilted my head toward Gwen whose lip was now quivering. "Tell Gwen you're sorry, please."

Vince rolled his eyes and mumbled, "Sorry."

I looked at the girl in the faded *Star Trek* tee. "And what do you say Gwen?"

"Apology accepted," Gwen muttered, turning a glare on Vince. "And I am *not* annoying."

"Gwen."

"Sorry, Miss Sally," she said. "Now can we hear the rest? What does Hagrid tell Harry he is?"

"He's a wizard," Becks answered.

As Gwen saw him, she smiled and waved like a mad woman. He grinned back.

"That's right," I said, flipping the book closed, "and I think it's picture time."

The kids groaned, and Vince said in a pitiful voice, "But Miss Sally, we didn't even get to the end of that chapter."

"We can finish it next week." Usually I tried to read them two chapters per session, but Becks was here now, looking like he had something to say. I wasn't sure I wanted to hear it, but my concentration was blown. "You guys just go up to front desk, and ask Miss Carranza for some paper and crayons. I'll be right over."

The kids got up, grumbling as they made their way over to the reference desk, and Vince shrugged, saying, "I'll just watch the movie anyway."

He hurried off, and only Gwen stayed behind.

Becks stepped forward. "Hey there Sal, Miss Gwen. How's everything going today?"

"Hiyah, Becks," Gwen said, bouncing on her toes. "Everything's good. Miss Sally did a great job reading, and I got all As on my report card. Except for gym," she muttered, "which isn't really a class anyway."

"Well, excuse me," Becks said, "but gym was my best subject in elementary school."

"Really?" Gwen eyed him suspiciously.

"Sure was."

"Oh, well, I didn't really try all that hard. Maybe I'll do better next time."

"I'm sure you will." He gave her one of his devastating smiles, and the ten-year-old looked like she was head over heels. Becks simply had that effect on women.

I stepped in, trying to save her from herself. "That's great, Gwen. You going to draw me another pretty picture today or what?"

"But I'm talking to Becks," she protested.

"Go on," Becks said. "I've got something I need to say to Miss Sally. We'll talk some more another time."

"Alright." Gwen sulked away, throwing glances at us over her shoulder.

"I really do like that little redhead," Becks said. "She reminds me of you, Sal."

I nodded. "We have a lot of things in common." Like the love of Trek and, oh yeah, the boy standing in front of me. "What's up?"

"Not here," he said. "Don't want anyone to listen in. It's kind of personal."

I tried to push down my fear as we weaved in and out of the rows.

Once we couldn't hear the kids' whispers anymore I stopped, turned back to him. He looked like he was nervous, thinking hard. The first was a new one on me. Becks hardly ever got nervous, and when he did, it usually meant something bad was coming.

"What is it?" I asked before I lost what little courage I had. No one ever really used this part of the library. We were completely alone. I was trying to decide whether or not that was a good thing.

"I want you to break up with Ash," he said.

Whatever I'd been expecting, it wasn't this.

"What?" I asked.

"I want you to break up with him, Sal." Becks looked uncomfortable, but he didn't flinch.

"Why?"

Becks's eyes shifted restlessly, looking at the books around us as if they might hold the answer. "It just doesn't feel right," he said finally. "You and Stryker are so different, Sal. He's not the one for you."

Mentally, I agreed but decided to listen and see where this was going.

"I mean, he's such a jerk," he went on. "And you're..."

"I'm what?"

"You're...you." I scowled, and he tried to backtrack. "No, no, I didn't mean anything by it. It's a good thing, Sal. A very good thing."

"How good, Becks?"

He frowned at me like I was the one not making sense. "The thing is, the two of you together...it's just wrong. Don't you feel that? I can't concentrate in school. I'm killing 'em on the field, but I can't get too excited about it because then I remember you're with him. You're never around anymore. I miss you so much; it's driving me insane and..."

"And?" I held my breath. One impossible thing had already happened today; was it too much to hope for another? Did Becks feel the same way I did? It sure sounded like it, but I was afraid to hope.

"Here's the truth, Sal." Becks held my gaze as I waited on tenterhooks. "Ash is no good for you. I know you haven't been with him long, but I think there's an easy way out. You could tell him you realized you've still got feelings for me. It'd smooth things over, and it's a believable lie. Then until graduation in a couple weeks, I'd go back to playing your boyfriend. Faking it should be easier this time around. We've already done it once."

My chest contracted, the air in my lungs releasing in one long exhale. This is what he'd had to tell me?

"What do you think, Sal?"

I thought I was having a heart attack, that's what I thought. It sure felt like I was dying.

"Good idea, right?"

Stupid, that's how I felt right then. Like the biggest fool in the world, and it was all my fault for thinking, even for a second, that Becks would—that he could—love me like that.

Tears trickled down my face, but I couldn't hold them back. Not this time.

"That's a horrible idea," I said, my laughter sounding like a sob. "It's the worst idea I've ever heard."

His eyes grew concerned, and he took a step forward, but I wouldn't let him any closer. I couldn't let Becks get any closer, or I might fall apart.

"Because you want to keep playing pretend when all I want to do is make it real."

He froze. "Why—"

"I love you, Becks," I said, the words ringing true even through my crying. "I've always loved you."

Becks rocked back, as if my confession physically knocked him off balance. The look of shock on his face didn't help things.

"I knew you never looked at me that way, but you must have had some idea," I said. "The way I'd always trail after you, how I wanted to be next to you, with you more than anyone else in the world. Our friendship's always been ironclad, Becks, but I've loved you from the start and never stopped. Even after I realized you could never love me back," I whispered.

One shoulder leaning heavily against the bookshelf, his eyes searched mine. Becks shook his head, speaking more to himself than to me. "I would have known. You'd have told me."

Another laugh/sob escaped. "I'm telling you now, Becks. Slytherins can be brave sometimes, you know."

"Sal, I...I love you, too."

My head snapped up, the tears forgotten. "What did you say?"

Becks locked eyes with me and repeated, "I love you, Sal. I always have."

"Don't," I said, taking a step back as he took another forward. "Please, don't do this, Becks."

"Do what?" he said and kept walking until my back hit the wall. I tried to look away, but he was so close, too close. "I'm saying I love you, Sal. There was just never a good time to tell you. I thought it'd ruin everything if I told you and you didn't feel the same. I've felt this way since the moment I set eyes on you. I just...never had the courage to say it out loud."

"Becks, please."

"I'm telling you the truth." Becks shook his head as his fingers ran along my cheek. "Why can't you believe me?"

The question was so similar to one I'd asked him in the past. Though that one had been about his stupid lucky scruff, the answer he gave worked just as good.

"I want to, Becks. Really, I do." The words tumbled from my lips. "It's just I'm not willing to take a chance on something so important and lose."

He scoffed, hand falling away from me, recognition in his eyes. "Jeez, Sal, that's not—"

"If I was wrong," I choked, crying again, "the fallout would be too painful."

"Sal," he said after a moment, "I don't understand."

I placed my hand against his face, feeling the stubble bite into my skin. Smiling a watery smile, I said, "I know you don't, Becks. It's like you and this beard. Sometimes you want to believe in things so bad you convince yourself they're true."

Becks went to respond, but I shook my head.

"But they're not, Becks. Don't fool yourself." I backed away. "I'm a big enough fool for the both of us."

When I told Mrs. Carranza I needed to leave early, she didn't question me. I must've looked awful because the woman usually wanted an explanation for everything. In the car, I turned the radio to a local station where they eventually started talking about Becks. Penn or UCLA, they said. They'd narrowed it down to those two top picks after the results this week. Their voices socked me in the gut, but it was like layering a scratch on top of a knife wound.

As I was walking in the door, Mom said, "Sally, I've got something for you."

Her voice had come from the kitchen, so I drifted that way, barely aware of my legs moving.

"Mom, I don't—" I stopped short, seeing her face.

Her eyes were so bright, jaw quaking with the force of her smile. Mom was radiating so much; it was like she'd swallowed the sun. In her hand was a large, white envelope with the Duke seal on the cover.

"Big envelope," she said, nodding, holding the package up high. "You did it, baby. You got in."

As she rushed forward, throwing her arms around me in a great big squeeze, I hugged her back, not knowing what else to do. Mom kept saying how great I'd done, how she'd always known I'd get accepted, how Duke was lucky to have me.

But the news didn't affect me the way I'd thought it would.

My confession had rocked the balance of my carefully constructed world. Becks knew—and he hadn't come after me. The memory of him lying, to both of us but mostly to himself, was...tragic. It was a good thing I was all cried out. I'd gotten into Duke, a dream come true, but the bigger dream had just exploded in my face. No matter where he chose, Becks was going away. It felt like that scene in *Star Trek* where Nero destroys the planet Vulcan, and there's nothing left but a big, smoldering black hole. My soul was that black hole, and even the thought of Duke couldn't fill me up.

Who knew it was possible to be so happy and so sad at the same time?

CHAPTER 17

I shifted back and forth, foot to foot, until I couldn't stand it another second. Looking back at the clock, seeing the time, my pulse ratcheted up another notch.

"Mom, you almost ready?" I called.

"Five more minutes," she said.

"I don't want to miss anything."

"We won't."

She'd said five minutes ten minutes ago, and we were already cutting it close. The game would start at seven on the dot. It was already thirty minutes till.

"Geesh," Mom said, stepping into the room, looking fresh as a daisy. "Why are you in such a hurry?"

"Mom, parking's going to fill up quick. The lot's always jammed for the championship."

"We'll get a space, Sally."

Yeah, I thought, probably somewhere in the next county over. She took her time applying her lipstick as I tried not to let the anxiety get to me. Broughton was good this year. Their team wasn't going to just hand over the state title. Chariot was going to have to be on their game tonight.

"Alright, ready," Mom said, swinging her purse over her shoulder.

"Finally," I said, grabbing my keys, practically jogging to the door.

Once we were in the car, I revved the ignition, rolling my eyes when Mom said, "Seatbelt." Of course, I put it on; I always wore my seatbelt, but she was flipping through radio stations as if we'd even have time to listen. It might've taken her twenty minutes to get to the stadium, but not me. Ten miles over the speed limit wasn't really speeding.

"Sally." Mom's stern tone said otherwise.

I eased it back to seven over. But seriously, this was the championship.

"Looks like Becks made his choice," Mom said casually. "I don't think anybody expected it to be UNC. They all thought he'd go out of state."

"I know," I spoke over her, "but the Tarheels are number one."

"Is that why he chose them?"

"I don't know, Mom. It's also close to his family."

"Close to you, too," she pointed out. "Duke's, what? Ten miles away from UNC?"

I shot her a don't-go-there look. "I'm sure that didn't even enter his mind."

Mom wouldn't back down. "And I'm sure it did."

How could it have? I thought. Becks didn't even know I'd been accepted. He'd been avoiding me ever since that embarrassing scene at the library—which was fine because I was avoiding him, too. Reaching out, I stopped on a station with lots of guitar and plenty of bass.

Becks had actually made the announcement yesterday, and like everyone else, I'd tuned in to see it. He hadn't called afterward. Though I'd picked up my phone a dozen times, I hadn't either. It was like we were strangers. We'd barely spoken, and whenever we did, it was always about nothing important. I missed him more than ever. We didn't have a lot of time before graduation, and if I hadn't said anything, if I'd never come up with that dumb fake boyfriend idea in the first place, we'd be spending every waking minute together.

Or at least I imagined we would have. Things were so screwed up. I could hardly remember the good old days when me and Becks were just me and Becks. Now with the whole love thing hanging over our heads, he'd gone mute, and I was just trying to hold it together. Sure, the schools were close, but what did it matter if we weren't even speaking?

As expected, when Mom and I arrived, we had to park about a mile away. There were no available parking spaces in the lot, so we'd had to park beside the curb a few streets down. They took our tickets as I tried to catch my breath. Man, that was a long walk.

"You made it," Hooker said as I joined her and Cicero at our seats.

"Barely," I said, looking around for Mom.

Her high-pitched whistle drew my attention, and I finally saw who she'd stopped to talk to. The Kents, everyone besides Becks and Clayton, of course, all looked back at me, waving with enthusiasm. I waved back, swallowing down my bitterness. Becks hadn't looked that happy to see me in days.

"Can you believe it?" Hooker said when I turned back to her.

"Believe what?" I asked.

I must've zoned or something while she was talking because she looked slightly annoyed.

"Becks," she stated like that said it all.

"What about him?"

Hooker stared at me like I'd sprouted an eyeball in the middle of my forehead. "Spitz, you've gotta be kidding me. Didn't you watch the news the other night? Or this morning?"

"Oh. Yeah."

"Well, why aren't you more excited?" She titled her head. "You and Becks'll be minutes away from each other. I mean sure, your schools are total rivals, but with all the worrying you've been doing, I thought you'd be over the moon."

"Yeah," I said sadly. "Me, too."

"Oh, come on," she huffed. "It's so obvious he's doing this for you. How can you not see that?"

I placed a hand over her lips. "Let's not talk about it, okay?"

Hooker scowled. "You're being a real dork. You know that, right?"

I shrugged. So long as we didn't discuss it, I wouldn't be reminded that Becks hadn't told me the news himself. I could forget that we weren't talking, pretend we could go on as we always had.

The players filtered out onto the field, and my eyes instantly went to Becks. His green and white jersey shined beneath the stadium lights, his face determined, jaw heavily dusted with five o'clock shadow, high-stepping to warm up his legs along with the other players.

He looked fantastic. Gone was the drooping, miserable shade of a person he'd been little less than a week ago. This was Becks in his element, shouting commands at his team, firing up the crowd. Chariot was here, and they were here to win. Becks's voice rang out again, strong and powerful.

I tried hard not to think about the fact that, up until recently, I hadn't gone a day without hearing that voice. Not since we'd met.

The first forty-five minutes were excruciating. Chariot ended one point up, but the lead was hard-won. Becks and Ash weren't playing any worse than they had at any other time during the tournament, but the Broughton team wasn't letting up. Every time we made a great play, they'd answer with one of their own. We had them on offense, but their defense was killing us. Running the ball up field, goal to goal, was nearly impossible. Their guys were everywhere. Whichever team won, by the end, they would've earned it no question.

At half-time, it was three to two, and I was nearly hoarse from shouting. Becks had scored two of those goals, Ash the other. Mom was back down there with the Kents, the brothers waving their arms around expressively, most likely reliving Chariot's best moments. There were certainly plenty to choose from.

"Dang, Spitz." Hooker elbowed me in the side. "He's like a man possessed."

I grinned proudly. Possessed wasn't the word. In the last play, Becks had done Rick Smythe's job, blocking the goal with his body, the ball rebounding off his chest. Phenomenon would've been more accurate.

"Becks is the best," I said, smiling. "There's no one better."

"Ugh, spare me." She made a face, leaning back against Cicero. He wrapped an arm around her, discussing that last block with the guy sitting behind him. "If you love him so much what was all that stuff at Mercedes's house? I thought it was over between you two."

"It is," I mumbled, wishing I hadn't said anything. Hooker was watching me carefully, her gaze too direct. I was worried if she looked close enough she'd see the pain I'd worked so hard to keep hidden.

"You don't sound so sure, Spitz," she countered. "If things weren't over, I'd have a few things to say. Number one would definitely be that you and Becks are acting like a couple of first-class idiots. Why can't you just tell him—"

Jumping to my feet, I decided it might be time for a bathroom break. She was obviously about to tell me all the reasons I should confess to Becks. Been there, done that. My heart still hadn't healed from the first time. The line to the ladies' room would be long, a welcome escape from Hooker's prying eyes.

They'd said there was going to be a special treat at half-time, but I had no desire to see it. That is until Becks stepped out onto the field, carrying a microphone, Ash on his heels, Clayton lugging a chair behind him. The sight of the trio was so unexpected I lowered slowly back into my seat, ignoring Hooker's exclamation of, "*This* is it? What a lame excuse for entertainment."

I didn't know it then, but she couldn't have been more wrong.

"Hey everyone," Becks said, voice echoing over the loudspeakers. "Enjoying the game so far?"

The words were met with a loud roar of applause and a couple of boos. Naturally, those came from the Broughton side.

"Yeah, me, too." Becks exaggerated wiping sweat off his brow and being out of breath, like he'd really been working hard—which he had. The crowd laughed. "You all are probably wondering what I'm doing out here."

"Yeah," Ollie hollered, "what the hell are you doing, Becks?"

That got a few snickers. I watched as Leo pulled him back down, smacked him in the head, and then moved my eyes back to Becks. What the heck's he doing? I wondered. He should've been using this time to rest and recharge. Instead he was out here showboating for the fans.

"Good question, Ollie, and I'm about to tell you." Becks grinned as the crowd grew silent, waiting to hear what he'd say next. "Everyone knows I'm a little superstitious. The proof's right here," he said, pointing, "on my face. But sometimes you got to risk something if you want to get a better return."

Murmurs went up as Becks sat down in the chair, and Ash pulled a razor out his pocket, holding it up so everyone could see.

My hands went to my lips, realizing just what he intended to do.

"What is it?" Hooker said, laying a hand on my shoulder. "Spitz, you alright?"

I hardly knew. He wouldn't...would he?

"Don't do it, Becks! Don't do it!" one fan cried.

Searching up and down the rows, Becks met my eyes, our gazes locking, mine shocked, his determined. His mic caught the words and threw them out for all to hear, but the words were really for my ears.

"This one's for you, Sal."

Someone gasped—or a whole bunch of someones actually. I might've been one of them. Next thing I knew, Clayton had lathered Becks's cheeks and chin, making sure to cover the entire lower area of his face. Ash moved in after him, leaning down to do the honors.

Before he made the first stoke, Ash spoke into the microphone. "And the idiot's letting me do it just to prove how serious he is. Don't fall for it, Spitz. Call me instead."

Ash's invitation went in one ear out the other. I was too focused on the so-called idiot I loved.

Becks got shaved right there, any luck that might've been in that beard falling away with each scrape of blade on skin. It took less than five minutes, but the whole time the crowd seemed to hold its collective breath. When it was done, Becks stood up and pounded Ash on the back like guys do sometimes, and The Whip returned the gesture.

Like I said before, guys = strange. Period.

"Thanks everybody," Becks said, looking right at me, before Clayton stole the mic for his own special announcement.

"Sally Spitz," Clayton said, scanning the audience as my face grew hot. I sunk down lower in my seat, but he still spotted me, not too hard since a few others were looking too. "There you are, girl. Just wanted you to know, if we lose this thing, it's on you."

Gee, thanks, Clayton. If people hadn't known it was me before, they sure knew it now. I couldn't look anywhere without meeting a glare thrown by one of Chariot's many diehards. I took note of the exits just in case things started going south.

"I don't get it," Hooker said, her face a question. "Why'd he say that was for you? All he did was get his stupid facial hair shaved."

"Don't know," I lied, smiling as I turned away— looking straight into the eyes of another glaring fan. I dropped the grin, didn't want to provoke the woman, but I was beaming on the inside. Hooker didn't have to understand. Like Becks said, that performance was for me, and I knew exactly what it meant. My broken heart tessellated (a great SAT word, meaning to mend), and it didn't matter if half the stadium attacked. Becks's confession had given me wings. I could fly out of there if I had to.

The second-half was even more brutal than the first. Broughton got ahead, four to three, with just minutes remaining. The menacing looks got worse, and Hooker moved down a few seats, fearing for her safety. It took a team effort, but with an assist from Becks, Ash tied it up. In a real nail-biter, especially for me, public enemy number one in the CHS section, Becks knocked the final goal in, making an impossible shot, one only he could've made.

At the whistle, everyone jumped up, cheering, screaming. The stands shook as hundreds of people raced for the stairs. It felt and sounded like an earthquake rolling through. I tried to meet Becks right after—but it seemed like every person in Chariot rushed the field. There was no getting around the wall of bodies as the stadium emptied out. TV crews and reporters, family members, the fans, it was crazy. By the time I made it to the stands' railing, I couldn't even see Becks in the sea of people.

That is until he was lifted high into the air on the shoulders of his team.

Look at me, I thought. Please, look at me, just once, so I'll know we're okay.

And then he did.

It was only for a moment, but our eyes found each other above the crush of people and held. Everything else melted. It was just Becks and me. The next second he was whisked away as the crowd rolled on toward the dressing rooms while I was still stuck in the stands, but it didn't matter. Just before he'd been carried off, Becks had given me the most desperate look— like he didn't want to leave me as much as I didn't want him to go.

I knew I was smiling like an idiot but couldn't stop. Didn't want to. I wasn't nervous anymore. I knew we were going to be okay. Better than. And I also knew, with a certainty that couldn't be shaken, that Becks *would* call, and we would talk, and things would be right again.

Setting the volume to high, I put my phone in my pocket and tried not to check it every five seconds.

⸜⸝

When Becks finally called, it was 4:27 a.m.

I'd fallen asleep in my room but got blasted awake by an earful of the *Star Wars* theme.

"Becks?" I said, suddenly standing. "Are you okay? What's wrong?"

"I'm at the door."

"What?"

"I'm at your front door," he repeated, louder but still whispering, "outside your house. I couldn't wait until tomorrow."

"Okay," I said. "Be down in a sec." Throwing on my Yoda snuggie, I tiptoed to the front door as quickly as I could, not wanting to wake Mom. When I opened it, Becks said, "Thanks," then shot past me into the living room, barely meeting my eyes. I closed the door carefully, flipping the lock, wondering what all that was about.

Guess I was going to find out here in a second.

I turned on a lamp then took the seat next to him on the sofa. Becks was just sitting there, smiling right into my eyes, like it wasn't two hours before dawn.

"Sorry, I'm so late. I just managed to escape Clayton and the boys. Aren't you gonna congratulate me, Sal?"

"Huh?" I said.

"On the game." He leaned back, making himself comfortable. "You never said anything about the game. Everyone else and their mother talked to me about it, but I wanted to get your take."

"At four thirty in the morning," I deadpanned.

"If it means hearing your voice, then yeah," he said. "Four thirty sounds good to me."

I kept the giddiness contained, face the mask of disapproval.

"What were you thinking?" I said, poking him in the chest. Becks seemed surprised, but I was just getting started. "How could you have risked the championship—the *championship*, Becks—just to pull a stunt like that? Why would you do it?"

"Ah, Sal, you loved it."

"I did not." I crossed my arms. "That was just about the dumbest thing I've ever seen."

"Don't you mean the sweetest?" His arms came around me, and when I allowed it, Becks smiled. "C'mon, Sal, don't be mad. You know I did it all for you."

"You did it to impress people," I corrected.

"No," he said, "I did it to impress you. Did it work?"

Relenting, I placed a hand on the smooth skin of his face. There was nothing I liked better than a clean-shaven Becks, but this time it meant something different, something more.

"Why?" I asked again.

He linked his hands behind my back and pulled me closer. "I was pretty sure you wouldn't believe me unless I did something drastic. You wouldn't listen, so I decided to show you how much I love you."

"A championship's a lot to wager," I said, my heart soaring. He'd said it again, and this time I was listening. I was hearing him loud and clear, and I desperately wanted to hear him say those sweet words over and over.

"Not if I get you out of the deal." Becks stared at me, expression serious, eyes on mine. "I love you, Sal. I never said anything because I thought you knew and just didn't feel the same. I couldn't risk losing you, our friendship. I figured we'd always be 'just friends.' When you asked me to be your fake boyfriend, I swear my heart stopped. This is it, I thought. My one chance. Even if we weren't really together, I decided to make the most of it." He paused to make sure I was listening. "But you have to know. Every word I said, it was all true. Every word. You are my girl, Sal. I love that you're so smart but still a little crazy. I love your freckles." I caught my breath as his fingers skimmed my nose. "I love that your favorite movie is possibly the worst movie on the planet. God, I love it when you talk German to me. I have no idea what you're saying, but I love it. When you told me you loved me, too..." He shook his head, a look of awe on his face. "I've been really stupid, but I'm putting a stop to it right now."

My eyes filled at his confession. I blinked them furiously, not wanting to ruin this beautiful moment by blubbering all over myself. *Becks loved me!* It was so unbelievable, but the truth of it hit me hard as I saw the look in his eyes.

"Sal, don't cry." Using his thumb, he gently brushed away the first teardrop to fall. "There's only one thing I know—have always known—that I wanted out of life. And it's you."

The bawling really started then, and Becks cursed, tugging me to him. I ignored the tell-tale creak of a stair and the following sigh, which told me Mom was definitely up and listening. From the quiet whimpers—

not mine—I thought she might be crying, too. After a moment, during which he continued to rub my back, he said, "You okay, Sal?"

"Yeah." Sniffling, I pulled back, but Becks didn't let me go far. With all Becks's pretty words running wild through my head, I'd almost forgot about his big collegiate announcement. "So...UNC?"

"Heard you were going to Duke." Becks shrugged. "UNC offered me a full scholarship."

I gave him a look. "Didn't everybody?"

He just laughed. "What can I say? The head coach said they need me." Becks looked down then back up at me. "And I need you."

I melted into him. How did he always know just what to say? "I love you so much."

"I know." Leaning closer, he dropped his voice to a whisper and said, "I'm your Huckleberry."

And he was, I thought, as he kissed me breathless. He was my Huckleberry, my Han Solo, my one, but most of all he was my Becks and I was his Sal. That was the truth.

It didn't get any better than that.

ACKNOWLEDGEMENTS

This book almost didn't get published, so I'd like to give a heartfelt thank you to everyone who encouraged me to keep writing, keep going, and never give up. To my mom who has always given me her love and full support. To Colleen who gave me my very first *Harry Potter*—as you can see, HP not only got me reading but brightened my world just like it did Sally's. To Pat who loved Becks and never let me get down on myself or my dreams. You are not only my aunt, best friend and editor; you are my favorite person of all time. You three are my heart. Thank you for filling my life with love and humor and all the best things. I love you.

To any and all of my literature teachers, thank you for teaching me the beauty of words and how to use them.

To Stephanie Mooney, thank you for giving my book such a gorgeous cover. It's perfect.

To my dancers, thank you for making me want to come to work each day.

And to you, the person who is reading this book, from the bottom of my heart: Thank you. I'm so thankful that you decided to read Sally and Becks's story. It's because of you that they are no longer languishing on my computer screen. It's because of you that they have a life beyond my imagination. I hope you enjoyed *Adorkable* as much as I enjoyed writing it. And if you're still looking for your Becks, never fear. He's out there. And he's probably looking for you, too.

ABOUT THE AUTHOR

Cookie O'Gorman writes stories filled with humor and heart for the nerd in all of us. Fiery first kisses, snappy dialogue, smart girls, swoonworthy boys, and unbreakable friendships are featured in each of her books.

Cookie is a hopeless romantic, a Harry Potter aficionado, and a supporter of all things dork. Chocolate, Chinese food, and Asian dramas are her kryptonite. Above all, she believes that real life has enough sorrow and despair—which is why she always tries to give her characters a happy ending. *Adorkable* is her debut novel.

COOKIE O'GORMAN

Whether it's about her books or just to fan-girl, Cookie would love to hear from you!

Website: http://cookieogorman.com

Twitter: http://www.twitter.com/CookieOwrites

Facebook: www.facebook.com/cookieogorman